"I mean it, Da

She widened her e
"I hadn't planned o

"I know what you're doing," Oakes said, his voice harsh. "You're trying to lure me in, messing with my head. Trying to get me to break."

"Oh, Oakes." She cupped his face with her gloved hand. "I would never want to break you."

"I'm not going to kiss you," he told her gruffly. But he was pulling her toward him slowly. So slowly she could stop him at any time.

"If you say so."

"But if I *do* kiss you," he said, a desperate man fighting a losing battle, looking for a way to justify his actions, "it's only to prove, again, that there's nothing there."

But his words were weak. How could they be anything but when he was drawing her nearer, his arms wrapped around her waist.

"If that's what you need to tell yourself," she whispered.

It was. He wished he could believe it, too. Eyes on hers, he lowered his head and pressed his mouth to hers.

Dear Reader,

Thank you so much for picking up a copy of *Winter's Kiss*! If you're a return visitor to Shady Grove, welcome back, and I hope you're enjoying the In Shady Grove series. Hello and welcome to all new readers. The town of Shady Grove is near and dear to my heart as it's based on my hometown—the town where I've lived my entire life, met and married my best friend, and raised our children. I'm so happy to be sharing with you all the very best of what makes small towns so wonderful!

I love everything about the holidays: the decorations and music, the food and family time. I even love the sappy commercials! So when I decided to write Oakes and Daphne's story, I knew they'd need a bit of holiday magic to achieve their happily-ever-after. Thanks to a winter storm that strands them in Shady Grove over Christmas, they find that magic—along with the strength and courage to fall in love.

Charming, nice guy Oakes Bartasavich is a good man trying to do what's right. He puts others first and never rocks the boat. Too bad he's about to be hit by a tidal wave in the form of Daphne Lynch! Daphne is irrepressible, fun and always follows her heart. And her heart is telling her that Oakes is the only man for her. Now she not only has to convince him she's right, but that together, they can weather any storm life throws their way.

I loved writing Oakes and Daphne's story and returning once again to Shady Grove and catching up with the people there. I hope you'll look for the next In Shady Grove book out in August 2016 where Zach Castro, the last Bartasavich brother, finds love and his own happy ending with Shady Grove resident Fay Lindemuth.

For more about future releases and a listing of all my books, please visit my website, bethandrews.net, or drop me a line at beth@bethandrews.net. I'd love to hear from you.

Happy reading!

Beth

BETH ANDREWS

Winter's Kiss

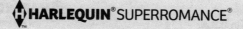

HARLEQUIN® SUPERROMANCE®

Recycling programs
for this product may
not exist in your area.

ISBN-13: 978-0-373-60932-1

Winter's Kiss

Printed in U.S.A.

While writing *Winter's Kiss*, the seventh book in her popular In Shady Grove series, Romance Writers of America RITA® Award winner **Beth Andrews** drank copious amounts of iced coffee, finished off several bags of Dove dark chocolates and shed many a tear over her youngest daughter's high school graduation (though she isn't saying whether those were happy or sad tears). When not drinking coffee and eating dark chocolate...oh, and writing, of course...she can be found cheering on the Pittsburgh Penguins, scrolling through Instagram or reading a good book with a happy ending. Learn more about Beth and her books by visiting her website, bethandrews.net.

Books by Beth Andrews

HARLEQUIN SUPERROMANCE

In Shady Grove

Talk of the Town
What Happens Between Friends
Caught Up in You
Small-Town Redemption
Charming the Firefighter

The Truth about the Sullivans

Unraveling the Past
On Her Side
In This Town
His Secret Agenda
Do You Take This Cop?
A Marine for Christmas
The Prodigal Son
Feels Like Home

Other titles by this author available in ebook format.

For Trevor and Hannah Grace.
Thank you for the best present ever!

PROLOGUE

IF SOMETHING SEEMS too good to be true, Daphne Lynch's mother had always told her, then it probably is. Especially if that something is a man.

Hard-earned wisdom from a woman who'd been burned not once, but twice by men who'd swept her off her feet only to stand by and watch as she landed flat on her ass.

Daphne knew her mother had reasons—valid ones—to feel the way she did. To want to protect herself from being let down again. From being hurt. But Daphne didn't want to live life that way. Afraid to trust. Afraid to love.

Life was about taking chances. Seeing the good that was out there and, most importantly, believing in that good.

So when she'd received an email from her father over a year ago—the first time she'd heard from Michael Lynch in six years—she'd been cautious. She may be only seventeen but she wasn't stupid. Far from it. And she hadn't forgotten what he'd done to her and her mother. What he'd done to Zach. She couldn't. Just as she wouldn't forget what type of man he'd been.

But she'd also been curious. Optimistic. Willing to give him a second chance. So she'd begun a correspondence with him over the last year. Hopeful, and eager even, to believe him when he'd said he'd changed.

Guess she wasn't all that smart after all.

Because it was now pretty clear that while Michael Lynch had changed physically over the last seven years—his face was puffier and more heavily lined, his once trim frame carried thirty extra pounds, his black hair was threaded with gray— the transformation was only superficial. The man approaching her was older and harder-looking, but he hadn't changed. Not really.

Not where it counted.

She glanced up and down the long, exterior walkway that circled George Grant High School's second-floor science wing and overlooked a pristine, tranquil courtyard. No one else was around. Exactly how she'd wanted it. She'd arrived at school early, checked in with the headmaster and asked for permission to slip outside for some privacy to go over her speech. Bad idea. She should have stayed in the cafeteria, where her classmates were assembling.

Sitting in a patch of warm sunlight on one of the wooden benches that lined the school's wall, she watched her father walk toward her, his gait unsteady enough to have him reaching for the railing of the banister every few steps, his face unshaven. Her fingers curled around her note cards, bending the edges. She prayed like mad she was wrong. That he was walking that way because he'd hurt his leg. That he sported a gray, bristly beard and disheveled hair and clothes because he'd been sick and unable to properly take care of himself.

"There she is," Michael said. "Class valedictorian!"

His slurred words bounced off the side of the building and floated over the green grass and immaculate flower beds below, scaring two robins into flight. He stopped in front of her, his eyes rimmed red, the stench of alcohol emanating off of him.

Crap. She glanced at the heavens. Thanks for nothing.

Guess she wasn't getting any help from God. Not with this. Her father was here, right in front of her, big as life and completely wasted.

Daphne swallowed and slowly got to her feet. "What are you doing here?"

He grinned and she had a glimpse of what he must have looked like before she was born, before the drink and drugs and his pack-a-day habit had taken its toll. A glimpse that told her, exactly, why her mother had fallen for him in the first place. It seemed not even moms were immune to a pretty face.

Her mom had been more susceptible than most.

"You didn't think I'd miss my baby girl's graduation, did you?" he asked.

"You've missed every other major event or milestone in my life," she pointed out. Including the ones during the time when they actually lived in the same house. Birthdays, dance recitals and softball games to name a few. Times when she'd actually wanted him there. Until she'd realized she was better off without him. "So, yeah. I thought you'd miss this one. Especially as you weren't invited."

This was all her fault. She never should have told him about being named valedictorian. Shouldn't have mentioned the date of her graduation. And since she was on a roll, she may as well add "being secret email pen pals for the past fourteen months" and "believing he was sober" to her list of mistakes.

Stupid list. It just grew and grew and grew.

"Now is that any way to talk to your father?" His tone remained friendly, if a bit quieter, but his eyes narrowed, warning her to be careful. Reminding her exactly what he was capable of.

She took a step toward the door leading to the cafeteria. Her one saving grace was that if she screamed, someone would hear. Would come to see what was happening.

Well, probably. If she yelled really, really loud.

Except, once they came, she'd have to explain why Michael was here. Who he was.

Her classmates and teachers would all get a firsthand look at who she'd come from. Her mother, currently sitting out in the blazing Texas sun, waiting for the graduation ceremony to begin, would know that Daphne had been emailing Michael for months. She'd be disappointed. Angry. But that wouldn't compare to how upset Zach would be once he found out.

And her older brother would find out. No doubt about that. Her mother never could keep a secret. Zach would know how stupid Daphne had been. How she'd betrayed him.

She couldn't let that happen.

So no screaming or asking for help. She got herself into this mess. She'd get herself out.

"You shouldn't be here," she told her father as she took another step away from him.

"I'm not here to cause any trouble. I just wanted to see you. It's a proud day for a father when his only daughter graduates at the top of her class."

The worst part? She almost believed him. Wanted to trust he told the truth. How pitiful was that? Maybe her mother had it right. Being cynical really was the way to go. Zach had certainly embraced that concept.

"I don't want you here," Daphne told him slowly. Concisely. She lifted her chin. "I mean it. Leave. Or else I'll tell security to escort you off the premises."

Because when you went to one of Houston's snootiest private schools, you could make demands like that. Even if you were there thanks to a scholarship and the generosity of a family that wasn't your own.

Michael held up his hands as if to show he was harmless, but she remembered the damage those hands could do. The sharp crack of his open palm across her mother's face. The sickening thump of his fists pummeling Zach.

The memories, combined with the smell of Michael's body odor and the stale cigarette smoke clinging to him, made her stomach turn. She breathed shallowly through her mouth until the nausea passed. Zach. He'd been her confidant and best friend her entire life. Her protector. He'd kept her safe, was a solid, strong presence, there to lean on when things got tough, lending a shoulder when the only solution was a cry-fest. Whenever she made a mistake—and sometimes it seemed as if she did nothing but—he stepped in, took over and fixed it.

He fixed her. Always.

Thank God he wasn't here to see this screwup.

Because today's mistake came in the form of six feet of what she knew could quickly turn into a mean, belligerent drunk. A ghost from their past she was sure Zach only wanted to forget.

And she'd practically invited Michael back into their lives again. Into her life. As if she'd forgotten how he'd hurt Zach. How Michael had taken his anger and bitterness out on him. How Michael had hated her brother for the simple reason that Zach was another man's son.

Tears stung Daphne's eyes. Sweat formed between her breasts. Oh, God, what had she done?

"I don't mean any harm," Michael said. "If you want to me go, I will. I just… I wanted to see you. Tell you how proud I am. I mean…look at you." He gestured to her black cap and gown. "You're all grown up. Graduating today and starting college in the fall. You're doing real well for yourself."

She raised her eyebrows. She was seventeen. If by "well for herself" he meant the minimum wage she earned at the fast-food restaurant where she worked, then yeah, she was kicking butt and taking names. Unsure what to say, she fell back on the manners her mother and Zach had instilled in her. "Thank you."

But instead of getting him to move on his way, her words seemed to please him. He stepped closer and she shifted farther away, realizing too late he'd maneuvered her back against the wall, blocking her escape. "See, the thing is, I've hit a…rough patch…and could use your help."

"My help?"

He nodded. "Five grand should cover it."

Her eyes widened. "You want me to give you five thousand dollars?"

"Seems the least you can do, seeing as how I supported you all those years."

Her jaw dropped. He hadn't been a part of her life since she was ten. Even before her mother kicked him out, he'd spent his wages on booze and drugs. Not on his family. "I don't have five thousand dollars," she told him.

"You can get it easy enough."

"Uh…no. I can't." Her *duh* may have been silent but even a drunk like him could hear it being implied.

"But we both know you can." He edged closer and she shrank back, hating her cowardice. Her weakness. "Come on now. You're a smart girl. Figure it out."

And she knew what he was saying. "You think Zach is going to give me five thousand dollars?"

"If you ask him he will. He'll do anything for his baby sister."

She shook her head, the corner of her mortarboard scratching the wall. "No. Not this."

"Why not? We both know he has it. And more."

Yes, her brother had money. Lots and lots of it thanks to being one of four sons of the superrich Clinton Bartasavich, Sr. But Zach refused to use the money in his trust fund on himself, preferring to make his own way in the world.

Letting his father know he wanted nothing from him.

"Even if I thought Zach might agree to this, I would never ask him to give me that much money," Daphne said, though she knew without doubt that he would. If she told him she needed money, he'd gladly hand it over. Would take care of her, just like he always did. "I'm not some charity case going around with my hand out, letting other people take care of me."

She worked for everything she'd accomplished—following the example Zach had set for her. It hadn't been easy earning the spot of valedictorian, but she'd done it by studying twice as much, twice as hard as her peers. All while working double shifts to pay for trips to the mall and to keep gas in the ancient Subaru she'd bought after her sixteenth birthday.

She wasn't like her father.

And her point couldn't have been clearer if she'd jabbed her father in the heart with it.

Michael grabbed her arms above her elbows, his fingers digging painfully into her flesh. "You think you're better than me?" he whispered harshly, his foul breath washing over her. He shook her. Hard. Rapped the back of her head against the wall with a sharp crack, dislodging her graduation cap. She grew dizzy, fear coating the back of her throat. He yanked her forward, lifted her onto her toes. "I'm your father. You owe me." Another shake, this one snapping her teeth together. "You ungrateful little bitch. You're nothing, you hear me? Noth—"

His words were cut off, his hands wrenched from her as a rocket slammed into him, pushing him into the wooden-slat banister across from her.

Gulping in air, Daphne took a shaky step away. She stared, wide-eyed and confused at her father, now bent backward over the railing, his face pale, his hands desperately clawing at the forearm currently lodged, quite solidly if she did say so herself, against his throat.

No, it hadn't been a rocket that had saved her. But a man. A handsome, dark-haired, broadshouldered man in a tailored, grey suit who'd come at Michael like some bastard-seeking missile sent by the wrath of God.

"Are you okay?" Oakes Bartasavich asked her over his shoulder, all calm and collected, as if slowly crushing another person's windpipe was just one of those things he did every day.

Maybe she was concussed. Hallucinating. Or else she'd stepped into some alternate reality, where Zach's older half brother, a mild-mannered bajillionaire law student who used his words instead of his fists, swooped in and saved the day.

"Daphne," he said, his voice a bit sharper, his green eyes narrowed. "Are you hurt?"

"Yes."

His expression darkened to something very scary and un-Oakes-like before he turned back to Michael. "You son of a bitch," Oakes hissed, leveraging more of his weight against her father's throat, practically bending him in half. Michael's eyes bugged out and he made horrible, gagging, gasping sounds.

"No, wait." Crap. She rushed over and touched Oakes's upper arm, surprised by how solid his muscles were, how…bulky. She had no idea he was so built. She tugged on his sleeve until he looked at her. "I meant, yes, I'm okay. I'm not hurt."

But he didn't seem to be getting it, just stared at her, rage in his eyes, his mouth a grim line. Was he in shock? Or pushed over the edge? Either way, it was up to her to talk him down. She stepped closer, sort of…stroked his arm, trying to soothe him out of this temper. Trying to bring back the man she knew. "Oakes, I'm not hurt. Really. Please let him go. He's not worth it."

Not worth Oakes getting into trouble over, or worse, being arrested for assault or whatever people got arrested for when they attacked drunks on the grounds of a private high school.

Finally, thankfully, Oakes blinked. He stepped back and lowered his arm. Michael sagged against the banister.

"Call 911," Oakes told Daphne.

"What? No." She shook her head. "No, no, no."

He speared her with a narrow, dark look. Who was this man? Oakes was usually all smiles and charm. In the four years she'd known him she'd never, not once, seen him get even remotely angry. He was always patient, laid-back and... well...even. No ups or downs for Oakes Bartasavich. He was like the calmest of lakes. Placid.

And now he looked as if he wanted to slam her father's head against the concrete floor, oh...a dozen or so times.

"He assaulted you," Oakes said in a tone most people used to explain things that are obvious. The sky is blue. The sun rises in the east. "He should be arrested."

"Assaulted?" Michael repeated, his voice raspy. "You attacked me." He drew himself up, obviously feeling confident, if not downright cocky, now that Oakes hadn't killed him. "The only one getting arrested will be you."

Oakes whirled on her father. "You had your hands on her."

"We were just having a little disagreement,

that's all." Michael glanced at her. "Isn't that right, Daphne?"

Both sets of eyes were on her. Waiting. Both expecting her to do, to say, what they wanted.

One of them would be disappointed. She was sorry it had to be Oakes.

"I just want him to leave," she told Oakes softly, refusing to lie outright to him about what had happened. "Could you…could you please just make him leave? Like I said, he's not worth the trouble."

"You heard her," he told Michael. "Get out of here. Now."

Michael smoothed back his greasy hair. Attempted to straighten his shirt, but nothing short of a miracle would accomplish that. Edging away from Oakes, he stopped by Daphne. Spoke quietly. "We're not done, little girl."

She flinched, wanted to move, but was frozen. Luckily, Oakes wasn't. He stepped between them, all big and broad and protective. A wall between her and her mistake. "You know who I am," he said to her father.

It wasn't so much a question as a statement, but Michael sneered and answered him anyway. "You're one of them Bartasavich bastards." He inclined his head toward Daphne. "Like her brother."

"You know who I am," Oakes repeated. "So you know what I'm capable of. My stepfather is a judge. My father has connections across the country. If you so much as look at Daphne again, if you so much as come close enough to breathe the same air as her, I will make sure your life is more of a living hell than it already is. There's no place you can hide from me. Do you understand?"

"I ain't scared of you, boy. Or your family."

But he looked scared. He looked terrified.

"If that's true," Oakes said, "then you're even dumber than I thought."

Michael swallowed before his face twisted and he turned back to her. "You're the one who's not worth it," he told Daphne before pushing past her and walking toward the exit sign.

She watched him go, her arms hugged around herself.

You're not worth it. What if that was true?

Oakes touched her shoulder, his hand warm and light. "Are you sure you're all right?"

She faced him and his hand dropped away. "You know." Her voice was tight with unshed tears so she stopped. Cleared her throat. "You know who he is."

"I suspected," he admitted. "When I got a better look at him."

Oh, God. Heat bloomed in her face. She was probably as red as a freaking stoplight. "How?"

He shrugged, all elegant and out-of-place on a school walkway in his expensive suit. "I recognized him from the few times he was with your mom when she dropped off or picked up Zach from Dad's house."

Zach had been forced to stay with his father, Clinton Bartasavich, every other weekend and at least one holiday a year until he'd turned eighteen. She guessed it made sense that Oakes, along with his and Zach's two older half brothers, had been there, too.

"I'm sorry, Daphne."

She frowned. She was the one who should be apologizing. Begging for forgiveness, from him and Zach and her mother. "For what?"

"That your father tracked you here. Today, especially."

That was her out. All she had to do was stay quiet. Or, better yet, thank him for coming to her rescue, maybe make some vague comment about Michael showing up as if she'd been completely surprised to hear from him, see him, after all these years.

"He didn't track me down," she blurted. As usual, her words were well ahead of her thoughts. "I mean…he did track me down. But he didn't… *track me down*. You know?"

"No. I have no idea."

She curled her fingers into the material of her graduation gown. "It's just…he knew I was here because I sort of…told him."

He gave a slight head shake. "You told him?" he asked, his careful tone not hiding his surprise. His disappointment. "Why would you do that?"

His reaction killed her. Made her feel worse than ever. His question surprised her. Her mom and Zach would be more focused on *what* she'd done. Not *why* she'd done it.

If they found out the truth, Susan would lay the mother—no pun intended—of all guilt trips on her, one laced with plenty of maternal disapproval and heavy sighs. Zach, on the other hand, would get quiet. Never a good sign. The quieter her brother got, the angrier he was, and God help you if you were the one on the other end of that anger. After he gathered his thoughts, the silence would end and the lecture would begin. He'd tell her she had to be careful. That she couldn't trust everything that came out of someone's mouth—especially if that someone was male. He'd go into warrior mode, all overprotective and rigid.

Zach didn't think she could take care of herself. And that was why Oakes was in her life in the first place. When Zach had joined the marines, he'd asked Oakes to check in on her, to make sure she was okay, and Oakes, being the good guy he was, had gone above and beyond. Stepping into the role of big brother whenever Zach was deployed.

As if she actually needed—or wanted—two older brothers. She wasn't a freaking masochist.

"I didn't invite my… Michael here," she told Oakes. "I just…mentioned that I was graduating and that I was valedictorian and I guess he thought he'd…show up to see my speech or something."

No way could she admit the only reason her father had come, the only thing he'd wanted from her, was money.

He didn't want her at all.

"You *mentioned* it to him," Oakes said and she wondered if that was a lawyer thing, repeating everything a person said. Not that he was an attorney yet—he'd just graduated from the University of Texas at Austin's law school a week ago—but he must have picked up a few things during his studies. "So you've spoken with him before? Met with him?"

"No. I mean, we haven't met up or anything. Today was the first time I've seen him in years. I swear. But we have been communicating with each other by email for…a few months." Just because she was being honest didn't mean she had to be *totally* honest. "He said he wanted to talk to me. See how I was doing, find out what was going on in my life. He told me he'd quit drinking and I believed him." Her humiliation was so complete, she couldn't even look at Oakes's reaction to her confession. "Pretty stupid, huh?"

"Hey, hey," he said, his voice so much deeper than the guys her own age, the smooth timbre of it causing her stomach to tighten pleasantly. He took her chin between his finger and thumb, then gently raised her head until she met his eyes. "You are not stupid."

Tears threatened but she blinked them back. She could let them fall later, during the ceremony, when everyone would assume she was getting weepy and sentimental about the end of her childhood. "I was dumb to believe him. To trust him. I thought… I thought he'd gotten sober for me. So he could be in my life."

Oakes stepped closer. He smelled good. Some highly expensive cologne probably, but at least he didn't bathe in it like high-school boys did. "Your father is missing out by not having you in his life, but you? You are not missing a damn thing by him not being in yours. You don't need him." His voice lowered, but his eyes never left hers. "You are strong and independent. Smart and funny. Creative and beautiful. You are too special to ever forget that or doubt it—or yourself—for a moment."

Warmth suffused her. Oakes thought she was special. Beautiful. She'd had guys tell her she was pretty before, others had claimed she was hot or had commented on how her body looked in certain clothes, but no one had ever before called her beautiful.

Other than her mom and that definitely did not count.

She wanted to believe he meant it. But her mom's lessons had been ingrained after all.

Trusting was harder than it looked.

"You don't have to say that," she mumbled, leaning back so he wasn't touching her anymore. "I'm not a charity case."

"No one thinks you are."

She rolled her eyes. "Please. We both know the only reason I'm even at this school is because of your family's money." Zach wouldn't touch his trust fund for his own needs, but he had no problem spending his father's money on her and their mother. He'd bought them a house, paid their expenses and would be footing the bill when Daphne attended Rice University this fall. "Just like we both know the only reason *you're* here today is because Zach told you to come."

Oakes smiled, looking much more like his usual good-humored self. "As much as Zach likes to believe otherwise, he's not the boss of me. I don't jump to do his bidding."

Crossing her arms, she raised her eyebrows. "No?"

"Okay, maybe he did ask me to come," Oakes

said. "But only because he was upset he couldn't be here himself."

She was proud of her brother for serving their country, but there were times she wished he'd just stayed in Houston and gotten a regular job that didn't require permission to attend his sister's graduation.

But as disappointed as she'd been that Zach hadn't been granted leave, hearing Oakes admit he was there because Zach had asked him to be was somehow worse.

She'd worry about why that was later.

"Yeah, well, you did your brotherly good deed," she told him, bending down to pick up the note cards, which she just realized she'd dropped, and her mortarboard, which she placed back on her head. Then she said, "You don't have to stay for the ceremony. I'll be sure to tell Zach you attended."

She turned to walk away but Oakes caught her wrist. Tugged her back. "He asked me to come," Oakes repeated, "but I'm here because I want to be here. Though I would have preferred if you'd invited me yourself."

She frowned. "You wanted me to invite you? Why?"

"Because we're friends."

Friends. She let the sound of it roll around in her brain a few times. She'd never thought of him as a friend. Yeah, they hung out a few times a year, usually with her mom as some sort of chaperone because an older guy and a teenage girl held too many creepy *Dateline* implications. Could it be that all this time, when he'd taken her bowling or out to dinner, when he'd asked about her school, her interests and friends, it wasn't so he could report back to Zach, but because he was truly interested?

"Oh" was all she could manage, and even that was tough to get past the lump in her throat.

"Yeah. Oh." He reached into the inside pocket of his jacket. "And with everything that happened, I forgot the reason I came looking for you in the first place." He pulled out a long, narrow box tied with red and black ribbons—her school colors. "Here." She took the box, stared at it for so long he laughed and nudged her hand. "Open it."

She pulled off the ribbon and lifted the lid to reveal a gold elephant charm on a delicate chain.

"I know you like elephants," he said, taking the necklace from the box, "and I read once that they're a symbol of good luck so I thought you could wear it during your speech." He reached around her, fastening the necklace behind her neck before gently lifting her hair from the chain.

She looked up at him, unsure of how they'd gotten so close, but not able to move back so much as an inch. He'd come to her rescue, wanted to be at her graduation and had told her she was beautiful. Plus, he'd remembered she liked elephants and he'd bought her a present. And he looked so unsure, as if he was worried she didn't like it.

Daphne threw her arms around him and hugged him hard.

"Ouch," he said with a chuckle when the pointy corner of her mortarboard jabbed his cheek.

"Sorry," she said against his shoulder because it felt way too good being held against his solid body to even lift her head. Especially since he was hugging her back.

But after a few moments she knew she had to let go or things would be all sorts of awkward between them. She leaned back, meaning to smile at him, to thank him for, well…everything, but when she opened her mouth, nothing came out. He was close…like, really, really close. His hands were on her waist, her arms still wrapped around his neck, and their bodies pressed together.

Her smile slipped away. Their gazes locked. Held. For one heartbeat. Then two. His fingers tightened and she had to stop herself from not delving her own fingertips into the hair at the nape of his neck. She was afraid to move, afraid to do anything that would break this fragile moment. And that's exactly what it was. A moment. A very real, very intense one between her and Oakes Bartasavich—a man eight years older than her, who was already out of high school, college and law school. A true grown-up with a job and his own apartment and his life all mapped out.

It was the best moment of her entire life.

Until he blinked and stepped back, his hands falling from her waist. He grinned but it looked strained, especially with his jaw being so tight. Sweat dotted his upper lip. She wanted to say something flirtatious, something adult-sounding, but what came out was "You won't tell Zach, will you?"

He flinched, as if the sound of her brother's name—of *their* brother's name—was like a slap to the face. And she realized she'd just put Zach between them, between even the possibility of them.

Yes, her list of mistakes just kept on growing.

"About my dad, I mean," she clarified, in case he thought she meant about their embrace—and that was how she'd think of it from this day forward. Not a simple hug between friendly acquaintances, but an embrace between a man and a woman. An almost woman, anyway. "You know, about him coming here and me, uh, emailing him. Which I won't do anymore," she added quickly.

Oakes grabbed the back of his neck and she had the feeling she was about to have a firsthand experience of what a lecture from him would be like: polite, no doubt. Calmly stated and oh, so very reasonable.

And really, her day had been crappy enough, thanks all the same. No need to add on to the pile.

"Look," she said, stepping toward him, only to have him take a quick step back. And wasn't that interesting? Not to mention quite encouraging. "I promise not to have anything else to do with my father, and I hope you can promise to keep what happened here today our little secret."

His gaze flew to hers. "What happened here?"

"With Michael?" Oakes stared at her blankly. "Him coming here. You almost killing him. Any of this ringing a bell?"

He laughed. Not really a ha-ha-I'm-so-amused chuckle. More like a relieved, oh-thank-God-that's-what-you-meant laugh. "Right. Yeah. I promise."

He held out his hand—always the lawyer—and she shook it, let her palm linger against his for a moment longer than necessary, just to test this new, amazing reaction to him. She felt a definite spark from the contact.

Yep. Still there and very much real.

The headmaster appeared out of the double glass doors down the walkway and called Daphne's name. She'd have to think about that spark and her reaction later. For now, she had a speech to deliver and a diploma to get.

"I'd better go," she said. "Thanks for everything. Especially the necklace. And for coming today. It means a lot."

He smiled and her heart fluttered. "I wouldn't have missed it for the world."

She kept her own smile easy and light, gave a little finger wave then turned and practically skipped toward the door. Her mother was wrong. Good guys weren't too good to be true. And they didn't come any better than Oakes Bartasavich. There'd been a very real, very heated and adult connection between her and Oakes. A shared moment where everything between them had changed.

A moment where she'd fallen in love with him.

CHAPTER ONE

Six years later

OAKES BARTASAVICH CONSIDERED himself a lucky man. He was healthy, had a large and close-knit family and had recently made partner at one of Houston's most successful law firms—two years ahead of his original schedule.

And yet, despite all that good fortune, this was the first time he'd awakened at 3:00 a.m. to find a beautiful woman in a tight, short red dress on his porch, with a pair of sparkly silver high heels and matching purse in one hand.

Too bad. A man could get used to this.

Not this particular beautiful woman, he amended quickly. Another beautiful woman. One who was closer to his own age of thirty-one, whose ties to him and his family weren't so complicated.

Definitely not Daphne Lynch, with her dark hair, blue eyes and curvy, voluptuous body. Daphne Lynch, the twenty-three-year-old half sister of Zach Castro, one of Oakes's five half brothers.

Yeah. *Complicated* summed it up. And was the best possible definition of his family.

"Daphne," he said, his voice rough from sleep. He cleared his throat. Wished he'd thought to change into jeans, maybe pulled on a shirt instead of rushing to the door in his bare feet and a pair of thin pajama pants. There was definitely a chill in the early December air. "What's the matter? Are you hurt?"

"Nope. I'm just fine and dandy. I haven't been mugged or in an accident. I'm not being chased by a crazed lunatic or running from the cops." She patted his bare chest, her fingers cool against his skin, then lowered her voice conspiratorially. "I'm drunk."

"Yes," he said, taking in her flushed cheeks, glazed eyes and the way she was swaying, like a tree in the wind. "I can see that now."

Would have seen it right away, he assured himself, if he hadn't been so shocked by her presence. It was the dress's fault. The neckline was too wide and low, showing ample amounts of golden skin and the rounded tops of her full breasts. It was too tight, the gathered material clinging to her waist and hugging her hips. And it was way too short, ending an inch above midthigh.

"Well?" she asked, her hand now pressed to his chest, her pinkie rubbing the spot just above his heart. His body liked her touch way too much.

Stepping back, he grabbed her wrist and tugged her hand away before she noticed how hard his heart was beating. "Well what, Daphne?"

"Aren't you going to invite me in?"

Invite her in? As in inside his house? No. Better yet, make that hell no.

He was a smart man. A cautious one. Cautious enough to know that letting Daphne Lynch into his home at this late hour, in her current state, wearing that damn dress, would be the beginning of the end of his life as he knew it.

A life he liked just the way it was.

"Please, Oakes." Her voice was low. Sexy. Inviting. The hairs at the nape of his neck stood on end. His fingers tightened on her slender wrist. She shifted closer, her knee brushing his leg, her scent clouding his brain.

For a second, a brief, terrifying moment in time, he forgot all the very valid, extremely reasonable reasons why he shouldn't want her. All the problems that would arise should he give in to his baser instincts, the ones that had dogged him with increasing intensity over the past few years.

In that all-too-fleeting space of time, he allowed himself the luxury of imagining they were just two unattached adults with no crazy family connections. No shared siblings. No tangled ties to trip over. If he wasn't a Bartasavich, if she had a different mother, if Zach hadn't been born,

Oakes could take what he wanted. Could finally bend his head, press his mouth against hers and see if the spark he'd been doing his best to deny for six years would sputter and fade. Or burst into flame.

Daphne shifted. And shifted again, her left hip, then her right. "I really, really have to pee."

The breath he hadn't realized he'd been holding rushed out of his mouth on a short, surprised laugh. He needed to check his ego. She wasn't here to seduce him. She had to use the bathroom.

He'd go to his grave claiming he wasn't disappointed.

"Sorry," he said, opening the door wider and moving back. "Come on in."

She brushed against him as she stepped inside, the contact slight enough, he was sure it must have been an accident.

Too bad his body didn't understand that the brief feel of a woman's soft, fragrant skin and lush curves against him didn't require the beginnings of an erection.

"Uh...the bathroom's down the hall, first door on the right," he told her.

Already heading that way, she waved a hand at him, the ends of her dark hair brushing her shoulders. "I know where it is."

"Right." Of course she did. This wasn't the first time she'd been in his home. They were friends.

In a roundabout way. A very twisting, turning, convoluted way.

In the way that meant he shouldn't let his gaze drop, shouldn't tip his head to the side and take in how good her ass looked in that dress, shouldn't enjoy the sway of her hips. He jerked his eyes up but that wasn't any better. Again, he blamed the dress. Because instead of a back, one with plenty of coverage, it had only two straps twisted together to form an *X*.

And he was going to hell for wanting to trace one of those straps, for wanting, if only for a brief, crazed moment in time, to brush aside her hair and trail a finger up the back of her neck. For not being able to turn away until she'd closed the bathroom door behind her.

Damn Bartasavich genes. Always trying to get him into trouble. But he wasn't his father. Clinton Bartasavich, Sr. had spent his entire life taking what he wanted without thought or care to the consequences. Mostly because when you were one of the wealthiest men in the country, there were no consequences.

It would have been easy for Oakes to follow in Senior's footsteps. Entitlement came with the last name. Nothing was out of the reach of a Bartasavich, a belief that Senior fully embraced, especially when it came to women. Five of his six marriages ended due to his numerous infidelities, and he'd fathered four sons by three different women.

Oakes had no doubt his father's last marriage would have suffered the same fate as his previous ones had he not had a stroke over a year and a half ago. Senior's young wife hadn't been able to handle being tied to a man who could no longer take care of himself and had opted for a quick divorce—and the payout guaranteed in her prenuptial agreement.

Oakes was fully aware that he'd grown up extremely privileged, but his mother and stepfather had instilled in him a sense of gratitude for that life. Had taught him how important it was to give back, to help those less fortunate.

No, he wasn't his father. Never would be. And that was why he'd never take advantage of any woman, especially not this particular woman, not when she'd come to him for help.

Or at least to use his bathroom.

Feeling much better, he hurried down the hall, tripping over her sparkly shoes before righting himself and continuing on to his bedroom. He changed into jeans then grabbed a T-shirt from his dresser and yanked it on. Stepped toward the door…and remembered the feel of Daphne's hand on his skin. How soft her fingers were. How warm.

How much he'd enjoyed it.

He turned around, crossed to the closet and picked out a sweatshirt. A thick one.

He was tugging down the hem of it when he re-entered the living room and found Daphne curled up on the leather sofa, her legs tucked under her, her elbow on the sofa's arm, head supported in her hand.

"You need anything?" he asked.

She tipped her head back, her grin goofy and so sweet it made his chest ache. "Nope. It's all good."

He wasn't sure about that. He flipped on the lamp, illuminating her face, then scratched the side of his neck. Was it his imagination or were her lips glossier, redder, than when she'd first arrived? And in this light, he could see she'd done something to her eyes, one of those magic tricks women performed to make the usually guileless blue of them seem somehow smoky and mysterious.

"So everything's okay," he said slowly. "You're not hurt or sick and yet you're here. At my house. At three a.m."

She touched her upper cheek with her forefinger then slid it onto the tip of her nose, pointed at him with her other hand. A drunk playing her own game of charades. "Bingo."

"Any reason you're at my house and not your own?"

"Yep."

When she didn't continue, he sat on the coffee table in front of her. "Want to tell me what that reason is?"

"Your house is closer," she said, as if that made all the sense in the world.

"Closer to where?"

"To the club."

This was getting him nowhere. As a trial attorney with a high win record, he was used to asking questions and getting answers. He was damn good at it, too, if he did say so himself.

He eyed the woman currently humming a pop tune under her breath. Usually. He was usually good at it.

"I take it you went out tonight?" he asked.

He hadn't realized she was into the club scene. Then again she was young enough that it made perfect sense that she might enjoy spending her Saturday night being jostled by bumping and grinding strangers while lights flashed and the bass pumped.

He winced infinitesimally. He was thinking like a ninety-year-old man.

She sighed—the long, drawn-out sigh of the weary and put-upon. "I didn't want to. Nadine made me."

"Nadine?"

"My cousin. Actually, my other cousins were there, too. Julie and Michelle and Steph," Daphne said, ticking the names off her fingers. "But Nadine was the ringleader. She decided I needed to go out. They kidnapped me," she said, attempting to slap the arm of the sofa but missing and almost toppling into his lap. He caught her by her upper arms, helped her back onto the cushion then quickly let go. "They told me we were going out to dinner, that Julie needed a break from the twins but they lied and they... They took me against my will. Can I press charges?"

"It might be better if we hold off on any discussions about legal ramifications until we're both sober."

She tapped his knee twice, left her hand to settle there. "You're a smart one, aren't you? But then they don't give out law degrees just for being pretty. And when we have our talk about legal ramen...ramekin...whatever, we can discuss a civil suit against my cousins for being liars. For being no-good, rotten lying liars who lie. Don't believe them," she said as she suddenly clutched his hand, her voice taking on a desperate quality. "No matter what they say, don't believe a word of it. Ever."

"I won't."

"Promise?"

"Promise," he repeated solemnly because it seemed so important to her. Then again, alcohol made even the most mundane things exciting, the most minor issue important.

"Okay." She relaxed the death grip she had on him and eased back. "Okay then."

"Why don't we get you some coffee?" he suggested.

"Oh, I can't have coffee this late," she told him, her eyes wide, her gaze earnest. "It'll keep me up."

She was so adorable, he couldn't help but grin. "How about we try it anyway? See if it sobers you up a bit?" And hopefully, helps her be more clear and concise in her answers as to why she was there.

She returned his smile. "Okay. But I should help you," she said when he got to his feet.

She started to stand and he pressed gently on her shoulders until she sat back on the edge of the sofa. "I've got this." But he realized he was still touching her. The thin straps of her dress were silky, her skin incredibly warm under his palms. The ends of her hair tickled the backs of his fingers and he sprang back, releasing her. Was fervently glad he'd put on jeans as he shoved his traitorous hands into their pockets. "You, uh, just relax. And tell me the rest of your story."

"What story?" she asked, still smiling at him.

Holy hell, this was going to be a long night. "About how your cousins forced you to get drunk."

Laughing as if that was the funniest thing she'd ever heard, she fell back against the couch, breasts bouncing, bare legs stretched out. She had a low, throaty laugh, the kind that scraped pleasantly along a man's nerve endings.

"Don't be silly," she said, still chuckling. "They didn't force me to get drunk. They forced me to go to the club. After dinner they told me we were going home but instead, we ended up at The District."

The District being one of Houston's most popular dance clubs, less than a mile from here. "I stand corrected. Although I'm a little confused as to why you stayed at the club if you didn't want to be there."

"I was going to leave," she said as she got unsteadily to her feet, bringing their bodies much too close for Oakes's comfort, "but then the DJ played 'Uptown Funk' and it's impossible to hear that song and not dance so I *had* to get on the dance floor."

"Right." He tried to put some distance between them but only managed to collide with the coffee table when he stepped back. He shifted to the right then circled around the sofa. "None of that explains why you came here," he said as he walked behind the granite-topped island, which separated the kitchen from the living room. "Why you're not still with your cousins."

"It doesn't?"

A headache began to form behind his right eye. "No."

"Oh." She flopped back down, crossed her arms on the back of the couch and watched as he opened an upper cabinet for the coffee. "Well, I'm not with my cousins because Julie and Steph went home early—Julie's husband has to work in the morning and Steph's youngest has an ear infection. Then Nadine took off in a huff after getting into an argument with her boyfriend via text and the last time I saw Michelle she was dirty dancing with a leggy blonde in a leather miniskirt."

Frowning, he measured out coffee beans, dumped them into the grinder. "They shouldn't have let you drink so much if they were just going to ditch you. One of them should have made sure you got home safely."

She laughed again, but didn't raise her head from her arms. "I'm twenty-three years old, Oakes. I can drink as much as I like. And, anyway, I'm perfectly safe, aren't I?"

"Safe," he pointed out, pouring distilled water into his coffeemaker, "but not home."

Still not moving her head, she waved a hand. "I didn't want to go home. I wanted to see you."

His shoulders tensed, his fingers tightened on the plastic bottle. "What do you mean? I thought you just needed to use the bathroom."

"Why would I come here in the middle of the night *just* to use the bathroom?"

He had no idea and no, it didn't make sense when she said it like that. But neither did her dropping by his place, drunk, at three in the morning.

Then again, women were a mystery so what the hell did he know?

"What did you want to see me about?" he asked, turning on the coffeemaker. When she didn't answer, he turned to find her eyes closed. "Daphne?" Nothing. "Daphne?" he repeated louder.

She blinked at him then smiled dreamily. "Hmm?"

Right. This obviously wasn't getting him anywhere. "We'll put your coffee in a travel mug," he said, pulling one out of a drawer.

"Okay. Am I going somewhere?"

"Home." But that only brought up the issue of him getting her into her apartment—a third-story walk-up across town—and into bed.

She snuggled back down into her arms, shut her eyes. "Don't wanna," she murmured.

And getting her up the stairs and into that bed would be even more difficult without her cooperation. Hell. Being a nice guy just didn't pay some days.

"Life's tough that way," he said, not sure if he was talking to her about doing things she didn't want to, or himself for his incessant need to always do the right thing.

He headed toward the hall only to stop at the sound of someone knocking on his front door.

"If that's another drunk woman," he muttered, "I'll tell her the bathroom's closed for the night."

Daphne stirred. "Did I tell you I didn't pay the cab driver?"

He pinched the bridge of his nose. "No," he managed to say from between clenched teeth, "You failed to mention that."

But her head was back down, her eyes shut. Another knock, this time louder.

"One minute," Oakes called then hurried into his bedroom for his wallet. Two minutes later he'd paid the understandably irritable cab driver— adding a hefty tip—and shut the door. He leaned his head against the cool wood, gathering his thoughts. The scent of coffee filled the air. He'd dump some into the mug, haul Daphne to her feet and settle her into his car. Forty-minutes—fifty, tops— and he'd be back home and in his bed, trying to forget this ever happened.

But when he lifted his head and turned, he saw all those hopeful plans go up in smoke. Daphne was asleep. Or, passed out if the sound of her snores was anything to go by. And there was no way in hell he was carrying her.

Looked like he had himself an overnight guest.

He locked the door and shut off the porch light, then crossed to the kitchen and turned off the coffeepot before he got a blanket from the linen closet. As much as he wanted to, he couldn't let her stay crumpled up like that, her neck bent at an awkward angle, her legs curled under her. He wiped his tingling palms down the front of his jeans as he studied her, tried to figure out how to make her comfortable with the least amount of touching possible—though any contact seemed inappropriate given her current state.

Deciding to start at the bottom—and pray like hell the rest of her straightened out of her own accord—he wrapped his fingers around her ankles and slowly swung her legs around.

She snored on.

He went to encircle her waist only to yank his hands back when he brushed the silk of her dress. He considered slipping his arms under her, but didn't want to take the chance of accidentally touching her butt. Not when he'd admired it only a few minutes ago. He could take a hold of her shoulders, but that would bring him close to those amazing breasts, to her open mouth.

In the end, he settled on taking her by the ankles again, this time gently pulling her until she slid onto her back on the cushions. His plan worked great, except her dress had slid up, showing a great deal more of her bare thighs. Keeping his gaze firmly on her face, he unfolded the blanket over her, tucking one end under her chin, the other over her toes.

He straightened. It was easier to look at her with all those curves covered. Easier, much easier to remember how young she was with her face relaxed, her mouth open, one hand curled by her cheek.

Easier to remember all the reasons he shouldn't want her.

But he couldn't stop himself from brushing a loose lock of hair from her forehead, then letting his finger trail ever so slightly over her arched eyebrow before he turned off the light and went to his room. Yanking off his sweatshirt, he tossed it aside then fell facedown on his bed, his feet hanging over the edge. He pulled a pillow over his head, but that did little to help him forget about the woman on his couch. The woman he thought about way too often. The one woman he wanted above anyone else.

The one woman he could never have.

SOME KNUCKLEHEAD WAS singing along to a Mumford and Sons song. Loudly. And badly.

Daphne would have covered her ears but really, lifting her arms at what had to be an ungodly hour was just too much effort. She settled for pressing her face into her pillow. It might not mute the sound, but if she kept it there long enough, maybe she'd suffocate. Either way would end her misery.

The idiot chose that moment to attempt a bit of harmonizing with a particularly high note, causing her back teeth to ache. Talk about freaking torture. Honestly, some people were so rude. Singing this early with no thought or care that other people were trying to sleep.

Jeesh.

She snuggled farther into the mattress, but instead of the softness of her sheets, she encountered smooth, cool leather. Shifting her leg to the right, she bumped something hard. She frowned. That wasn't right. There should be ample empty space in her king-size bed. Of course Cyrus, her golden retriever, took up a great deal of it but that hadn't been his large, warm body, either.

Even racking her sleep-laden brain it took her a moment, surely longer than it should have, to figure out she wasn't at her apartment, wasn't all cozy and safe in her bedroom. She wasn't even in a bed.

As she processed that bit of reality, the events of last night unfolded in her mind, frame by frame, like a movie in slow motion. There was dinner with her cousins at her favorite restaurant, good food and lots of laughs, then that fateful trip to The District, where, despite being irritated that they'd tricked her into a night out, she'd danced and drank. And drank. And drank.

Squeezing her eyes shut harder, she remembered being hit on by a cute blond physical therapist, then later, by a darkly handsome electrician. When she'd declined to give either of them her phone number, Nadine had gotten on her case about turning down not one, but two potential soul mates, badgering her as only Nadine could until Daphne had blurted out the truth. That she had no interest in getting to know random strangers or taking part in the whole dating scene. Not when she couldn't stop thinking about one particular man she already considered a friend.

Oakes.

While she hadn't exactly been pining for him all these years, the possibility of them as a couple had never fully disappeared. It was always there, in the back of her mind. In her heart. Like a dream of the future for when they were both single and ready to act on the attraction between them.

When the time was finally right.

Last night, with her brain muddied by tequila and her pride stinging with the news of her ex's upcoming wedding, the timing had seemed perfect.

So, in the infinite wisdom of the inebriated, Daphne had decided the best course of action was to tell Oakes she'd fallen in love with him six years ago and still was in love with him today.

She groaned and pulled her knees closer to her chest, curling into a protective ball. Yes, yes, it was all coming back to her now. How very wise she'd felt about her decision. How comfortable with the plan to win over the man she loved with a heartfelt declaration. She'd ridden that wave of alcohol-induced confidence from the club all the way to Oakes's house, and had let it carry her up to his porch, pushing her into pounding on his door.

But now she slowly sank with the realization that showing up at his house, stinking drunk, at 3:00 a.m. might not be the best way to convince him that she was not just serious, but, more importantly, sincere.

For some crazy reason people in her life had a hard time believing she could be either.

The song changed but the singing continued, Oakes's usually pleasant baritone ruining "Little Lion Man" for her for life. A cupboard door opened then shut, and the smell of fresh coffee filled the air.

Ca-rapity crap crap. Once again she'd acted before thinking things through. If she wasn't careful, that could become a bad habit.

But she at least had figured out where she was and why her back and shoulders ached, and her left hand was numb. Seemed she'd ended her night by passing out on Oakes's couch. Great. Mystery solved. And since there was nothing she could do about the events of last night, couldn't undo them or wish them away, she might as well go back to sleep.

She'd deal with the consequences of her actions later.

Much, much later.

CHAPTER TWO

DAPHNE HAD JUST drifted off again when the scent of coffee grew stronger, as if the pot had grown legs and walked over to tempt her out of sleep. She was having a rather heated internal debate on whether or not she should lift her head to investigate this turn of events when someone nudged her shoulder. She didn't move and that someone did it again.

"Poke me one more time," she warned Oakes, eyes still squeezed shut, her face hidden in her folded arms, "and I will kill you. Slowly. And with great relish."

An idle threat, really, and one that didn't have much of a punch due to her being unwilling to lift her head from where it rested, quite comfortably, thank you very much. It didn't help that her tongue wasn't currently working—her words came out as a cross between a slur and a groan.

Plus, why kill him before he'd had the chance to see how awesome, adorable and amazing she was? He was the man she loved, after all.

At least, she was pretty sure he was.

She opened her eyes and peeked under her arm at him. Her heart sighed, one long, happy sigh. He wore the same faded jeans as last night and an Astros T-shirt, the soft material hugging his broad shoulders. He had a body on him, a surprisingly hard and muscular one, despite the fact that he sat on his rear for a living. His jaw was sharp, his nose straight and she knew that when he smiled, he had even, white teeth and a charm about him that went right to her gut. Dark hair and green eyes completed what was, all in all, one very pretty picture.

But she hadn't fallen for him because of his good looks. Or, at least, not only because of them. Yes, he was handsome—all the Bartasavich brothers were gorgeous, including her own brother, Zach. No, what set Oakes apart was his kindness. His warmth and generosity.

Her brain still foggy, her mouth feeling as if it had been filled with cotton, Daphne lifted her head. Realized she'd drooled in her sleep. Wonderful. She wiped the side of her mouth, making the move as casual as possible. How the heck was she going to convince him she was his soul mate after drooling on his sofa?

"You are alive," he said, the right side of his mouth lifted in a grin. "I'd wondered."

"Alive and well," she assured him, though her voice sounded rusty. She brushed her hair out of her eyes and tossed back the blanket, which she assumed he'd covered her with last night, before swinging her legs around, her bare feet connecting with the cool wood floor.

His gaze dropped and his mouth tightened before he jerked up his eyes to stare at a spot somewhere in the vicinity of the ceiling. She followed his gaze but there was nothing to see except white ceiling so she glanced down. Oops. Her dress had shifted and twisted and ridden up during her sleep. She hadn't flashed him everything God had given her, but it was pretty darn close.

Lifting her hips, she tugged down the material, making sure all was covered and right with the world. When she looked back at Oakes, her breath caught at the intensity in his gaze. The interest.

The attraction.

He blinked and it was gone, just...*poof*, and his expression smoothed out as if it had never been. She could relate. For years she'd gone back and forth over whether to embrace her feelings for him or pretend they didn't exist. But she knew, whatever choices they made didn't matter. They could fight the inevitable, could pretend there was nothing between them, but if they were meant to be—and her instincts were telling her they were—then they'd end up together. Eventually.

Still, it wouldn't hurt for her to give fate a bit of a nudge.

He held out his hand. Now, she was completely capable of standing on her own—she'd been doing so since she was a baby, after all—but she wasn't about to pass up the opportunity to touch Oakes, to test him, just a bit. Placing her hand in his, she let him tug her to her feet, making sure her breasts subtly brushed the hard planes of his chest as she did so.

He would have backed up, she knew, but he was trapped between her body and the coffee table, her fingers still curled around his. She rubbed her thumb over the back of his hand and slowly lifted her head, her hair brushing his chin. He went completely still except for the working of his throat as he swallowed.

"Thank you," she said, sounding like a breathy sex kitten.

Hey, if that's what it took to get him to stop pretending he wasn't attracted to her, she could go that route, complete with pointy ears, whiskers and tight catsuit.

Meow.

Their eyes met. Anticipation filled her, grew to an almost painful point, when his gaze dropped to linger on her mouth. He leaned forward. Her heart hammered. Her lips parted. Oh, God, this was it. The moment she'd been waiting for. He was going to kiss her. Well, that would certainly put an end to the whole I-see-you-only-as-a-platonic-nonsexual-friend act he pulled whenever they were together.

It wasn't quite the romantic scenario she'd fantasized about when she was seventeen and in the throes of a huge, heartbreaking crush on him. And maybe having him get this close to her when she undoubtedly had morning breath wasn't such a great idea, but if the man was finally going to kiss her after she'd waited six long years, she sure wasn't about to deny him simply because they weren't on a moonlit beach and she needed a mint.

She let her eyes drift shut.

Only to have them pop open when he gave her hand a friendly squeeze and slid free of her grasp. "No problem," he said, his voice gruff.

Then, as if to make sure her humiliation was complete, as if to drive home the fact that he found her harmless and cute, like a child, he patted her head.

The man literally patted her on the top of her head.

She didn't know whether to cry or punch him in the throat.

She settled on nipping the coffee cup from his hand as he raised it for a drink. Took a cautious sip before he'd even had time to blink or lower his arm back to his side.

"Ah, the nectar of the gods. And the only good thing about waking up in the morning."

"Please," he said, his tone all sorts of dry. "Help yourself."

Feeling a bit better, she sent him a cheeky grin and drank again, deeper this time now that she knew it wasn't blistering hot. Served him right after he'd gotten her hopes up only to cruelly dash them.

She gulped down some more, praying the caffeine kicked in quickly. The coffee could use a hefty dose of both cream and sugar but beggars couldn't be choosers—and she was well used to playing the part of beggar. "I don't suppose you're hiding a bagel on your person?"

"Excuse me?" he asked, his expression bemused.

"A bagel," she repeated slowly. Maybe he needed the coffee as much as she did. She handed the mug back to him. "Or a muffin? At this point I'd even take a scone." When he just stared at her as if she'd lost her ever-loving mind, she wrinkled her nose. "No, huh? Too bad. I'm starving."

"How about we start you off with some dry toast? See how that goes."

She made a face. "How about you slather some peanut butter on that toast and we'll have a deal." She eyed the coffee cup he still hadn't bothered drinking from. "If you're not going to finish that..."

He handed it back to her.

She wished it was that easy to get everything she wanted from him.

She headed toward his kitchen, crossed to the large fridge and opened it. Grabbed the half-and-half and poured a hefty amount into the cup.

"Sugar?" she asked. She'd been to his house before, of course. Plenty of times, the most recent being over the Fourth of July weekend when he'd thrown an impromptu barbecue and had told her to feel free to drop by.

They were friends, but not the kind who knew how the other organized his—or her—kitchen. More like the kind that texted every few weeks to check in with each other, met up for coffee or lunch once a month and invited each other to casual get-togethers.

That was all about to change. It was past time they discovered if they were meant to be *more*.

He joined her, reaching for the sugar bowl in an upper cabinet, his shirt riding up slightly to show the ridges of his stomach. She'd touched him, she remembered, her fingers tingling with the memory. Last night she'd slapped his chest, then had kept her hand there, had felt the smoothness of his skin, the coarse hair dusting his chest.

The first time she'd touched him in anything

other than a friendly, hey-we're-buddies-and-sort-of-but-not-really-related sort of way in years. Since her high school graduation.

Progress. At long, long last.

She added sugar to her coffee then gulped it down gratefully. "That's better," she murmured as Oakes poured himself a fresh cup. "Now, what about that toast?"

"I ordered from Pitter Patterson's Bakery," he said, mentioning the name of one of her favorite breakfast restaurants. "I thought you might want something in your stomach other than wine."

"You," she said, setting her cup down, "are a prince among men. Thank you. But there's no wine in my stomach. I don't drink it."

"You don't?"

Was that what the women he usually dated drank? Probably. He went for the socialite types or the well-educated, high-powered corporate woman. Tall, thin and blonde, though that one VP he'd dated two years ago had been a petite brunette, the kind who worked out regularly and was going back to school for her third degree.

Daphne shook off the feelings of inadequacy. She was just as good as anyone. Better than most, certainly, at least when it came to being good enough for Oakes. Now all she needed to figure out was if she was right for him. And if, as her instincts told her, he was right for her, too.

"Nope," she said. "Wine gives me a headache." Plus, she never knew what to order, what color went with her dinner or the whole sniff-sip-swish routine that went with drinking it. "The credit for last night's buzz belongs solely to tequila."

"Tequila?" he repeated, staring at her as if she'd admitted to downing an entire bottle of the stuff in one sitting.

"The other nectar of the gods," she assured him. "Anyway, I think I'll take a moment to freshen up before we eat. Be right back."

She grabbed her purse from the coffee table then padded barefoot down the hall to the bathroom. Flipped on the light, turned, and jumped at the sight of her reflection in the mirror. "Oh, dear Lord," she whispered, horrified, her hand going to her crazy, frizzy hair. It stuck out straight in spots, was plastered to her head in others.

"Seriously?" she asked God through gritted teeth, her gaze on the ceiling as though she could see through it to heaven. "You let him see me like this? Whose side are you on?"

No wonder the man hadn't wanted to kiss her.

Pulling a small brush from her bag, she attacked her hair, pulling the bristles through snarls that fought back valiantly. Too bad no amount of brushing could get the thick, naturally wavy strands to behave. Her makeup was long gone, except, of course, for the dark smudges of black eyeliner on her temples, the mascara caked on her lashes and rimming her lower lids. Sleep marks marred her cheek like a road map. She rubbed at them but that only made her face red.

Triple crap.

By the time she took care of personal business, washed her hands and face, tucked her hair behind both ears to get it to stop winging out like she had a bat on her head and went back to the kitchen, Oakes had set plates at the bar.

"Bless you," she told him fervently as he handed her a glass of orange juice. "Seriously, you are definitely going to heaven for this."

He poured juice into a second glass and as she sat she noticed he had silverware, cloth napkins, the whole shebang set out for them. Lessons from his mother, Daphne was sure. She didn't know Rosalyn Moore personally, but she'd gleaned enough information about the woman from Oakes to know she believed in making the best out of any situation—such as having an uninvited, overnight guest. She also put a lot of stock into making a good impression and keeping up appearances.

Daphne wondered which one of those had kept Rosalyn married to Oakes's father after he'd cheated on her with Daphne's mom.

Oakes joined her on the other high-backed

stool, his thigh pressing against hers for a brief moment before he shifted, ever so subtly away.

"Really, Oakes, thank you," she said, sipping her orange juice. He'd poured her more coffee and had the cream and sugar on the counter. "You're so sweet to take care of me this morning and for not kicking me out last night."

"We're family."

She squeezed her glass. Hard. They weren't family. Yes, yes, they had similar relatives but they were not related. Not in any way, shape or form. "You had every right to tell me to get lost," she said, wanting him to say something, anything, that would give her some hope, some idea that he felt what she felt. That he, too, wanted to take a chance on whatever this was between them. "No one would have blamed you."

He raised his eyebrows. "I'm not sure Zach would agree with you on that."

And that was not what she'd had in mind.

Zach. Right. The brother they shared. The bane of her existence and, she was fairly certain, the reason Oakes had yet to make a move on her. It was a tricky situation, undoubtedly. Oakes's father, the very wealthy, very powerful Clinton Bartasavich, Sr. had four sons: Clinton, Jr. and Kane, both with his first wife; Oakes with Rosalyn, his second wife; and Zach with Susan, who'd been Oakes's nanny at the time of the affair.

Rosalyn had eventually divorced Senior, after ten years and numerous infidelities on his part. She'd remarried and had two younger sons. Susan, too, had moved on, marrying Michael Lynch. And having Daphne.

Yes, sir. Tricky, tricky, tricky.

"I don't think even Zach could blame you if you'd turned me away," Daphne said to Oakes, although her brother did have a sanctimonious and judgmental streak, especially when it came to her. And a major stick up his butt when it came to the Bartasavich side of his family. "I mean, I did show up at your house in the middle of the night, drunk."

Oakes lifted a shoulder. Always a good guy, he didn't seem to want her gratitude. "It's no big deal." He turned, grinned at her. "Livened up my night, that was for sure."

She stared at her spoon, concentrated on stirring and stirring and stirring her coffee. Cleared her throat. "Yes, well, I shouldn't have done it." Especially now that she realized she could have easily interrupted something. What if he'd had a woman over? He'd been seeing Sylvie Green the past few weeks. Sylvie, with her shiny, golden hair and tiny waist. What if she'd been here, in his house, in his bed, when Daphne showed up?

She wasn't sure she could have handled that, not in her inebriated state.

Ah, the clarity of sobriety. Too little, too late.

"Anyway, I really appreciate you taking me in," she continued, the thought of him being with Sylvie making her sound less grateful and more annoyed. "It meant a lot to me."

"Like I said, I couldn't turn you away."

No, he couldn't. Not Oakes. Hadn't she counted on that, realized that even while drunk? He'd never do anything to hurt anyone.

"I'm still not sure how you ended up here, though," he said. "You said you wanted to see me."

Pretending it took all her concentration, she sipped her coffee. Had she said that? Well, at least she hadn't told him the real reason she'd come here—to declare what could possibly be her undying love for him.

Yay. One point for self-control.

"Did I?" she asked with what she hoped was casual curiosity. She forced a light laugh. "I must have really been out of it. The last thing I remember clearly was getting in the cab and telling the driver to bring me here as it was closer and I didn't think I'd make it home without passing out."

Lies, lies, horrible lies to protect herself, to save her from complete and utter humiliation.

He looked as if he was about to call her on her fibs when there was a knock on the door. "That must be the food," he said, heading to answer it.

Thank God. She gulped more caffeine. Blurting out that she loved him and wanted them to be together didn't seem like such a hot idea in the cold, harsh light of day. But she wasn't ready to go back to how they'd always been, either. For years she'd told herself that what she felt for Oakes was nothing more than infatuation. The remnants of a childhood crush.

But what if it wasn't? Surely a crush wouldn't have lasted this long.

She still thought of him often. Too often. Her heart tripped when she received a call or text from him. If they went too long between visits or chats she missed him. And when something happened in her life, good or bad, he was the first person she thought of telling, the person she wanted to share the news with more than anyone else.

She'd told herself to just get over it, to get over him already. Had tried to push her feelings aside. It wasn't as if she sat around waiting for him to notice her. She'd gotten her undergraduate degree and was now in grad school. She'd dated other men, had even had a short-lived engagement that had ended six months ago.

And when those relationships ended, she found herself right back to square one. Thinking about Oakes. Wondering if he was the one for her.

She used to believe that if she and Oakes were

meant to be, they'd end up together no matter what directions life took them in.

Now, though, she wasn't so sure letting fate lead the way was the best idea. What if this was their opportunity? She was single and Oakes and Sylvie had only gone out a few times so they weren't serious. Her drunken epiphany last night just might have been destiny's way of giving her a good swift kick in the rear and telling her to take charge.

She had to be smart here, though. Had to try and figure out what Oakes thought about her, about them, before giving away too many of her own thoughts, her own feelings.

He was too honorable to make the first move. He probably thought she was too young for him. And he wouldn't want to rock the boat where their families were concerned. Yes, it would take Zach, and their mothers, time to get used to the idea of them being together, but they'd all just have to deal. She'd been waiting six long years for Oakes to notice her as something other than Zach's younger sister and a friend.

It was time he noticed her as a woman.

She had to ease him into the idea of being with her. Get him to think it was the best idea ever.

Mainly, she had to let him think it was *his* idea. She knew all about men and how sensitive they were about being led to do something. He had to take the lead.

With some encouragement from her, of course.

"Here we are," he said, after shutting the door. He held up a large bag with the diner's logo on it. "Best breakfast this side of Houston."

"Let me help you." She slid to her feet, crossed to him in what she hoped was a slow, seductive sashay and not a clumpy, eager gallop. But damn it, she was starving and the food smelled really, really good. She took the bag, waved him back to his seat. "The least I can do is dish this out. And I hope you'll let me pay for it and whatever the cab cost."

"My treat and so was the cab ride." He grinned down at her, teasing and friendly. "But maybe next time you go out, you shouldn't spend all your money on drinks."

And the last thing she wanted was for him to look at her that way, as if she was some cute kid sister who'd gotten herself into a jam. "I didn't spend all my money on drinks. I switched purses before we left and my wallet wouldn't fit in my smaller one. I thought I'd grabbed my credit card and a fifty but my cousins were rushing me and I'd only put a ten in there along with my grocery store's rewards club card. Luckily, my cousins insisted on paying for dinner—as they should since they kidnapped me and all."

"How did you pay for your drinks then?"

"I didn't."

He followed her back to the counter, though he wouldn't let her take the bag. He set it down and faced her. "You have generous cousins. They must have really wanted to make sure you had a good time."

She laughed. "They can be generous, and they paid for a few rounds for all of us, but they weren't the only ones buying me drinks last night."

"They weren't?"

She smiled. Maybe she could get a reaction out of him after all. "No. There were some very sweet men there who insisted on supplying me with beverages."

He blinked. Blinked again. "You let some strange guy buy your drinks?"

She pursed her lips. "Actually, it was two guys. Strangers, yes, but I don't think they were strange. Christopher was really funny and Ray had that whole bad-boy vibe going on, which made the night interesting."

Oakes frowned, his eyes narrowed and she wondered if it was too soon to assume he was jealous, or if he was thinking of her with those other guys—not both at once, of course—when she could be with him.

"You shouldn't accept drinks from strangers at bars," he said, sounding irritated—very unlike easygoing Oakes. "Didn't your mother ever tell you that?"

"Not in so many words." Her mother knew she was capable of taking care of herself.

"I'm sure Zach warned you about it," Oakes continued, not like a jealous man at all, but more like a lecturing teacher.

Or big brother.

"Men who buy women drinks at bars," he continued in a voice way too similar to her freshman year lit professor's superior tone, "do it for one reason and one reason only."

"Really?" Setting her elbows on the counter, she cupped her chin in her hand and stared at him wide-eyed. "Do tell."

His frown deepened. "They see you looking like..." He waved a hand at her, going up and down as if to take in her entire person. "That," he finally said. "And they want to take you home."

She blinked, slowly and with great exaggeration. "Whatever for?"

He looked so uncomfortable, she almost felt sorry for him. Almost. "You know what for."

"A complete innocent like me?" she asked, hand to her chest. "Why, I haven't a clue."

"Sex," he growled from between his teeth. "They're hoping you'll sleep with them."

"No. That thought never crossed my mind. Thank God I have you here to set me straight on the nefarious ways of men in clubs." She rolled her eyes. "It may come as a shock to you, but I'm not a child. I've gone out to clubs and bars before." She lowered her voice and leaned forward. "I've even had sex before."

He stepped back so quickly, he almost tripped over the stool behind him. "That's... I don't need to know...you don't..."

She smiled. How could she not? He looked so horrified, but that wasn't all. He looked...stunned. As if the thoughts of her and sex had never co-existed in his mind before. But then she looked closer, saw a definite heat in his eyes behind the panic, and she wondered if maybe, just maybe, that heat wasn't the reason for the panic.

Maybe he didn't see her as just a friend or some sort of little sister after all.

Only one way to find out.

She moved closer. "I know exactly why those guys bought me drinks, what they were hoping to get from me. But I choose who I go home with. Who I sleep with, share my body with." At her words, his eyes dropped and raked over her body, before his jaw clenched and he yanked up his gaze once again. "I didn't go home with any of those men, didn't want to go with them. I came here. I came to you."

CHAPTER THREE

I CAME HERE. I came to you.

The words hit Oakes like a punch. Like the answer to a prayer, one he'd never been brave enough to say, let alone think about.

He was in serious trouble here. Because he was taking what she'd surely meant to be innocent words as some sort of overture. He was a man well used to women coming on to him. His looks helped, but he knew part of his appeal was his last name—at least before those women got a chance to know him. He also knew when a woman was tossing the ball in his court, giving him an opening, a chance to make a move.

And he wanted, badly, to do just that. To make a move on Daphne, to see how those curves felt pressed against him, how that mouth would taste.

He was wrong. He had to be. There's no way she was coming on to him. Daphne was his friend. Sort of. But more than that, more important than that, she was Zach's sister.

He gave her an awkward, brotherly pat on her shoulder. "I'm glad I could help. And that you had the good sense not to go home with some stranger."

Was it his imagination or did she look disappointed by his response? He couldn't analyze it, was afraid if he did, he'd come to a conclusion he didn't like. One that was purely a figment of his imagination.

"Ready to eat?" he asked, desperate to get back on solid ground with her.

As if the moment had never happened, she smiled. "Yes, please. I am starving."

He pulled the boxes out of the bag while she refreshed their coffee. He tried not to take in how good she looked in his kitchen, that red dress like a beacon calling his attention again and again. How comfortable she was here, barefoot in his house, all bright and cheerful as she chatted about some dessert she'd had last night.

He let her talk wash over him as he folded the bag and set it with the recycling. He had to get a grip. Yes, he found Daphne attractive. He was a man, wasn't he? And she was, well…she was Daphne. All curves and subtle sensuality. She was also smart and funny and full of energy. Last night when she'd been asleep on his couch was the first time he could remember seeing her so still. She always seemed amped up, lit up from some internal light, an inner spark.

But she was Zach's sister. Zach Castro, the only one of Oakes's brothers who kept him at arm's length. The man who was recovering from injuries sustained while serving with the marines in Iraq.

The only Bartasavich son not to take their father's name, who'd been raised as much as possible away from his older brothers. Zach had spent his entire life making his resentment toward his father and the rest of his family perfectly clear.

Not that Oakes could blame him. None of them could say they were close to their father. Clinton Bartasavich, Sr. wasn't an easy man to get to know or to love. In his younger years he'd been all about power and increasing his wealth. As the company that had been in his family for generations had grown, so had Senior's ego and his unhappiness with his personal life. Always searching for the next best thing, he cheated on his first wife—C.J. and Kane's mother—with Oakes's mother, taking advantage of her young age and adoration of him. That marriage, too, eventually failed after Senior's numerous affairs.

"I owe you for this," Daphne said, setting his coffee cup in front of him. "How about I take you to dinner next weekend?"

Have dinner with her, just the two of them? Yes, they ate out together, but usually coffee or lunch. Quick, casual meals that had a set time limit, and were held in open, bright and airy places surrounded by noise and people. But dinner was different. It was too dangerous. Too close to a date.

He tried to avoid this exact scenario with her as much as possible—had done so for the last few years, ever since he'd noticed she wasn't a little girl anymore. "There's no need. I'm happy to help. We're family, after all."

"You keep saying that," she said, opening the takeout box he'd given her, "but we're not."

"I feel like we are," he insisted, needing her to understand where he stood. She'd had a crush on him as a teenager, around the time he'd finished law school, and he didn't want a repeat of the awkward, uncomfortable experience they'd shared back then.

Zach had asked Oakes to look in on her and their mother while he was serving overseas and, as it was the first and only time Zach had ever asked him for anything, Oakes had been more than happy to do his younger brother a favor. And things had been fine until Daphne graduated from high school. But after that she took every opportunity to flirt with him—touching his arm or leg, flipping her hair and batting her eyes.

He'd been horrified. She was a child and he an adult. Thank God she'd gotten over it when she started college, but for a few months, it'd been torture.

Mainly because, as much as he hated to admit it, he'd found her attractive, too.

It had killed him that he'd allowed his baser instincts to get the better of him. That he'd been just like his father. He hadn't acted on his feelings, of course, but that hadn't made him feel any better. So he'd avoided her as much as possible and by the time they'd met up for coffee over Thanksgiving break during her freshman year at Rice, things between them were normal again.

They'd become friends and he didn't want to lose that friendship just because he was having some inappropriate, yet purely physical and normal, feelings toward her. It was simple science, really. She was a smart, beautiful, sexy woman.

And he was just a man.

She opened her breakfast and frowned down at the dry toast and scrambled eggs. "What's this?"

"I thought you might want something bland. To settle your stomach."

She eyed his omelet, loaded with cheese, peppers and sausage. "Why would I want something bland?"

"For your hangover. And you should drink more," he said, nodding toward the bottle of water he'd set by her elbow. "It'll help with the headache."

She laughed, the sound light and sunny. "Please. I'm Irish-Mexican. You insult my ancestors by such slander. I'm not hungover. I can handle my alcohol. I just…shouldn't have handled quite so much of it last night." She shoved her food aside and pulled his plate closer to her. Dug into his omelet. "Mmm…good, but needs hot sauce."

And she hopped down. He couldn't help but notice her dress riding up a bit so he turned his attention to his breakfast. Sighed, then switched it with hers.

Although he did scoop some of the hash browns onto his plate.

She came back, added enough hot sauce to her food to get his eyes watering—and he wasn't even eating it—then tucked in to her meal as if she feared it'd disappear if she didn't shovel it into her mouth as quickly as possible.

"That last shot of tequila hadn't been such a good idea," she said around a mouthful. She wrinkled her nose. "Well, the last two shots, really. Hindsight and all that, you know? Just once, I'd like to have a bit of foresight. An inner sense of worry or a niggling of doubt that warned me the wonderful, brilliant plan that popped into my head was really only misery in the making. Some sort of sixth sense to stop me from following said course. One to give me a moment's pause, time to sort through all my options and work out what I should do next. That would be wonderful and, I imagine, come in quite handy."

"You wouldn't listen to it," he said.

"What do you mean?"

"You don't like being told what to do. By anyone. Not even yourself. It's one of your flaws." He softened his words with a wink.

"I prefer to think of it as an independent streak. But you're right. I wouldn't have listened to any inner sense telling me not to drink, but I may have at least limited myself to two margaritas. Three, tops."

Margaritas, too? He wasn't even going to ask how many she'd had. "Sounds like you had a busy night. What with those men buying you drinks and all. But you still didn't have to accept them," he pointed out. "Unless they poured the alcohol down your throat?"

"Nothing like that. But they were nice. And it would've been rude to decline, right? Anyway, the only reason they were buying drinks was because of this dress. If I'd showed up in jeans and a T-shirt without the makeup, they wouldn't even have noticed me."

He doubted that. But she was right about the dress. She looked all curvy and soft in that little bit of silk. "We men are but simple creatures."

"No kidding." She poured the entire container of syrup over the half stack of pancakes he'd been looking forward to. "That's why we womenfolk love you guys so much."

He used his fork to slide a pancake from the bottom of the pile onto his plate. "We aim to please. So tell me..." he said, wondering about something he hadn't yet gotten a clear answer on—a question that had become extremely important to him. Or at least, her answer to it had. "Why did you come here? And before you tell me it was only to use the bathroom or because it was closer and you were too tired to sit in the back of a cab for the ride to your place, remember I am an attorney and therefore have learned how to spot lies."

Picking up a piece of toast, she avoided his eyes. "You want the truth?"

"That would be an interesting twist to this entire experience."

She nodded. "Okay, here it is. I came here for you."

DAPHNE NIBBLED ON a triangle of toast as Oakes stared at her, mouth open, eyes wary. Huh. Not so thrilled with the truth now, was he?

"What do you mean?" he asked, brave man that he was. But he looked as if he was bracing himself for her answer.

He wasn't doing much for her ego.

He'd said he wanted the truth and she'd given it to him, but now one of life's greatest, deepest and hardest to answer questions played in her mind.

Continue with that whole honesty thing or…?

Or lie like a dog on a hot summer's day?

She set down her toast. Yeah. She was going with option number two. Though she wasn't against combining the truth and a lie for something in between. It was easier to keep track of a fib if you threw a bit of fact in there as well.

"Let me tell you a story," she began.

He raised his eyebrows. "I'm going to need more coffee for this," he muttered as if listening to one of her entertaining tales was some hardship.

"Hey," she said as he stood up, handing him her cup to refill as well. "I'll have you know my stories are very well told."

"They are," he agreed, pouring coffee into their cups and rejoining her. "They're also long. And are filled with repetitive, and at times, irrelevant information."

She waved that away. "Now, don't get all lawyerly on me. No one likes that. Sit back and relax and drink your coffee. You wanted to know why I came here, but before I can get to that part, I have to start at the beginning."

"I already know all that. Your cousins tricked you into going out to dinner then forced you to go to a club where several men—"

"Several? I'm flattered. But it was only the two."

"Where two men vied for your attention—"

She snorted. "Believe me, it wasn't my attention they were vying for."

He frowned and she noticed his fingers had gone white on his cup. She hid a smile behind her own mug as she lifted it to take a sip.

"You got drunk," he continued in what she assumed must be his professional voice. Laying out the facts as he knew them in a deep baritone. "The cousins who took you to said club all left you alone to your own devices. You had enough sense to get a cab, but had to go to the bathroom and didn't want to travel the distance from the club to your apartment so you, in a moment of clarity, gave him my address. Have I summed up your previous statement clearly?"

She blinked. God, but he was so freaking cute with his courtroom tone and wide shoulders. Smart, funny and good-looking. Was it any wonder she was stuck on him?

"That was very concise and, yes, that is accurate," she said, turning to face him then crossing her legs. His gaze dropped, briefly, to the movement before he brought his attention back to her face. "But what I didn't tell you was the reason my cousins got it into their tiny brains that I needed a night on the town, one that preferably ended with wild, kinky sex with a stranger."

"Your cousins wanted you to hook up with a stranger?"

She lifted a shoulder. "Well, not all of them. Two were for, two were against. Nadine and Steph were hoping I'd meet my soul mate. But they all agreed that I needed a night out, that I needed to put myself out there."

"Because?"

This was the tricky part. The embarrassing part. "They think I'm heartbroken over Ricky."

"Ricky? As in your ex-boyfriend?"

"Ex-fiancé," she corrected primly. They may not have been engaged all that long but he had proposed and she had worn the diamond he'd given her. That made him her fiancé—even if only for a few short months. "He's back in town."

She watched him carefully but there was no stiffness to his shoulders. No jealousy tightening his features.

Too bad. She could use some encouragement here.

"Has Ricky contacted you?" Oakes asked, again in lawyer mode. "Does he want to get back together?"

"He's contacted me," she said slowly, "but not to get back together." Though when she'd broken up with him six months ago, she'd imagined him trying a bit harder to get her back. Guess she was easy to get over. "We met for coffee the other day and he told me he's getting married."

"I see."

"I'm fine," she told him because he was looking at her with sympathy. As if she was someone
to be pitied.

Well, why wouldn't he pity her? He thought—
as everyone did—that Ricky had been the one to
call off their engagement.

Probably because that's what she'd told them
all.

"I'm sure you are," Oakes said quickly. Too
quickly to be believed. "But if you need anything," he said, giving her hand a pat, "you know
I'm here for you, right?"

Her throat tightened. She did know that. It
wasn't just because he cared about her. It was
because he was that kind of guy. The kind who
was always there for people, for his family and
friends, someone they could count on, could lean
on.

And she was going to take horrible advantage
of that very trait, one she found super sexy and
one of the many reasons she was attracted to him.

And she was almost certain he was attracted
to her, too—he just needed some help realizing
it. And if that took a teeny, tiny bit of manipula-
tion, a few half-truths and some serious acting
chops on her part, then so be it.

She sighed, hoped it was the long, drawn-out
sigh of the brokenhearted. "Thank you. I know

I shouldn't be upset about Ricky moving on, it's just…it was a shock." Partly because she'd never thought he'd return to Houston from Dallas, where he'd moved after their breakup. Or that he'd find someone else so quickly. Someone he wanted to spend the rest of his life with after he'd begged her to come with him. When she'd told him she couldn't marry him, he'd acted devastated. Had insisted she was his one true love and he'd never get over her breaking his heart.

She'd felt horrible. Ricky was a great guy and she'd hated hurting him but it seemed he'd managed to rebound nicely from his heartache.

"The worst part," she continued, "is that he and his new girlfriend—fiancée—are getting married in a few weeks and, if you can believe this, he invited me."

"That's very…"

"Movie-of-the-week, I know. I don't think he did it to be vindictive or to rub my nose in it, though." She chewed on the inside of her lower lip thoughtfully. "I mean, he said all the right things, about how he knew it might be awkward, but that he still cared about me and hoped we could be friends and still be a part of each other's lives…"

"You don't believe him?"

"I believe he believes it. The only logical conclusion I could come up with was that Jenny—

his fiancée—thinks Ricky and I need the closure that my witnessing their wedding to him would provide."

Oakes grinned. "Glad that psychology degree is paying off."

"Hey, if I can't psychoanalyze ex-fiancés, what's the point?"

"You're not going to his wedding, are you?" Oakes asked.

"I don't want to," she admitted. Fact was, she'd rather pour hot sauce in her eyes than attend. "But I'm afraid if I don't, Jenny—or worse, Ricky—will think I'm not attending out of spite. Or because I'm still in love with him."

Oakes studied her, his gaze intense and searching. "Are you?" he asked quietly.

"Of course not."

"All I'm saying is it's only been six months since he broke things off—"

"Us splitting up was for the best," she said, realizing she sounded like a jilted lover trying to act as if she was fine and dandy with being dumped. Guilt pricked her about not clarifying *who*, exactly, had done the breaking up, but she couldn't tell Oakes the truth about her and Ricky. Not without giving too much away. "We weren't meant to be. It happens."

Oakes took her hand in his, held it lightly. "No

one would blame you if you still had feelings for him."

"Oakes, I said that I'm over him. I'm twenty-three years old—old enough to know my own feelings."

That Oakes thought she didn't was another blow to her ego and one of the reasons she couldn't admit to her feelings for him. He'd never believe her. Would think this was a continuation of the crush she'd developed on him as a teenager or that he was some kind of rebound.

"Seems to me you said the same thing when you got engaged."

Her face heated. No fair throwing her own words back at her. "I loved Ricky—at the time—and thought marrying him was the right thing to do. Turns out I was wrong."

"I hate to say I told you so—"

"Not as much as I hate to hear it," she said in a faux sweet tone.

"But I did suggest you might be rushing things with him. You were too young to make such a huge commitment."

"I wasn't too young. But I did let it happen too fast." She and Ricky had met at the end of her junior year at Rice, where he'd been a teaching assistant. Being with him had been easy. Maybe too easy. Too…comfortable. When he'd proposed on Valentine's Day she'd thought it cheesy and romantic and had let herself get swept away with the idea of being in love.

And she had loved Ricky. Just not enough. And not in the way a woman should love the man she'd agreed to marry. When he'd accepted a position at a small, private college in Dallas and asked her to move there with him, she'd realized her mistake. She'd broken off their engagement but had told everyone he was the one who'd ended things between them.

It had seemed the lesser of two evils at the time. Her family and friends were all very supportive, very sympathetic. But she hadn't fibbed to get sympathy. She'd done it to protect herself.

If the truth came out, she'd have to explain why she broke up with Ricky. And it wasn't as simple as her making a mistake in accepting his proposal in the first place.

She'd done it for Oakes.

She'd realized that if she went with Ricky to Dallas, if she let herself get swept along with wedding plans and building a future with him, she'd have to give up her dreams of being with Oakes.

She couldn't do it. She couldn't let Oakes go. Not without knowing, for sure, whether or not they were meant to be.

She squeezed Oakes's hand then slid free of his grasp. She didn't need his pity, even if Ricky had moved on rather quickly. "Not that I don't appreciate your advice—"

He snorted. "You don't appreciate my advice."

"True. Mainly because I don't need it. What I need is a favor."

"Why am I suddenly nervous?"

"Don't be such a baby. I'm not asking for a kidney. I came up with the perfect solution to my problem. In order to stem any gossip or speculation, I attend the wedding…"

"That's your perfect solution?" he asked after a moment. "I have to tell you, I really thought you'd come up with something a bit more…inspired. Or at least interesting."

"You didn't let me finish."

"You stopped talking."

"I was pausing for dramatic effect."

He leaned back, waved a hand. "Then by all means. Continue."

"As I was saying, I go to the wedding…"

"You want me to do a drumroll?"

"No need. I'm imagining one in my head. Anyway, my point is, I go with you as my date." She lifted her arms in a gesture of *ta da!*

"You want me to take you to your ex-boyfriend's—"

"Ex-fiancé."

"—wedding?"

Men. So clueless. "Yes. If I go alone, I'm either

the humiliated, sad, pathetic ex, there to weep over the loss of the groom, or I'm there to win him back. Neither option is appealing. But if I show up on the arm of one of Houston's most eligible bachelors—"

"I thought we agreed to never mention that again," he muttered.

And he was blushing. Gorgeous, smart and humble? He really was a dream come true.

"It's not like I'd bring along copies of the article or anything." Last winter a local magazine had run a piece on the city's hottest bachelors under thirty-five. Oakes, to his chagrin, had come in at number two. "Though I might bring it up in conversation. Only if there's an opening."

"Daphne," he said in warning.

"I'm kidding." Sort of. "Look, if you go with me, it helps me save face and gives both Ricky and me closure."

No one would ever doubt she was over her ex if she showed up with Oakes. Including Ricky and Jenny.

But more importantly, it would be a great chance for her and Oakes to spend some quality time together.

He studied her, as if trying to sense any hidden meaning behind her request. She kept her gaze on him, her expression open. Hopeful.

"If you think it will help," he said, "then sure. I'd love to take you to your ex's wedding."

She gave a soft whoop of delight. "Hooray! Thank you, thank you, thank you. Don't worry. I'll make sure you have a good time."

"I don't doubt that." He began clearing the bar. "And I'll do my best to play attentive date. Just tell me when and where to show up."

"The ceremony and reception are both taking place at the Sam Houston Hotel the day before Christmas." She got to her feet and set her silverware on her plate. Noticed his frown. "What's the matter?"

"I can't go with you," he said, sounding regretful. "Kane and Charlotte are getting married that same weekend."

"Oh," she said, wondering why she hadn't known the date of his brother's wedding. Probably because she wasn't invited to it and Zach had never mentioned it was taking place on Christmas Eve.

The depth of her disappointment surprised her. It wasn't as if she'd never see the man again. But her spontaneous plan had been so perfect. She'd take Oakes as her date to the wedding, saving face with Ricky and spend a lovely evening with Oakes as nonfriends. The romance of the wedding, she was sure, would help loosen Oakes's inhibitions where she was concerned.

Oakes patted her arm as he passed by, his other hand carrying his dirty plate. "I'm sure you'll find someone else to go with you."

She made a noncommittal sound. It wasn't as if she had low self-esteem—Zach often accused her of having too much. Finding a date wasn't the problem. Both men from last night had given her their numbers, telling her to call if she changed her mind. But she couldn't imagine asking a man she barely knew to attend her ex-fiancé's wedding with her.

That screamed of desperation and by God, she wasn't there yet.

Besides, if she asked them to do this favor for her, she had no idea what they'd want in return. With Oakes, she didn't have to worry about how much payback would cost her.

Plus, and this was a biggie, she didn't want to be with any other guy—not any more. Not even for an evening. She wanted Oakes.

And suddenly a new plan, an even better one, started to take shape in her mind, and she realized that she could still have him.

"Eureka!"

At the sink, he glanced over his shoulder at her. "Did you just discover gold?"

"Pretty darn close." She gathered her plate and cup and carried them to the sink. Standing at his elbow, she leaned against the counter. "I just had the best idea ever. It'll take some planning, but then, what brilliant idea doesn't?"

He ran the water, began rinsing dishes and setting them in the dishwasher. "Planning is good. But not exactly your strong suit."

Oh, if he only knew. "I plan for the important things." She pushed away from the counter and paced the length of the room, brushing his back as she passed. "We'll need to check flights, which I'm sure won't be cheap, especially for a holiday weekend. Plus I'll have to find accommodations. And I'll need to buy a few things," she muttered, making a mental checklist. "A winter coat and maybe boots." She stopped to find him staring at her curiously. "I'm assuming there's going to be snow? So, yeah, boots for sure."

He shook his head, totally confused. "What are you talking about?"

"Snow. In Pennsylvania, where Kane lives."

"It snows there in the winter," he said slowly, reaching to shut off the running water. "Why?"

He didn't have to look so suspicious. Or so worried.

She smiled. "Because I've changed my mind. The favor I want from you isn't for you to go with me to Ricky's wedding. It's for you to take me with you to Kane's."

CHAPTER FOUR

OAKES LOOKED SHOCKED, as if she had indeed not only requested a kidney, but also insisted he lay back so she could dig it out of him right now. "Excuse me?" he asked.

"I could go with you to Kane's wedding. It's a great idea." The more she thought about it, the more she began to believe it. Knowing body language was an important part of any conversation, she leaned forward, hoping to convey her need and earnestness, and ticked off all the ways her plan was brilliant. "It's the same weekend as Ricky's, which means I'd have a legitimate excuse not to attend his nuptials and, if I go with you as your plus one, no one in Houston can say I'm heartbroken or missing Ricky's wedding because I'm still in love with him or spiteful. It's the perfect solution."

"Perfect." The word said he agreed but his muttered tone suggested otherwise. "Except for the fact that Kane's wedding is in Pennsylvania."

"Even better."

A change of scenery would do them good. It

might be easier for Oakes to stop seeing her as only Zach's little sister, as only a friend, if they were away from Houston. Unfortunately, they couldn't escape the Bartasavich family entirely as most of the family would be at the wedding in Shady Grove, but she and Oakes would have plenty of time and opportunity to be alone.

She'd make sure of it.

"Weren't you invited to the wedding yourself?" Oakes asked as they both sat back down.

"Nope. Why would I be?"

She barely knew Kane or C.J., Oakes's older brothers. Oh, they'd spent some time together at the hospital when Zach was first brought back to the States after he'd been injured. But it wasn't as if she had anything in common with C.J.—Clinton Bartasavich, Jr.—the current CEO of Bartasavich Enterprises, who was so far out of her tax bracket, social sphere and peer group, they might as well be on different planets. And the same was true with the long-haired, tattooed Kane, who preferred biker boots over power suits and owned and operated a bar in Shady Grove, Pennsylvania.

Oakes shifted. Cleared his throat. "I thought you and Charlotte had become friends."

"We did. Sort of. Just not the type of friends you feel the need to invite the other to an out-of-state wedding that's taking place on Christmas Eve."

Daphne liked Charlotte Ellison, Kane's fiancée.

She was smart and funny and it had been great having an RN with them in the hospital to cut through all the medical terms. She'd been extremely patient about explaining things to Daphne and her mother. But it wasn't like they'd become BFFs after spending a few days together—even though those were important days in Daphne's life.

Realizing Oakes was grasping at straws, looking for any reason not to take her with him to Shady Grove, she frowned. He wasn't doing much for her ego, that was for sure. "Do you...do you already have a plus one for the wedding?"

A distinct possibility given that he was seeing Sylvie. But Daphne couldn't imagine Oakes bringing some woman he was casually dating halfway across the country to his brother's wedding.

Talk about a commitment.

"No," he said slowly, in that way people did when they were trying to find an excuse to get out of doing something they didn't want to do. "I hadn't planned on bringing a date."

She laid her hand on his knee. "But there's no reason you can't bring one, right?"

She let her hand linger on his leg. It was nice, touching him, feeling the warmth of him through his jeans. But mostly she liked how he reacted to her touch. As if it made him uncomfortable and not in a he-found-her-repulsive way, but the opposite. He must have felt the spark between them, too, and was fighting his baser instincts for all he was worth.

A girl could dream, right?

He brightened suddenly and she would have bet her last dollar that he gave himself a silent *eureka*.

And that made her nervous.

"You can go with Zach," he said. Just as he'd done last night, he covered her hand with his briefly and then slid it away from his person. But she noticed his fingers hadn't been completely steady. "I'm sure he'd be thrilled to take you."

"As you're well aware, Zach is never thrilled to do anything. But you're right. He would take me. *If* he was going."

"Zach isn't going?" he asked. "Why not?"

She shrugged. "Says he's not up to traveling."

As excuses went, it was a valid one, seeing as how he was still recovering from his injuries and in rehab, learning to live without the use of his right arm and leg, both of which had been amputated.

But it was still an excuse.

Zach went out of his way to have as little to do with his father's side of his family as possible. And if that meant missing his brother's wedding, then so be it. Though out of all his brothers, Kane was the one Zach seemed to like the most, but that wasn't saying much. About the only two people in the world her brother cared about were her and their mother.

"I'm cutting him some slack and not bugging him about it because he has been through a physically and emotionally traumatic event," Daphne continued. "But I think what's really stopping him is that he doesn't want to travel in the wheelchair." He hadn't been fitted for prosthetics yet and still used a wheelchair to get around. "I don't think he wants people feeling sorry for him."

Oakes exhaled heavily, shoved a hand through his hair. "Yeah. I can understand that." He got to his feet, stepped away, then turned again. "Is this the real reason you came here last night? To ask me to take you to the wedding?"

No. She'd come to tell him she loved him, wanted to marry him and have his babies.

Thank God she hadn't confessed those things.

Damn tequila. Not only was it some sort of legal truth serum, but it also gave people delusions of grandeur.

"You think it's a bad idea?" she asked, wide-eyed and innocent. "Us going together?" He opened his mouth, probably to say yes, but she kept right on talking. "Because I think it'll be fun. I'm a great date, honestly. I promise you'll have a good time."

"What about the holiday? Won't your mother

be upset about you not being home for Christmas?"

"She'll understand my reasons. Plus, I can fly back early Christmas morning, be home in time for dinner."

He was going to say no. She could see it in his eyes, in how he held himself, so stiffly and unyielding.

She stood, crossed to stand in front of him. "Please, Oakes," she said softly, not realizing until this very second how badly she wanted him to say yes. How much she needed him to say yes. If the moment they'd shared six years ago on her graduation day was the beginning of her feelings for him, the beginning of their friendship, then this moment, right here, right now, was the turning point. His decision would either take their relationship to the next level...or leave them to crash and burn without ever having a chance. "Please."

He scratched the side of his neck. Sighed, then nodded. "I'd love to have you with me at the wedding."

He wouldn't. That much was clear in his conflicted, tight expression. In his unenthusiastic response. Guilt nudged her. Hard. She shoved it aside. She had nothing to feel guilty about. She wasn't tricking him. Wasn't lying to him.

Aren't you?

Stupid inner voice. *No one asked you.*

Still, she kept the hug she gave him brief, didn't press her advantage—or her breasts—against him, choosing to step back quickly. "Thank you. You won't regret this. And, if you ever need a favor, I'm your girl."

He shoved his hands into his pockets and gave another nod. Rocked back on his heels. "What are friends for?"

She kept right on smiling. "Indeed."

"I already have my flight booked, but can probably get you a seat on it." He took his phone out, checking the information. "Once it's all set, I'll text you the travel and hotel details."

"That's okay. I can book my own flight, get my own place to stay."

"You're my guest. I'll handle it."

Meaning he'd not only make the reservations, but also pay for them. All her travel expenses and, she was sure, he'd insist on footing the bill while they were in Shady Grove.

That was not what she was after here. She didn't want his money, didn't care about the size of his bank account. His family and his wealth were actually part of the problems standing between them. She refused to take advantage of him that way.

"I'll book my own flight," she told him, not quite sharply but sternly enough for him to know she was dead serious. "And my own hotel room. Both of which I will pay for, on my own."

"Daphne, it's not a problem."

It was. Too many people saw only dollar signs when they looked at him. Saw only what he and his connections could do for them.

She saw him.

"Oakes," she said, mimicking his indulgent tone, "you're doing me the favor here, remember? I should be offering to pay for *your* airfare and hotel. But, since that's well out of my financial range, I'll just finish cleaning up here instead."

Clearing the bar, she gave herself a mental pat on the back.

She'd done it. She was going to Shady Grove with Oakes. No, that hadn't been her original plan, but in all honesty, her original plan had sucked and the backup she'd come up with on the spot hadn't been much better. This one, though, was a keeper. They'd get to spend an entire weekend together instead of just one evening. She was certain that once they were out of Houston, they'd be able to connect on a different level. One that left friendship way behind.

OVER AN HOUR later Oakes pulled into a driveway across town. He'd just dropped off Daphne at her apartment and was due at his mother's house to watch the Texans' play the Patriots with his stepfather and younger half brother, but before he enjoyed some quality family time, he had to visit the one and only member of his family who couldn't stand him.

Actually, Zach was the only person, period, who didn't like Oakes.

He hated to admit how much that bugged him.

Still, Oakes may be easygoing, but he didn't back down from doing what was right. Even if it threatened to ruin a perfectly good Sunday.

One that had started with a gorgeous woman with messy dark hair, wearing a clingy, wrinkled red dress, eating his breakfast and somehow convincing him to take her halfway across the country to his brother's wedding.

Not that she'd needed to do much convincing. He was nothing if not accommodating, especially to the people he cared about. It was a trait he usually took pride in—being there for his family and friends. At this moment, though, that particular trait seemed less like a good quality and more like a glaring flaw.

C.J. was always telling him that his generous nature was going to get him into trouble one of these days. But Oakes hadn't listened. For one thing, C.J. was generous in his own right—mainly with his opinions, most of which rolled off of Oakes's back. For another, C.J. was most like their father and if there was one person Oakes wanted to be as opposite from as possible, it was Senior.

His father was selfish, self-involved and arrogant. He didn't do anything for anyone unless there was something in it for him. So, of course, when Daphne—his friend—had asked Oakes for a favor, he'd wanted to do all he could to help... even if it might cost him his sanity.

He really, really hoped she didn't wear that red dress to the wedding. Not when all he could think about was peeling it off of her.

He climbed out of his car, shoved his hands into his coat pockets and hunched his shoulders against the cool, winter breeze. Time for some damage control.

He followed the walk toward the neat, ranch-style house. Multicolored lights lined the windows and a fat, green wreath with a huge red bow decorated the door. A six-foot-tall, blow-up Santa, complete with red cheeks and a jolly smile, hefted a bag of toys at the far corner of the house, while ceramic versions of Mary and Joseph, kneeling on either side of a peacefully sleeping Jesus, took center stage in the front yard. Though it was daytime, the sun shining brightly, a spotlight had been left on, pointing directly at the trio.

Climbing the three steps up to the small front porch, he sidestepped a quartet of plastic carolers—hands holding song books, mouths open in an unsettling way—and rang the doorbell. A dog barked from inside but other than that, there were no hints of movement. He glanced at the driveway. Only his car and Zach's pickup. During their drive to her apartment this morning, Daphne had explained that her mother would be at Mass until past noon, then she called Zach to tell him she'd be by in a few hours to pick up her dog, Cyrus. Oakes couldn't imagine his brother dog-sitting, but after she'd hung up, Daphne had said that Zach and Cyrus had bonded since the accident.

Probably because Cyrus couldn't talk. Zach preferred quiet.

Oakes pressed the bell again, heard a definite *ding dong*, then more barking. But no footsteps. No voice calling that they were coming.

Good thing he was a patient man.

He leaned back against the siding and crossed his legs at the ankles. The wrought-iron railing to the right had been removed so that a wide, wooden ramp could be installed to accommodate Zach's wheelchair. The doctors said it would be at least another month before Zach was ready to be fitted with prosthetics, but Oakes didn't doubt Zach would eventually walk again under his own power. Until that time came, Susan had done everything she could to make her house accessible to her son.

The barking got closer, followed by a male

voice saying something that had the dog quieting. Oakes pushed away from the wall and turned. The door opened only a few inches, but Cyrus squeezed his big body through, his tail wagging fiercely when he spotted Oakes. He barked, two quick yaps, then pressed his quivering body against Oakes's leg.

Oakes stumbled a step before catching his balance. He crouched. Scratched behind the golden retriever's ears. "Hey, bud. Hey, boy." Cyrus attempted to give him some love in the form of sloppy licks, but Oakes leaned back and gently shoved the dog's head away. "No French kissing, remember? We talked about this. I'm just not into you that way."

Cyrus sat on his haunches, barked as if to say Oakes didn't know what he was missing, then almost knocked him over in his zeal to sniff at the carolers.

Oakes straightened to find the door fully open and Zach watching him, his dark gaze hooded. Zach's black hair was longer than it had been in years, the ends brushing the collar of his faded USMC T-shirt. A full beard covered his cheeks and chin, though it did nothing to mask the gauntness of his brother's cheeks, or the scarring on his right temple. He wore grey sweats and his left foot was bare. His right foot was gone, along with the lower half of his leg and his right arm, all the way up past his elbow.

"Cyrus, go," Zach told the dog.

Taking his cue, Cyrus raced down the ramp, sniffed all four of the tires of Oakes's car before deciding to pee on one.

Oakes pursed his lips as the dog drained his seemingly huge bladder on his tire. "New trick you taught him?" he asked Zach.

"No trick. Dog just has good instincts. What are you doing here?"

Zach was, as always, less than happy to see any member of the Bartasavich family. Oakes tried not to let it bother him. No sense getting angry about it. He couldn't change Zach. Couldn't change what the real problem was—the circumstances of Zach's birth.

Though if anyone had a right to be touchy about Zach coming along, it was Oakes. His mother, after all, was the one who'd been duped, the one who'd trusted Susan Lynch with caring for her son, only to have that trust thrown in her face when a nineteen-year-old Susan came to her saying she was pregnant with Senior's child.

Still, it didn't matter what Zach's particular problem with Oakes was. His brother had issues with every member of the Bartasavich family—he just seemed to have the biggest issue with Oakes.

And that was why Oakes was here today—to

make sure Zach wouldn't have a problem with Daphne going to Shady Grove with him. It was the least he could do, Oakes figured, and if the situation had been reversed and he had a younger sister who was going to be traveling halfway across the country with one of his half brothers, or even a friend, he'd want to be told about it.

Not for the first time he thanked God he didn't have any sisters, only a niece. And Estelle had Kane, her father, to worry about her. To look after her. Even if it was from a distance, as Estelle lived in Houston and Kane was in Shady Grove.

"Just thought I'd drop by," Oakes said smoothly. He may be a nice guy, but that didn't mean he couldn't lie when needed. "See how you're doing."

"I'm fine," Zach said, then whistled for the dog.

Cyrus ran up the ramp and slipped into the house and Oakes knew if he didn't enter, Zach would simply shut the door on his face and go on with his day as if Oakes had never been there.

Some days this particular brother bugged the hell right out of him.

Still, he'd cut the guy some slack. He'd lost a lot—not just his arm and leg, but the military career he'd always planned on.

Zach used the hand control to back up his motorized wheelchair and Oakes took the opportunity to step inside the entryway and shut the door behind him.

Zach's flinty gaze went from Oakes to the door and back to Oakes. "I'm getting ready to watch the game," he said flatly.

Oakes checked the time on his phone. "It doesn't start for another forty minutes."

To settle the matter—and because it'd be a cold day in hell before Zach offered him a seat—Oakes brushed past him and walked down the short hall to the living room and sat on an armchair in the corner. He'd been in the house only once before, when Zach was finally discharged from the hospital. Daphne had asked him and C.J. to help move furniture around, making it easier for Zach to maneuver through the house in his wheelchair. But as soon as they'd finished, they'd left, not wanting Susan to know they'd been there.

Bad blood. So much of it between Susan and Rosalyn, Zach and…hell…most everybody he was related to. At least on Zach's end.

Forget Senior's business acumen, what he really excelled at was hurting people. At least, he had until his stroke. Now he couldn't even feed himself.

Oakes wasn't sure if that was karma or overkill. No one deserved to be stuck inside a useless body, unable to communicate or take care of themselves. Not even his father.

Now, Oakes took the time to check out the house where Zach and Daphne had been raised.

It was small, but warm and well-maintained. A far cry from their father's huge mansion, or the roomy, open house where Oakes himself had grown up with his mother, stepfather and younger brothers.

The living room, like the rest of the house, was bright and airy and colorful, the walls a muted green, bursts of color coming from pillows on the sofa and the paintings on the wall. A tall leafy plant stood in a sun-drenched corner, while a large, flat-screen TV on the wall flashed the Texans' pregame show.

The soft whir of a motor grew louder and a moment later, Zach rolled into the room.

Oakes grinned and settled deeper into the chair, a man not going anywhere. "It's good to see you. How's the rehab progressing?"

Zach steered the chair to a spot next to the couch, turned it so he faced the television. "Fine."

"You look good."

The only response to that was a low sound in the back of Zach's throat.

But Oakes had spoken the truth. When Zach had first arrived stateside after the explosion, they hadn't thought he would make it. He'd been severely hurt, had internal injuries and burns, not to mention the loss of his arm and leg. But he'd pulled through. The bruises had faded, the burns had mostly healed, leaving only a few scars, and he seemed to have accepted his limitations.

Oakes had been worried that Zach would fall into a depression. Never exactly happy—not even as a kid—he'd been prone to moodiness and melancholy, been bitter and resentful about his lot in life. Pissed at the world in general, the Bartasaviches in particular. With all the news about military personnel returning home without enough support and guidance, suffering from their external injuries and PTSD, Oakes had worried Zach would have trouble finding his strength, his new purpose in life.

He'd been wrong. Zach had not only found some inner strength, but he'd also become determined to live as normal a life as possible, going so far as to push away any offers of help.

Still, it wasn't easy seeing his brother in that chair. Oakes wanted to fix it, as he knew his older brothers wanted to, as well.

"Spit out what you came here to say," Zach said, his eyes on the local sports anchor, who was discussing the Texans' offensive line. "Before the game starts."

No invitation to stay and watch the game. Then again, Zach would probably rather invite Oakes to take a quick trip to hell than to spend a few hours in his company.

Not sure where to begin, Oakes shifted in his

chair, hoping inspiration would strike. When it didn't, he forged ahead. "I heard you're not attending Kane's wedding."

"Word gets around fast."

That was it. No explanation. No excuse, though he sure as hell had a couple of good ones. "I'd be happy to travel with you if—"

"No."

"Are you sure? Kane will want you there and—"

"He'll survive," Zach said dryly. "It's good for a Bartasavich to hear the word *no* from time to time. Keeps them humble."

Irritation climbed Oakes's spine. He ignored it. He'd always given Zach leeway, had let him lash out, and he sure as hell couldn't change that now, not when his brother had been through so much.

"If you came here to talk me in to going," Zach said, "you've wasted your time."

"I didn't. I came to tell you I'm taking Daphne. To the wedding. In Shady Grove," he added, just to be clear.

That got his brother's attention. Zach turned—first his head, then his upper body, then finally, slowly, his wheelchair—and narrowed his eyes. "What?"

"I've asked Daphne to be my plus one at Kane's wedding," Oakes said, deciding Zach didn't need to know Daphne had actually invited herself to fill that position. "I thought you should know."

"Why?"

That stunned him. "Excuse me?"

"Why did you think I should know?"

"Because she's your sister."

Zach nodded. "She is my sister. But she doesn't need my permission to go on a date." He raised his eyebrows, the expression reminding Oakes of their father—a comparison he was sure Zach would hate. "Unless you're the one asking for my permission?"

Oakes sighed. He couldn't win with Zach. Sometimes he wondered why he even tried. "Not permission. I just thought it would be…considerate. Letting you know. Guess I was wrong."

"Guess you were," Zach said quietly, watching him intensely, as if trying to figure something out.

Oakes stood up, hands in his pockets, but there was nothing more to say. "See you around," he simply said, but he knew that he wouldn't. Not unless he made the effort to seek out Zach.

No response, not that Oakes expected one. He walked out, stopping to give Cyrus a pat on the head before heading back out into the crisp day, feeling uncertain and unsettled, as if he had unfinished business.

It's good for a Bartasavich to hear the word no *from time to time.*

An image of Daphne as she'd looked last night on his porch flashed through Oakes's mind, then one of her this morning, her makeup rubbed off, her hair a mess. Want hit him, hard and piercing, in his chest. He rubbed the area over his heart. Blew out a heavy breath.

No one, not even a Bartasavich, could get everything he wanted. Not all the time. So, yeah, Zach had been right. It was good for a Bartasavich to hear the word *no.*

But that didn't mean he had to like it.

CHAPTER FIVE

"IT WON'T WORK, you know."

At Zach's words, Daphne studied her mother's huge dining room table. She was silently counting place settings and chairs. "It'll be fine. If we get any extras, we'll set up a card table or two in the living room."

They never knew how many people were going to show up to their mother's weekly Sunday dinner. Some weeks it was relatively peaceful with only a dozen aunts, uncles, cousins and assorted neighbors. But that one week a few years ago when Zach was home on leave they'd maxed out at fifty-two guests. Thank goodness it had been late spring and they'd been able to set up extra tables outside.

"I'm not talking about dinner," Zach said, something in his tone warning her she was about to get an earful. The only problem was, she couldn't imagine what she'd done to earn herself one of Zach's lectures. "I'm talking about you going after Oakes."

Oh, well. That. Yep, that would definitely put Zach into lecture mode.

She folded a napkin, her movements slow and deliberate. "First of all, I don't care for your tone. Second of all, what is that even supposed to mean? Going after? You make me sound like I'm a bounty hunter or something."

And how, in all that was good and holy, had he found out? She hadn't even properly celebrated her successful first step in her budding, possible relationship with Oakes, let alone told anyone about it.

"Don't play dumb," Zach told her, but his tone had improved, wasn't quite so low and harsh. "It's beneath you."

That was her big brother. Always building her up, always telling her she could do anything, be anything she wanted.

Always thinking she was better than she was.

"You're right." She set down the napkin. Picked up another. "It is beneath me. I take it you've somehow heard about my accompanying Oakes to Kane's wedding?"

He nodded and her brain went into overdrive. The only two people who knew about it so far were her and Oakes. And while she'd certainly planned on letting her family know she would be out of town the weekend before Christmas, including Christmas Eve, she hadn't planned on sharing that tidbit until she absolutely had to.

Preferably the night before she left.

So that meant...

"Oakes told you?" she asked.

"He stopped by a few hours ago. Said he thought I should know."

She wasn't sure whether to laugh at Oakes being so predictably nice, so forthright, or be pissed that he'd run to their brother and basically tattled on her.

Something to figure out later when Zach wasn't watching her so closely.

She shoved a handful of forks at him. "If you're going to be in here, at least make yourself useful."

He took the forks in his hand before setting them down on the table so he could pick one up at a time, even that easy movement not coming naturally. He was right-handed—or had been right-handed. Now he had to relearn everything— signing his name, eating, reaching for a door handle. Stupid, everyday things that most people took for granted he had to stop and think about. Figure out how to make it work.

But he was here. Alive and, while not exactly whole, not even close to being broken.

He was her hero. Always had been. Always would be.

He spread a napkin on his lap then put the forks

on it before moving around the table, using his left hand to work the wheelchair then stopping at each plate to place a fork next to it. She turned her attention back to folding the napkins, had to bite her lower lip to stop herself from telling him never mind, that she'd set the table. She hated seeing him struggle, even a little bit, but she knew he had to learn how to do things for himself. That he wanted to.

Even if it took him twice as long as it would have before his injuries.

She wouldn't coddle him like their mother and grandmother, wouldn't try to do everything for him, wouldn't try to make his life easier. His life wasn't going to be easy. But he was strong enough to get through it—was strong enough, smart enough and stubborn enough to succeed on his own. And he deserved to have that sense of pride, of accomplishment that came with overcoming a huge, life-changing obstacle.

Just like he'd always taught her to be strong, to be independent. To think for herself and make her own choices. He'd always believed in her, always supported her decisions, even when he knew she'd end up crashing and burning.

He'd always been there to cheer her on to victory. Or to lend a helping hand in getting back on her feet. So she would now do the same for him.

However, if he changed, turned into some overbearing, overprotective, bossy older brother, she would swiftly kick him in his shin. And not feel bad about it one bit.

"So Oakes told you I asked him to take me to the wedding?" she asked when Zach was on the opposite side of the table.

He paused, his head lifting like a predator catching a scent of prey.

Or a brother catching a whiff of a lie. "He said he invited you."

Of course he had. Oakes, always so sweet, probably thought he was somehow protecting her by not telling Zach what really happened. Sweet, but seriously misguided.

She folded the last napkin. Slid the pile of knives toward Zach. "He probably didn't want to tell you that I showed up at his door at three o'clock this morning. Drunk. Or that I asked him to take me to Kane's wedding so I wouldn't have to suffer the humiliation of being in Houston when Ricky gets married."

"Ricky's getting married?"

At least someone hadn't known how quickly her ex had moved on.

"Yep. In two weeks. People are already placing bets on whether or not his fiancée is pregnant."

"And it bothers you?" Zach asked in a quiet, contemplative tone. "Ricky moving on?"

She bristled. Her feelings were no one else's

business, not even her brother's. She did have some pride after all and she refused to…to…pine for her ex.

Though she had set herself up to play the part of the rejected, dumped fiancée.

She really should have thought this through more.

"Of course not." She kept her gaze averted, focused on a fork he'd just put down. "I'm… glad Ricky's found someone who can make him happy."

Zach snorted.

She slammed her hands on her hips. "And what, exactly, is that sound supposed to mean?"

"Just that you're full of shit."

"Thank you, so much, for your support, brother. I thought you'd be thrilled to see how well I'm handling this. Weren't you the one who told me Ricky wasn't good enough for me?"

"Ricky's an idiot. You were lucky he broke things off with you."

If Ricky *had* broken things off, that might be true. "It didn't feel lucky," she said.

"Ricky wasn't for you." Zach studied her intently. A lesser woman would have squirmed under his scrutiny but she knew his tricks. The heavy, see-through-you-to-your-soul looks, the I-have-all-day-to-wait-for-you-to-say-something-incriminating-or-to-blurt-out-the-truth silences, the flinty, man-of-few-words act. He wouldn't break *her*, by God. "And neither is Oakes."

Ah. So that's what he was getting at. "Is this the part of the conversation where you expect me to deny being interested in Oakes?"

"Yes," he said, the word coming out like a bullet. "And as forcefully as possible."

She batted her eyelashes at him, keeping her mouth firmly shut.

"Aw, hell," he said on a drawn-out sigh. "I knew it."

"Knew what?"

"That this whole wedding thing was one of your schemes."

She rolled her eyes. Glanced behind her at the open doorway when she heard the back door open, followed by the sound of her Aunt Regina's and Uncle Lonny's greetings as they entered the kitchen. "I'm not a cartoon villain, Zach. I don't scheme. I plan. There's a difference."

He snorted. "You plan your diabolical schemes."

Her lips twitched. "Diabolical? Big word. Are you studying for the SATs?"

He flushed. "I've been doing a lot of reading," he said, his tone defensive.

"And it's improving your vocabulary. But your imagination is working overtime. Look, it's very simple. If I'm not in Houston then our cousins can't ambush me again into going out and searching for a replacement Ricky. Nor do I have to worry about everyone expecting me to burst into tears at the mere mention of his name. Like I already mentioned, attending Kane's wedding will save me from a weekend of humiliation and awkwardness." She patted his shoulder. "It's a win-win-win situation."

"Is that what you told Oakes? Because he's just gullible enough to buy it."

"He's not gullible, he's...nice. You should try it sometime."

"You fed him a line of bullshit and he fell for it. Because we both know you're not afraid to tell our cousins *no* or to refuse to go to Ricky's wedding, regardless of what people might think. No one forces you to do anything."

Why did he have to know her so well? "True. My big brother taught me to stand up for myself," she told him with a grin.

"Only because I knew I wouldn't always be around to save you from yourself and your schemes when they backfired. Which they always do."

"Okay, first of all, stop saying schemes, it makes you sound like some sort of cheesy, low-rent superhero. Secondly, my plans don't always backfire."

"Just usually."

She set down a spoon with a sharp crack. "Well, usually isn't always, is it?"

And the important plans, the ones she'd worked hard on, like being accepted into graduate school and getting that internship at an inner-city high school, had worked out just fine, thank you very much.

And so would this one.

"Look," Zach said, "we all know you had a crush on Oakes—"

"Had. As in past tense. As in over six years ago." The voices in the kitchen grew louder, meaning more and more people were arriving. "A crush I got over the moment I laid eyes on Curt Nelson during freshman-year seminar."

"Exactly," Zach said, as stubborn as always. "You're too old and too smart to confuse a teenage crush with something more."

"You're right. I *am* too smart to confuse the two."

She knew he didn't mean to be insulting but, damn it, he was. She was an adult and she made her own decisions, something he'd always encouraged. It wasn't as if she'd mooned over Oakes from the time she was seventeen. She'd had boyfriends. Several. Curt had lasted through spring break her first year of college and she and Louie Delcagno had been together a year before they broke up and she met Ricky.

For God's sake, she'd even been engaged. So no. No mooning. No pining. She'd known that while she was in school a relationship with Oakes was out of her reach. Though it hadn't been easy, letting go of the dream of being with him. Especially since she'd always believed that if she worked hard enough, she could have whatever she wanted.

"All right," Zach said in a tone she knew was supposed to inject calm into the situation. Or, more accurately, into her. "You don't have a crush on Oakes. Great. But it's not fair for you to use him to get out of town. Just don't go to Ricky's wedding. You don't owe him or anyone else anything. Not even an explanation."

"I know." She sat in one of the chairs. "Do you really think I'm using Oakes?"

"You asked him to take you to a wedding in Pennsylvania."

It sounded bad when Zach said it. "I'm paying my own way. And maybe, maybe this will give us—me and Oakes—a chance to…get to know each other better."

Zach went still, eerily so, and for a long period of time. She held the edge of a butter knife under his nose and he jerked his head back. "What are you doing?" he said.

"Checking to see if you're still breathing."

He swiped the knife from her. "You just said you don't have a crush on him."

"I don't. Crushes are for children. Although I suppose you could, technically, define my feelings for Robert Downey, Jr. as a crush…"

"Can we stay focused?" Zach asked, though how he managed to do so while barely moving his lips was a mystery.

Focus, yes. Right. "I have feelings for Oakes." Real, true feelings. "I think… I think I'm in love with him."

Zach paled. "Not. Funny."

"I would never joke about love. There's something between us. Something real. What's wrong with exploring that, seeing where it leads, if it leads anywhere?"

"And tricking him into taking you to Pennsylvania will accomplish that?"

"It'll give us a chance to be together without being reminded, every day and in every way, of our very complicated relationship. It'll give us a chance to get to know each other as Daphne and Oakes, two unattached people. Not as Daphne, your younger sister. Or Oakes, your older brother."

"Half brother."

Zach always reminded everyone that Oakes, Kane and C.J. were his half siblings. It was his way of separating himself from them. Making them seem less important.

Oakes never did that.

Just one of the many differences between the two men she cared for most in the world.

"You're making a mistake," Zach told her flatly.

"If I am, then it's my mistake to make. My heart I'm risking," she told him quietly.

He shook his head. "Don't fool yourself. The Bartasaviches are hard. Cold. You want to believe Oakes is different, but he's not. He'll use you up and toss you aside when he gets bored or something better comes along."

"Oakes would never hurt me."

"He's a Bartasavich."

And that, in Zach's mind, said it all.

"Yes, he's a Bartasavich," she said as a cheer went up in the living room. The Texans must have scored. "So are you."

"Don't rub it in."

She couldn't help it. She grinned. Leaned down to hug him, a hug he returned with his good arm. "I'll be fine." Straightening, she winked. "Oakes won't know what hit him."

She walked out to greet the rest of her family as Zach muttered, "That's what I'm afraid of."

OAKES SAT ON the edge of his mother's sofa, his bottle of beer held loosely in his hand, dangling between his knees, his eyes glued to the large, flat-screen TV on the wall. The center snapped the ball and Tom Brady fell back. J. J. Watt shook off one Patriots linesman, then a second.

"Go, go, go," he muttered as Watt bore down on Brady, then made a flying tackle, sacking the Patriots quarterback. "Yeah!"

He surged to his feet almost simultaneously with his stepfather, Michael, and seventeen-year-old brother, Gregory. They exchanged high fives. There were still eight minutes to go in the game, plenty of time for Brady to pull one of his amazing comebacks, but right now, the Texans were up by six.

The Patriots called a time-out.

"Your turn for snack run," Gregory told Oakes. Greg was a perfect blend of his parents, with Michael's dark auburn hair and their mother's blue eyes. He was tall and lanky, like his father, but he might still fill out the way Dusty, their twenty-year-old brother, had once he'd graduated from high school. He handed Oakes the empty chip bowl. "More guacamole. And see if Mom made those bacon-wrapped shrimp."

Since it really was his turn for a snack run, Oakes would take the bowl. But first he had something to do. He reached up—hating that his youngest brother had three inches on him—and slapped Greg upside his fat head.

"Ow." Scowling, Greg rubbed the spot. "What the hell was that for?"

Oakes grinned. "You forgot to say please."

It was his job to make sure his younger brothers didn't get too cocky for their own good.

Not that he'd ever been able to get through to Zach.

Greg turned to Michael, who'd retaken his seat in his recliner. "Dad! Did you see that? He assaulted me."

Michael considered his son's argument. At sixty, he looked ten years younger, despite his receding hairline. He nodded once, looking very much like the hard-ass judge he was, a decision having been made. "Overruled."

And he flipped up the leg rest, leaned back and laughed at a beer commercial.

Greg shoved the empty bowl at Oakes again, forcing Oakes to take it. "Please get me some more goddamn guacamole."

"Gregory Michael," their mother said sharply as she walked into the den carrying a tray of assorted appetizers, including the shrimp Greg wanted. "That had better not have been you cursing!"

Greg blanched. Michael might have the authority to send criminals to prison but every male in the house knew Rosalyn was the one you didn't mess with. She was tough as nails, a true Southern belle who didn't take any sass, always wore lipstick and doted on her husband and sons.

When she wasn't boxing their ears to keep them in line.

Rosalyn set the tray on the glossy coffee table then straightened and raised one eyebrow at her youngest. "Well?"

Greg glanced around, but Michael ignored his son's pleading look and helped himself to more food. From behind Rosalyn, Oakes pointed at Greg then used that same finger to make a slitting motion across his throat.

Greg's mouth flattened but then he grinned. Oakes was surprised a cartoon lightbulb didn't appear over the kid's head with whatever brilliant idea he'd come up with. "No, ma'am, it wasn't me. It was Oakes."

Michael snorted. "Son," he murmured, "you'd best learn to either keep your voice down if you're going to cuss, or get better at coming up with a believable lie."

"Oakes," Rosalynn declared, her hands on her slim hips. She was a woman not to be messed with in her demure, Sunday-best dark green knee-length skirt, cream-colored sweater set and the pearl necklace Michael had given her on their first anniversary. She skewered her youngest with a look guaranteed to make a man's—or, in this case, an almost man—balls shrink. Oakes almost felt bad for Greg.

Almost.

"Do you expect me to believe," she continued, "that it was Oakes I heard, clear as day, taking the Lord's name in vain? On a Sunday—a holy day, mind you. In my house?"

Greg, eyes wide, cocky grin nowhere in sight, swallowed audibly. "I'd sure appreciate it if you did. Believe it, I mean."

Rosalyn's sigh was a work of art—part aggrieved female surrounded by idiotic males, part disappointed mother, wondering where she went wrong. "Michael," she said, turning to her husband, "I expect you to do something about this."

Michael nodded solemnly. "You can count on me. Soon as the game's over, I'll take him out back to the woodshed."

Though her stance remained unyielding, her lips twitched. "We don't have a woodshed."

"I'll get right on building one," Michael promised. "After the game."

"Why?" she asked the heavens, adding to the drama in her tone with a good old-fashioned hand toss. "Why must I be surrounded by men?"

"You're extremely lucky in that regard," Michael said. "But not—" he grabbed her hand and pulled her onto his lap "—as lucky as we are."

"Michael!" she squealed, tugging her skirt down, her cheeks pink. "Mind yourself!"

"Yes, ma'am," he said, sounding much like Greg had a moment ago. He nuzzled her neck.

"Now, darlin', you know we'd be lost without you."

She swatted at him halfheartedly. "Oh, now, go on with you. Finish your game. And let me up, I have dinner to prepare."

But she softened her rebuke with a smile and a kiss to his forehead. Greg rolled his eyes and attacked the snacks, but Oakes leaned back and grinned. That, *that* was what he wanted when he got married. A partnership like they had. He knew love played a big part, so did mutual respect, but the commonalities between his mother and stepfather couldn't be discounted.

They were the same age, had similar backgrounds, tastes and personalities. They supported each other's goals, parented as a team and never took the other for granted. Even their few differences—Michael's let-it-be personality often annoyed Rosalyn, who could worry about anything and everything and usually did—complemented each other.

They weren't perfect, Oakes thought as Michael helped Rosalyn to her feet then gave her a light swat on her rear, and their marriage wasn't perfect, but it was the closest Oakes had seen to it. He may have been only ten when his parents divorced, but even then he'd known their relationship was dysfunctional at best. Senior was too selfish to be a true partner. He took advantage of Rosalyn's love and trust, focusing solely on his own needs, thinking he could make up for his mistakes with expensive gifts, an abundance of charm and false promises.

It had worked, too. For far too long. Until his mother had found the strength and resolve to leave him. She'd been rewarded with a second chance and had shown Oakes what a healthy, loving, long-lasting relationship looked like.

Now he was starting to think it was time he found one of his own.

An image of Daphne flashed through his mind. Not of her barefoot on his porch, or smiling drunkenly at him from the couch, but of how she'd looked this morning sitting next to him at the bar, her face clean, her hair wild. He was attracted to her. He refused to feel guilty about it. Mainly because he'd never act on it.

Even if he hadn't been able to get her off of his mind for more than fifteen minutes at a time today.

"I was hoping you'd bring Sylvie to dinner today," his mom said, dragging him back to the present moment. Bringing his thoughts to the woman he should have been thinking about. "She's such a lovely young lady."

Sylvie was lovely. Lovely and intelligent and interesting. They'd met at one of his mother's fund-raising events, had hit it off immediately.

When the evening had wound down, he'd asked her out, knowing instinctively she was a woman he could have a future with. They not only had common interests, but also shared a social circle and had similar backgrounds. Sylvie was the perfect match for him. Even his mother approved.

As she should have, considering she'd been the one to introduce him and Sylvie to each other.

And while he'd never worried about whether or not his mother would like the women he dated, he was at a point in his life where marriage, children and the future were on his mind. And that future would be a hell of a lot smoother if his mother and wife got along.

"It's a little too soon to be inviting her to family dinners," Oakes said as the game resumed. "Maybe after the holidays."

After they'd gone out a few more times. Right now things between them were casual, which seemed to suit them both. There was no hurry. They had plenty of time to figure out where they were going. They could take things as slow as they needed in order for them both to be sure, to be certain of what they wanted.

Love wasn't something you stumbled into. It took time to grow. It needed nurturing and effort. Marriage was too big, too important, to rush into. There was no room for error. There could be no mistakes, no confusing lust with love. Anything worth having was worth waiting for.

And why that brought Daphne to mind—again, damn it—he refused to ponder.

"Oh, but that's weeks from now," Rosalyn said. She sounded disappointed, but at least she drew the line at out-and-out pouting. "I suppose I don't have a say in the matter."

Although it was a statement, she made it sound like a question. "No," Oakes told her with a laugh. "You don't."

"Fine. But at least tell me how things are going with you two. As the person who introduced you, I feel a certain ownership in your relationship."

"Please don't ever introduce me to a girl, Mom," Greg said, not taking his eyes from the game. "I get enough questions about my love life without you claiming ownership—" still not looking at her, he made air quotes with his fingers "—in any of my relationships."

"Good call," Oakes told his brother. "Wish I would have thought of setting up that stipulation a few years ago."

"Yes, I'm a horrible, nagging, meddling mother," Rosalyn said, her tone as dry as dust. "Introducing my son to a beautiful, intelligent woman. What a monster I must be."

He slid his arm around her shoulders and squeezed. "I appreciate you introducing Sylvie to me. But there's nothing to tell. We're taking things slow."

Rosalyn laid her hand on his cheek. "Honey, I love you, but someone needs to light a fire under your ass."

He choked out a laugh.

"Mom!" Greg said, half horrified, half impressed his usually gentile mother knew how to swear. "And on a Sunday."

"Hush now," she told her youngest. "I'm talking to your brother." She set her sights on Oakes. "Now listen to your mama. Slow is all well and good for some things. Not when it comes to matters of the heart. A woman wants to be wooed. She wants to be swept off her feet. She wants the man she's interested in to pursue her, actively and intently. You need to make a gesture. It doesn't have to be grand or over-the-top, just something to let Sylvie know she's a priority for you. You should ask her to Kane's wedding."

He shifted, like a guilty kid trying to get away with something. "I'm not taking Sylvie to Kane's wedding. We've only been seeing each other a few weeks."

"Oakes, it's been over a month. Long enough for a trip away together."

"It's in two weeks. On Christmas Eve. She probably already has plans."

"Even if she does, I'm sure she'd much rather

spend the weekend with a handsome, successful, interesting man." She patted his cheek, smiling at him warmly.

"Guess that leaves you out then," Greg told Oakes with a cocky grin.

Looked like someone needed another lesson in manners. "Good one," Oakes replied, deadpan. He leaned down, pretending to help himself to a pesto-and-tomato-topped cracker, but paused to speak directly into his brother's ear. "But let's just remember which one of us has sex," he said in an undertone. "Regularly. With real live, actual women."

Greg flushed. "Showoff," he muttered.

"Just speaking the truth, son," he said, giving Greg a harder-than-necessary slap on the shoulder. Then another. "Just speaking the truth."

Okay, maybe he wasn't having sex as regularly as he'd like, but the point was he could. In truth, he'd gotten over the whole meaningless hookups and one-night stands long ago. They'd never really been his speed anyway. He wasn't ashamed to admit he wanted more than a few hours of sweaty satisfaction. He was ready to settle down. He already had the house, now all he needed was the perfect woman.

And to stop thinking about Daphne Lynch.

"Mom, I can't ask Sylvie—"

"Of course you can. Make it clear you'll be

back on Christmas day and that you'll pay for separate rooms so she doesn't think it's some sort of booty call—"

"My mother just said *booty call*," Greg murmured, sounding dazed. "She used it incorrectly, but still… I'm going to need massive amounts of therapy now."

Rosalyn ignored him. "I'm sure Sylvie will say yes."

It wasn't what his mother said so much as how she looked when she said it that had Oakes groaning. "Please tell me you didn't mention this already to Sylvie."

"Well, we did run into each other the other day at lunch and the subject of the wedding may have come up in casual conversation," Rosalyn said, too innocently to be believable, "but nothing specific. I just gathered, from her responses, that were you to invite her to be your guest at your brother's wedding, she would be more than happy to accept."

He liked Sylvie. He really did. But he wasn't ready to spend the entire weekend with her, halfway across the country at Christmas, no less. "I can't invite her," he repeated. He pressed his lips together, debating how much information to share. His conscience told him to spill it all, that she'd find out eventually. And his head warned him that if she heard it from someone else, there'd be hell to pay. "I'm already taking a guest."

"I hadn't realized you were seeing someone besides Sylvie," she said, not sounding too thrilled with the idea. "Who is this mysterious woman?"

He sighed. "I'm taking Daphne."

As he feared, she looked shocked. And hurt. Damn it. This was what he was trying to avoid. "I see," she said weakly.

"I don't think you do." He kept his tone gentle. Took her hands in his, discovered her fingers were like ice. "I'm taking her as a favor, that's all."

She pulled her hands free. Linked them together at her waist. "But you're still...seeing her."

"We're friends." And though he knew that hurt his mother, him being with the daughter of the woman who'd had an affair with her first husband, he wasn't about to let Daphne's friendship go. He couldn't. "What happened between Susan and Dad wasn't Daphne's—or Zach's—fault."

He'd kept his tone gentle but she still flinched. Straightened her shoulders. "I need to check on dinner."

He moved to stop her from leaving the room but his stepfather rose, shaking his head as he caught Oakes's eye. "I'll help." He squeezed Oakes's shoulder as he passed him then said softly, "She'll be all right."

Oakes hoped so. The last thing he ever wanted

was to hurt her. And while he understood why she clung to her anger over her father's betrayal, that didn't mean he agreed with it.

It was time—past time—they all moved on.

He was more than ready to look ahead. To focus on the future instead of the past. The past was where his parents' mistakes lived on, haunted him. Their choices influenced his decisions. It was where anger and resentment resided, like a living, breathing beast, needing to be fed constantly.

He was damn tired of being a slave to it.

And in the spirit of moving on, as soon as he got back from Kane's wedding, he'd refocus. Step up his game where Sylvie was concerned. He knew what he wanted. A wife and kids. A career he found both stimulating and satisfying. A home filled with love and laughter, like the life he'd had here. One with no fights and accusations. No crying and heartbreak. Just honesty and trust.

And peace.

He really wanted peace.

His ideal life was out there. His for the taking. He was a Bartasavich, after all. Nothing was beyond his reach. All he had to do was go and get it. And he wouldn't let anyone get in his way.

Even if he had to be as selfish and single-minded as his old man.

CHAPTER SIX

LATER THAT EVENING, Oakes opened his door. Raised his eyebrows. "Am I experiencing déjà vu?"

Daphne grinned, her hair smooth and shiny, her eyes bright, a casserole dish in one hand, a plastic container in the other. "Nope. This isn't a repeat visit. It's a return visit. And this time," she said, lifting the items in her hands, "instead of begging for favors, I come bearing gifts."

The scent of something spicy caught his attention. "Then by all means, come in."

Having learned his lesson last night, he kept plenty of space between them as she stepped inside. He shut the door and wondered about the sense of anticipation filling him. The tension arising within him at the sight of her.

The happiness and excitement.

He grabbed the back of his neck and squeezed. Hard. He was acting like a teenager seeing his crush in the hallway. Exhaling heavily, he turned to her. Grinned. "Not drunk then?"

"Sober as a priest. Well, not Uncle Carlos, obviously, as he loves his whiskey, but sober as a priest who doesn't drink. Or really, anyone who doesn't drink. I even drove myself so you don't have to play cabbie and take me home. See? This is totally different from last night."

He was glad. Just as he was glad she had on jeans—even if the dark denim molded to her curves. But she was wearing a Texas A&M sweat-shirt and her face was clean of makeup, which made her seem younger than her age, a good re-minder that it hadn't been all that long ago when she'd been a coed.

"Here," he said, realizing she was standing there holding the containers, a sexy, knowing smile on her face—please, sweet Jesus, don't let her know what he was thinking. "Let me take those."

"Mom sent some leftovers," Daphne explained as he took the dishes. "Dinner and dessert."

"Your mom sent me dinner?"

"Well, technically, she didn't give them to me so much as I boxed up a few things myself." And that made a whole lot more sense. "But I'm such a kindhearted, generous soul, I thought I'd share. Although, I'm guessing your mom already made sure you're well stocked up on Sunday dinner leftovers."

"You're right," he said, opening the fridge. He stepped aside so she could see the neatly labeled containers his mom had sent home with him after dinner. By the time they'd all sat down to eat, Rosalyn had been herself again. No guilt trips—though she could throw a mean one when provoked. No drawn-out silences. No snide comments.

His mother was a forgiving soul. No holding grudges for Rosalyn. She preferred to suffer in silence. Or, more often than not, pretend that any unpleasantness never happened in the first place.

It was how she'd been able to put up with a lying, cheating husband for over ten years.

"I'm pretty sure my mother doesn't think I can feed myself, either," he told Daphne.

She laughed and the sound, deep and husky, hit him in the solar plexus. "I wish my mom would think I wasn't capable. Instead of sending me home with food, she hands me recipes and tells me I need to cook more and eat out less. Abuelita thinks I'm going to get fat—it runs on my grand-father's side of the family, she likes to tell me—if I don't start cooking healthy, homemade meals."

He couldn't stop his gaze from going to her body, taking in the shape of her hips and thighs, the curve of her waist. He cleared his throat. "I'm sure you don't have to worry about that."

She wasn't stick-thin like most of the women he dated, but she was far from fat. She was curvy and voluptuous, like a pinup girl. A fantasy. One he shouldn't indulge in.

"You're sweet. And speaking of you being sweet," she said, pulling something from her pocket, "here's the money I owe you."

He stepped back. Held up his hands. "I don't want your money, Daphne."

"Well, you don't need it, that's for sure," she said with a teasing grin, only one of a few people he knew well enough to joke about his coming from not one, but two very wealthy families. "But I always repay my debts. Just one of those stubborn traits I picked up from Zach."

Something about the way she said their brother's name, about the way she looked at Oakes as if waiting for his reaction, put him on edge. "It wasn't a favor," he said. "I wanted to help you out last night."

And he figured she could use all the cash she could get. He knew Zach had offered to pay her grad school tuition, but she'd refused, claiming he'd helped her more than enough by funding her private high school education and undergraduate degree. Which meant she was putting herself through school now. Oakes doubted she made much at her internship and her second job as a fill-in receptionist at a dental office.

She made a humming sound, the kind women made when they were trying to get you to believe they were thinking something through, but really, had already made up their mind—mainly that whatever you'd said was dead wrong. "Well, now you can help me by taking this money and letting me pay you back."

She was stubborn and once she dug in her heels, there was no sense arguing.

Besides, he hated losing at anything, especially an argument, and if it could be avoided by giving in, then he figured that wasn't a loss, but smart strategy.

He took the money, careful not to let their fingers touch just in case any of that insanity from last night or this morning was still lingering, and he felt a tingle or got hit by a shot of awareness. "Thanks. But you didn't have to come over here tonight to deliver this. We're going to see each other in two weeks."

Daphne leaned against the counter, making herself right at home in his kitchen once again. "Actually, our trip to the wilds of Pennsylvania is why I dropped by."

The silky tone of her voice warned him something was up. Something that did not bode well for him.

Nothing if not cautious, Oakes meant to take a moment, to choose his next words carefully. Instead, all he could do was stutter.

"You dropped by because of the trip?"

"You're repeating things I say. Are you okay? Am I speaking too fast for you?"

He shook his head. "I'm just…confused."

She confused him. Then again, his own feelings confused the hell out of him these days. It wasn't a sensation he felt often. He always knew what to do, what to say, how to handle any situation. It was what he was best at—reacting, adapting, making the most of any situation. Making the best of it.

But with Daphne he felt at a loss. Out of his element. And that not only annoyed the hell out of him, but also pissed him off good.

"No need for confusion," she told him. "I just thought we should discuss a few things."

He winced. Her tone, if possible, got sweeter.

Scary how a woman could lace her words with sugar as she ripped out a man's throat.

"Such as?" he asked warily.

"Such as you running to tell Zach that I'd asked you to take me to Kane's wedding."

Shit. That's what he was afraid of.

He grinned. When in doubt, pull out the charm. It had worked for him most of his life—only his mother was immune and even that happened on rare occasions. "I hadn't realized Zach couldn't be trusted with the details of a private conversation. But then, he'd always been something of a tattletale."

Must be a younger-brother thing. Gregory had spent the first twelve years of his life tattling on Dusty and even Oakes, while he still lived at home.

"And I didn't tell him you asked me to take you," Oakes continued. "I told him I invited you."

"Right. Always the gentleman, trying to protect others. But he wasn't tattling. I think he was concerned about why you would take me. I explained the whole thing, how I talked you in to it, that I took advantage of your kindness, knowing you wouldn't be able to say no."

And that made him sound like the weak-willed wimp his older brothers—and probably Zach— thought him to be. "Just because I'm not as arrogant as C.J., don't have long hair and tattoos and ride a motorcycle like Kane and didn't serve in the marines like Zach," he said, irritation making his words clipped, "doesn't mean I can't say no when I mean no."

He was getting tired of people thinking that because he was a nice guy, a good guy, that he didn't have a freaking backbone.

"Duly noted," she said then inhaled deeply. "But be that as it may, I'm still going to do you a favor since you did one for me last night. I'm giving you the option of opting out of our agreement."

His eyes narrowed. What was this? "When I give my word, I keep it."

She knew that. She knew *him*. Why would she think he'd renege on their agreement?

"Oh?" she asked way too innocently for it to actually be an innocent question. "Because I figure the reason you told Zach was so you could get out of taking me."

"I told him because I didn't want things to be weird between him and me. As you know, we're not exactly close and I didn't want this to cause problems. I didn't want him to think I was taking advantage of you."

"Like I said," she murmured, "sweet. But, you see, here's the thing—Zach trusts me. He trusts my judgment. Most of the time, anyway. He knows I'm an adult. A fully grown, intelligent, independent woman who makes her own choices and her own way in life. I don't need him to make decisions for me or to tell me what I can do, where I can go or who I can go with. I don't need anyone to do that." Now she looked at Oakes in disappointment, as if he'd somehow let her down. He hated it. "I thought you knew that about me by now." She stepped toward him and it took all his willpower not to step back. As if she was stalking him and he was in grave danger. "I don't need another big brother, Oakes," she said quietly. "I don't *want* another one."

He was nervous, which was crazy. He wasn't in any danger. This was Daphne. He'd known her since she was ten. Had watched her grow up. Had watched over her. And during those years he had felt a certain responsibility toward her. Had thought of her like a little sister.

Until she'd graduated from high school and their relationship changed. Somehow, despite her attending college and him starting a career, they became friends. Unlikely friends, but true ones, nonetheless. And he refused to do anything to risk losing that friendship.

He needed to remember all that when faced with her curvy body, when looking into her blue eyes, when hearing her light laugh. He couldn't help but be attracted to her. He was alive and breathing, a red-blooded male who found her bright and witty and so damn beautiful it made him ache.

But he wouldn't act on his attraction.

There was no faster way to ruin a perfectly good platonic relationship between a man and woman than having sex.

"Of course I know you're intelligent and capable," he told her, but he drew the line at denying he wasn't trying to act like another brother to her. He wasn't big on lying. "My visit with Zach had nothing to do with you."

She cocked a hip. Tipped her head to the side, showing the long line of her neck as her hair slid over her shoulder. "No?"

"No. Like I said, I went there because I wasn't sure how Zach would react about the two of us going to the wedding together. I thought I was being considerate to my brother. That's all."

"I see," she said and, like with his mother earlier, he wasn't sure if she really did or not. "Well, now that that's cleared up, I think the only question that remains is…do you want to take me to the wedding? No recriminations, no tears or tantrums or hurt feelings if you don't."

This was his way out, one she was handing to him on a silver platter. But he couldn't take it. As he'd told her, when he gave his word, he kept it.

No matter what.

Sometimes being honorable and trustworthy was a pain in the ass.

"I would love to have you as my date to my brother's wedding," he said, knowing it was true.

And why wouldn't it be? She was great company. Bright and funny and fun. Plus, she needed him. He wouldn't let her down. He'd just have to ignore any inappropriate thoughts he had about her, would grit his teeth and endure the sweaty, sexy dreams that always seemed to follow any time they spent together. He'd treat her like he would any other friend. One he didn't touch. Or fantasize about. Or want to kiss.

No problem.

"Are you sure?" she asked. "Because the last

thing I want is to force you to do something you'd rather not do."

"I'm positive."

"Okay. Well, that's good because I'm really looking forward to it." She smiled, looking relieved, and he knew he'd made the right decision. "I've never been to Pennsylvania. I hear it's very…green."

"It is," he told her, especially the small town of Shady Grove, where Kane lived, outside of Pittsburgh. "I'm not sure how much green we'll see in the winter, though. When I was there for Kane and Charlotte's Valentine's Day engagement party, everything was covered in snow."

"Really? I've never seen snow. I mean, only the dusting we've had on occasion. I bet it's pretty. And perfect for a Christmas wedding."

"It's pretty enough. If you like wet shoes, slippery roads and freezing temps." He'd almost put his rental car in a ditch driving to the airport after the engagement party.

"I'll be sure to bring boots and a warm coat. Plus, you don't have to worry about my safety on the roads. I'm an excellent driver," she said in her best *Rain Man* imitation before winking at him and turning toward the door.

He had the strangest, strongest urge to reach for her, to take her elbow lightly and ask her if she wanted a drink. Or if she had time to watch a movie or just sit and talk for a while.

He wanted to ask her to stay.

Dangerous thoughts. The kind that could get a man into deep, deep trouble. The kind that could lead him to a place he should avoid. A detour that could destroy all his plans. Could mess up his calm, careful life and endanger the future he'd always dreamed of.

He watched the sway of her ass, the swing of her hips as she walked away, and thought she just might be worth it.

He shoved his hands into his pockets, his fingers curling into fists, and followed her. She opened the door and stepped out onto the porch before facing him. "I still don't believe you, by the way."

He stiffened. Had she somehow sensed his reaction to her? Had he given himself away? "About what?"

"About why you really went to Zach. You were hoping he'd get angry."

Oakes frowned. That made no sense. "People don't get angry with me," he told her, shooting for amused but afraid he sounded more irritated. He may not be his father's favorite son—Senior didn't play favorites, not when he loved himself above everyone else—but Oakes was the favorite Bartasavich brother. The one his family all turned to when they needed help or a calming influence. He wasn't like C.J., whose arrogance and bossiness rubbed the rest of their family the wrong way. Hadn't deserted his family and stayed away for years like Kane. Didn't use bitterness and resentment to keep others at arm's length like Zach.

"I'm not sure if I should agree with you because that's true," Daphne said, "or step back to give your ego more room."

He flushed. He wasn't egotistical. Was he?

"I'm just saying that it makes no sense for me to antagonize Zach." Not when he'd spent his entire life trying to get Zach to stop hating him.

A cool breeze lifted the ends of her hair, had the scent of her shampoo surrounding him. "Okay, I take it back. You didn't want him mad at you. But you did want him to put his foot down. To demand you tell me you changed your mind and couldn't take me to Shady Grove after all. Admit it, you went there hoping he'd stop us from going. Then you wouldn't have to go back on your word, but you could still get out of taking me to the wedding."

Oakes opened his mouth to deny it but the words stuck in his throat. It was rare times like this when he wished he was more like his father, spouting lies and half-truths, all in the name of protecting himself.

She stepped forward, laid her hand on his chest.

His heart jumped underneath her fingers. "It's okay," she said quietly. "I know you're scared of me." She looked up at him through her eyelashes, but there was nothing demure about the wicked grin on her face as she rose onto her toes and whispered her next words in his ear. "You should be."

He stood, still as stone, the blood rushing in his head, his body hardening from her closeness, her touch, as she lowered to her heels and trailed her fingertips down his sternum before turning and walking away.

She was wrong. He wasn't scared of her.

He was terrified.

GRACIE WEAVER KEPT humming Christmas carols under her breath.

It was driving him nuts.

Luke Sapko ground his back teeth together and scrubbed harder at the toilet. It wasn't that he had anything against Christmas songs—although they'd been playing them nonstop at the stores and restaurants since the day after Halloween. It was the fact that Gracie's humming was so cheerful that drove him nuts.

He clenched his fingers around the handle of the toilet brush so hard, his knuckles turned white. If he had to scrub toilets—and not even the toilet he used at home, but a toilet that strangers used—the least fate or God or whoever was running things could do was let him do it in peace and quiet.

"I'm going to get started on the Blue Room," Gracie said, packing up her bucket of cleaning supplies.

"Whatever," Luke muttered, then ducked his head when she frowned at him. He hadn't meant to sound so ticked off. He needed to do a better job of hiding his emotions.

Gracie sure was doing a good job of hiding hers.

Then again, maybe she wasn't hiding anything. There he was, pretending all was right with the world, that he had no worries and was happy with how things were between them, when, in reality, he wasn't sure how he felt.

Or what he wanted.

He shook the water off the toilet brush, dropped it in his bucket. That was the problem, wasn't it? He wasn't sure what he wanted, or at least, he hadn't been sure last summer when he and Gracie had become friends.

He'd gotten hired at Bradford House, a bed-and-breakfast in Shady Grove, as part of the housekeeping crew. He hadn't even known Gracie worked there until he'd arrived on his first day. They'd gone to school together since preschool and while they hadn't exactly been friends, he'd always thought she was nice. Smart, too. But what really made her stand out was how unique she was. Quirky, his mom called it. Though some of the other kids at school preferred the term *weird*.

It all seemed to roll off her back, though, and he admired that about her. Sometimes he thought he worried too much about what other people thought, about how they perceived him, no matter how hard he tried not to.

So he and Gracie had become friends over the summer, which was easy enough to do because she was fun, even though at first she'd acted cool toward him. As if she didn't like him, which, to be honest, hadn't happened all that often in his life.

But then his girlfriend cheated on him and they broke up and Luke's feelings for Gracie changed. Grew. He'd started liking her as more than a friend...

Too bad he'd messed it all up.

He may not have thought he and Kennedy, his ex, would wind up getting married, but he'd thought they'd last through high school. It was a blow, discovering she'd not only cheated on him, but that she'd done so by hooking up with his best friend, Drew.

His now *ex*-best friend, Drew.

From the moment Luke found out about Kennedy and Drew, Kennedy made it clear she wanted Luke back. As angry as he'd been, he'd still had feelings for her. So when Gracie showed up at his house one hot August afternoon and admitted that she liked him, he'd been thrilled—and totally confused.

He'd told her he and Kennedy had been talking, were considering getting back together. She'd handled it gracefully, but had told him that it would probably be better if they didn't try to resume their friendship. At least, not right away. He'd had no choice but to agree.

And now it was four months later and the best way to describe their relationship was friendly acquaintances. The kind who smiled and said Hi when they saw each other in the hallways at school, who chatted casually about the freaking weather or weekend plans while at work.

It sucked.

Luke carried his supplies out into the hallway. He'd liked it better when they were closer, when she used to tell him things. When she'd come over to his house and watch a movie, or he'd go to hers and they'd hang out with her little brothers.

He'd liked it a lot better when she trusted him.

Now she only spoke to him when necessary and always in a polite, friendly tone, a distant one that grated on his last nerve.

He stepped into the Blue Room. As the name implied, it was very blue. Soft blue walls that reminded him of what his own room had looked like when he was a kid, a blue-and-white quilt on the double bed, deeper blues in the throw rugs covering the wide-planked, hardwood floor. Bradford House did a brisk business in the summer and into the fall, but not so much in the winter. Not many people wanted to spend their weekends in Shady Grove when it was freezing out and snow covered everything. They weren't close enough to a ski resort to draw in that crowd and the snow-mobilers usually stayed at one of the small motels outside of town, where they were closer to the woods and trails.

But now it was closing in on Christmas and apparently there was some big wedding taking place in town this weekend and Bradford House was booked from today until Sunday. And that meant overtime for him, which was good, but also more time spent with Gracie, which was not so good.

Maybe he should stop whining and make the most of it. Even if he wasn't sure what he wanted from her.

He walked into the bathroom, which was also blue, bluer and bluest, to find Gracie scrubbing the bathtub. Even though no one had stayed in the room for the past two weeks, they needed to clean it as if it had been occupied just this morning. So Gracie was bent over the edge of the tub, her hips swaying with her movements. Her long, floaty top had risen, showing the backs of her thighs in her tight, dark leggings. His entire body went hard. Bam. Just like that.

Sometimes he really hated being a teenage boy. At least now that he was closing in on eighteen he could control his body's reactions better, could stop things—namely his burgeoning erection—before they got out of hand.

Still, he felt almost guilty thinking of her as an object of lust. His mother would kill him if she thought he saw females as only bodies with soft, sweet-smelling skin and all those interesting curves, from boobs to waists to hips and thighs and ass.

What could he say? He was a guy. A damn lucky guy, who'd had sex regularly during the two years he and Kennedy had been together. A guy who hadn't had it since he and Kennedy hooked up one night late last summer while trying to work things out.

They hadn't. Worked things out, that is. He didn't trust her and had realized he'd never trust her again. Their second breakup wasn't as dramatic as their first, but at least so far, it had stuck.

Despite Kennedy still texting him almost-daily, sexy, flirtatious texts that let him know she still wanted him.

Sure, he could go back to her, if only for the sex. Or he could hook up with someone else. Plenty of girls were into him. Came on to him at parties or flirted with him in class. But he didn't feel right about going out with them just to get laid.

And that reasoning was why he'd backed off from pursuing something with Gracie after he'd kissed her when they'd babysat his nieces. It had been right after breaking up with Kennedy, and before Gracie had admitted her feelings for him. He shouldn't have done it. Shouldn't have rushed things between them and risked their friendship. He hadn't wanted to use her to get over Kennedy. Didn't want to be the type of guy to use any girl that way.

He'd done the right thing by backing off. By making sure he really was over Kennedy. And had lost Gracie's friendship in the process.

As if sensing him behind her, she stiffened and slowly turned, giving him enough time to avert his gaze to somewhere way more respectful and send her a wide-eyed, innocent look when he finally met her eyes.

He cleared the tightness from his throat. "Want me to clean the mirrors?"

"You mean so I'm stuck with the toilet?" she asked, but there was a slight teasing note to her voice, a small smile on her mouth.

He couldn't help but smile back. "I did the last one," he pointed out.

"Right. Fair is fair."

That was Gracie. She wasn't into drama or playing games. She was honest and levelheaded. She wasn't like other girls his age. Even the clothes she wore were different, usually thrift-store finds, her outfits thrown together in a very bohemian way. She rarely wore jeans, preferring skirts or dresses, long or short, that she layered with colorful stockings or leggings.

Today she had on a floaty floral top over her leggings and a pair of pink camouflage combat boots. Her long, supercurly brown hair was pulled back into a ponytail. She stood and used the back of her gloved hand to swipe a loose curl from her forehead, but it just fell right back.

He wanted to offer to help, wanted to reach out and take that curl between his finger and thumb, maybe rub it for a quick second, feel its softness, release its scent. He knew her shampoo smelled sort of minty, but still sweet.

He fisted his hands and watched as she took off her glove and tucked the curl behind her ear.

It immediately sprang free.

She poured cleaner into the toilet. "Did you get your application sent in to Pitt?"

And this was what they'd been reduced to. Conversations about college applications, homework and lame teachers. He hated it.

"I'm still working on the essay," he said, which wasn't a complete lie. He was working on it. In his head. He'd just yet to actually start writing it. "What about you?"

She nodded. "Two weeks ago."

Two weeks and he hadn't known? Then again, they rarely talked in school. Though they shared two classes and a study hall, she seemed content to pretend they didn't know each other at Shady Grove High and he didn't want to do anything to make her feel uncomfortable. Plus, now that the B and B wasn't very busy, they rarely worked the same hours, not like they had during the summer.

"I'm sure you'll get in," he said. Pitt was tougher to get into than most people realized, but Gracie's grades were excellent, as were her SATs.

Something else they shared.

"Thanks. It would be nice, though I'd probably have to commute and I was hoping to have the whole on-campus, away-from-home college experience."

Gracie's family wasn't exactly hard off, but her dad and stepmom had six other kids, all boys including a set of identical twins, and all under the age of eight, so her options for college were limited. "Did you apply anywhere else?" he asked, remembering she'd wanted to look in to schools outside of the Pittsburgh area, even though her parents had told her she had to go to school in-state to save money.

"Penn State," she said. "The University of

Pennsylvania—which is probably a long shot, considering it's Ivy League and probably way too expensive even if I did get in. Are you thinking of applying anywhere else?"

"Dad wants me to try a few smaller schools, see about playing hockey, but since I haven't played in the past two seasons, I doubt any college coach, even at a small school, will bother giving me a chance."

He'd quit hockey at the beginning of last year to play football instead.

His parents and older brother and sister had all told him he'd regret quitting. They'd been right.

And he'd lick the toilet brush before ever admitting it.

Gracie stopped cleaning the toilet to study him. "I hadn't realized you wanted to play hockey at the college level."

He shrugged. "I used to want it. Until I realized how much work it would be, playing a sport at that level while trying to keep my grades up."

Especially since he had no freaking clue what he wanted to do with his life. A common question people—adults mostly—loved to ask high school seniors.

She looked as if she wanted to say something, but then her phone, which was on the counter next to the sink, buzzed. And buzzed. She tugged off her gloves and he picked up her phone to hand it to her. He couldn't help glancing at the screen. His fingers tightened on it and he had to force himself to let go when she reached for it with a grateful smile.

"Hello?" she said before pausing. "Oh, hi." She turned her back to Luke. Another pause. "Actually, I'm working right now. Can I call you later?" Pause. "Okay. 'Bye."

"I didn't know you and Bryce Dennis were friends," Luke said.

Her cheeks pink, she turned off her phone. Set it back on the counter, but had to reach around him to do so. The flowery scent of her soap filled his nostrils and he inhaled deeply, shutting his eyes at the soft brush of her inner arm against his side, the slight pressure of her hip against his thigh before she stepped back. "We have AP Gov together," she said as if that explained everything.

"So he was calling about homework?"

She raised her eyebrows. Probably because he'd sounded pissed off. "Not that it's any of your business, but he called to talk to me. We...talk sometimes."

Luke had no idea what that meant. Girls. Why couldn't they just say what was on their mind, what they were thinking? "I figured that," he said, sounding like a brat and feeling weird...sort of uptight and antsy and jittery. "Considering I just heard you talking to him on the phone."

"Oh. Right." She lifted her slim shoulders. She was so tiny compared to him. Compared to most people. Petite, his mom had called her after she'd been to his house that first time. Like a pixie. And that was what she reminded him of, with her colorful outfits and her huge hair that seemed to float around her shoulders. "I meant that Bryce and I are *talking*." Her voice was matter-of-fact but she kept her attention on making halfhearted swirls inside the toilet bowl with her scrub brush. "We've gone out a few times."

Luke blinked. Blinked again. There was a roaring sound in his ears, like a freight train was rushing by inside his head. "You're Bryce's girlfriend?"

"We're not exclusive or anything," she said in that way she had of sounding carefree, as if she had everything figured out. "I guess if you had to classify it or define it, the correct term would be that we're dating."

They were dating? And no one had told him? What the hell?

Shady Grove was a small town and the high school was even smaller. He should have heard talk about them seeing each other. But then, he and Gracie didn't run in the same crowd—a fact she'd tried to point out to him last summer, but he'd brushed it aside because he thought all of that bullshit about popular kids and jocks and nerds and geeks not interacting was stupid.

Mainly because it had never applied to him. If he wanted to be friends with someone, he was friends with them. But that hadn't stopped him from spending the majority of his time with the kids who had the same interests. Kids he'd been friends with almost his entire life. The same crowd he was still a part of that included his ex-girlfriend and his ex-best friend. Athletes and cheerleaders and members of student government.

So, no, once he took a minute to think about it, it wasn't a shock that he hadn't heard about Gracie being with another guy.

But it still pissed him off.

"Oh. That's…great," he said, and fully expected a bolt of lightning to strike him dead for the lie. "Bryce is a good guy."

The worst part? That he actually was a good guy. There was nothing wrong with Bryce. He was a decent kid, played soccer, was marginally popular and well-liked by most people.

"Yeah, he is nice. I'm not sure we have all that much in common, though," she said.

Luke's heart lifted. "No? Well, I guess I could see that. I mean, he's really into soccer."

She wrinkled her nose. "Soccer is about the only thing he's into at the moment. That and watching reruns of *American Horror Story* on

Netflix, but that doesn't matter." She lifted her chin as if he'd pushed her buttons. "I think maybe what people say about opposites attracting might be true after all. Not for long-term or anything, but for shorter relationships."

He didn't like hearing her call dating another boy a relationship. And he couldn't help thinking her comment about opposites attracting was directed at him since they'd had plenty in common, and look how that turned out.

"So I guess you'll be going to the dance with him, then?" he asked.

The school was putting on a Winter Wonderland dance on Christmas Eve.

"Yes." She hit the brush against the toilet bowl to remove the excess water. "Are you going?"

He tugged his gloves on harder than necessary. "I don't know. Probably." And he turned his back on her and squirted the mirror with glass cleaner, his movements jerky as he wiped it clean.

He was so stupid. He'd been thinking about asking Gracie to go to the dance with him, had thought it might be a good way to ease back into the way their friendship used to be. Now she was going with someone else.

He'd waited too long. And he'd lost her again.

CHAPTER SEVEN

WELL, OAKES HAD been right about one thing, Daphne thought as she climbed out of the car that the bed-and-breakfast had provided to bring her from the airport in Pittsburgh to Bradford House—there definitely wasn't much green. As a matter of fact, everything was white. The ground was covered in snow, as were the rooftops and several vehicles that obviously hadn't been moved in a few days.

Snow fell softly from the sky now, dusting her hair and coat—a coat that wasn't equipped for the cold weather—despite her earlier vow to Oakes that she'd bring one. But at least it looked damn good.

Her feet were frozen before she'd even reached the porch of the Victorian house. As a lifelong Houstonite, she was seriously out of her element in the frigid temperature and snow.

She gratefully stepped inside a warm and welcoming foyer. A wide staircase to her left, with a glossy wooden banister, curved as it went up before disappearing on the second floor. There was a large mirror over an antique dry sink in front of her with an arrangement of huge red poinsettias in a white pitcher-and-bowl set. Aaron, the driver, came in behind her and set down her luggage.

"Thank you," she said, handing him a generous tip. She'd learned on the ride that he had two kids in college and worked as a driver to help make ends meet. "I'll be sure to ask for you on my return trip."

"You do that," he said with a toothy grin and she had a feeling that had he been wearing one of those jaunty, chauffeur caps, he would have tipped it. "Have fun at the wedding."

"I will," she assured him, then waved as he went out the door. Leaving her bags where they sat on the floor beside an ornate wooden bench, she helped herself to one of the dark chocolates in a bowl next to the flowers and walked down a short hallway.

The scent of gingerbread reached her as she stepped into a small dining room. Tables were set up to the left, scattered around the room, several in an alcove surrounded by floor-to-ceiling windows, the scene of softly falling snow outside reminding her of a snow globe.

She shivered. Who knew snow came with such bitter, bitter cold temperatures? She'd rather have rain. Though what they usually ended up with a few times a year in Houston was ice. Maybe snow wasn't so bad after all.

There was a small plaque marked Office next to a closed door, but since she wasn't sure whether she should knock or just walk in, she went with her instincts—and her nose—and ignored it completely, heading instead for a large wooden door on the opposite wall. She pushed it open and stepped into paradise.

Or, a very warm, very cozy kitchen with a large center island topped with dozens upon dozens of several varieties of Christmas cookies.

"If I'm dreaming," she murmured to the heavens, her hands in prayer, "don't wake me. Not until I've had at least one of each. Amen."

"Am I supposed to say 'amen,' too?" a soft voice asked. "Or is that only if I'm actually praying?"

Daphne turned and saw a petite teenager in a loose, floral top that hit her midthigh, a pair of black leggings and pink boots. "Excuse me?" Daphne asked, realizing the girl was looking at her expectantly.

"You were praying," the teen reminded Daphne. "And I wasn't sure if I needed to join in at the closing or not." She wrinkled her nose. "I've never been to church—well, other than for my grandpa's funeral, but I was four and I don't think that counts since they had to take me out of there for trying to swim in the holy water—so I'm not all that familiar with the rules. Do you need an 'amen' from me to make your wish come true?"

Daphne grinned, liking this kid already. "One 'amen' is plenty. I doubt God's all that worried about a proper closing salutation, anyway."

The teen nodded then turned to take a tray of cookies out of the oven. Daphne edged closer to the island and yes, okay, closer to the cookies, too. "If you made all of these and they're half as good as I'm imagining, I'm applying to be your best friend for life."

The girl set down the tray of baked cookies, put a tray of unbaked wreath-shaped cookies in the oven, then shut the door. "They're delicious. At least, that would be my guess. Unfortunately, I already have a best friend. Though at the moment, she's mad at me for not skipping work to go shopping with her in Pittsburgh. But you can be best friends with Damien," she continued, using a spatula to move cookies to a cooling rack. "He's Bradford House's cook and the one who actually makes the cookies. I'm just baking them for him because he got called away unexpectedly."

"Tell me, does Damien look as good as these cookies smell?"

The girl pursed her lips, obviously putting some serious thought into Daphne's question. "He's not traditionally handsome," she said after a moment. "More like Dwayne Johnson handsome.

Big. Built. Bald. And he has an unfortunate habit of wearing do-rags while he cooks. I mean, when I say bald, I mean the man's head is one, round, shiny, smooth ball. Believe me, there's no hair up there to fall into the food, so I say give the bandanas back to the eighties, where they belong."

Daphne laughed. "I could live with bald, and even a do-rag or two, if it came with wicked baking skills. Forget him becoming my new BFF. I'll just have to marry the man."

"He's already engaged."

Daphne sighed and sat herself down on a stool at the counter. Set her chin in her hands. "Just my luck. I'm always a day late and a dollar short."

The teen nodded solemnly, as if she, too, had that issue. "And in this case, you're also the wrong gender." She paused, perhaps for dramatic effect. "Damien's gay."

"Yeah, I figured that out with the whole *wrong-gender* comment." God, but this kid was a kick. How she took everything so literally. Enjoying herself, Daphne slipped off her coat and set it on a stool. "Maybe I could convince him to switch back to the home team."

The girl studied Daphne and Daphne had an insane urge to smooth her hair, as if she was serious about trying to convert some probably very nice gay man all so she could enjoy his...cookies.

"I don't think that's how it works," the teen

finally said. "I mean, I know some ultracon-servatives think you can make it go away with prayer or therapy or whatever, but I'm pretty sure Damien was just born that way. And believe me, wishing that someone will change for you is noth-ing but wasted effort."

"Such cynicism for one so young," Daphne murmured.

"I prefer to think of it as hard-earned wisdom."

"That a girl." Daphne offered her hand over the cookies. "I'm Daphne Lynch."

The girl set down the spatula and wiped her palm on the hand towel draped over her shoul-der, then shook Daphne's hand. "Gracie Weaver."

"It's very nice to meet you, Gracie. Now, are you going to offer me a cookie or ten or do I have to beg?"

Gracie chewed her lower lip, a frown marring her adorable face. "I don't know," she hedged. "Cookies are supposed to be for guests."

"Well, then, it's my lucky day because I am a guest. Or I will be as soon as I check in." She chose a plump sugar cookie with extra icing. Bit the head off of good old Saint Nick. "Mmm...good."

Gracie observed her with wide eyes. "I guess you're not used to being denied something you want."

"Not true," Daphne said around a mouthful of cookie. "I've been denied many, many things over my lifetime. Though, you're right, not by my own doing. The secret to getting what you want is to know when to push for it, when to beg for it and when to just…reach out and take it."

And with that she helped herself to a round, crinkly chocolate cookie with a dusting of sparkling sugar.

"You seem to have the taking part of the equation down," Gracie said without any judgment or rancor, simply making an observation of what was going on around her. She nodded toward the little wreath cookies. "Try a spritz cookie. They melt in your mouth."

Setting the chocolate cookie on the napkin Gracie handed her, Daphne took a spritz, bit into it. Groaned. "Oh, my God. Where have you been all my life?" she asked the rest of the cookie. Then devoured it.

"Yeah," Gracie said, watching Daphne with an intensity that bordered on creepy. "Those used to be my favorite."

"Used to be?"

"I'm vegan," the teen explained, not sounding so happy about her lifestyle choice now that she was faced with a plethora of cookies she couldn't eat. "So no buttery, eggy cookies for me. Damien promised he'd modify the recipe for me, but so far all three of his attempts haven't worked out. I mean, unless you know of someone who actually wants to eat cookies that taste like a combination of cement and sawdust."

"You could always have one little bite," Daphne said.

Gracie seemed tempted but then shook her head, and made herself busy dropping rounded table-spoons of dough onto a cookie sheet. "No. It took me almost a year to go completely animal-free and I don't want to ruin it now by backsliding."

Daphne admired her dedication. She'd never had very much willpower herself. And that fact probably explained the ten extra pounds she carried.

It was that whole unable-to-deny-herself-what-she-wanted thing.

"Please tell me guests are also allowed coffee," Daphne said, spying the full pot on the counter next to an industrial-sized stainless-steel fridge.

"They are," Gracie said, adding one more dough ball to the tray before getting a mug from a glass-fronted upper cabinet and pouring coffee into it for Daphne. "Are you here for the family Christmas party or the society wedding?"

"Thanks," Daphne said, taking the cup. "The wedding."

Gracie gestured to a tea set complete with chilled cream and sugar cubes. "Relative of the bride or groom?"

Daphne poured cream into the cup, added two

sugar cubes, stirred and tried it only to add one more. "Neither, actually."

"Then you're a friend of Charlotte's?"

"Not really."

Gracie frowned and tugged at a loose curl by her temple. "I doubt you're a friend of Kane's. I mean, no offense or anything if you are, but he doesn't seem like the type of man who has friends. Let alone a female one."

"Good instincts," Daphne told her. Kane was bad boy through and through, from his long hair, to his tattoos, to his penchant for motorcycles and not taking any crap from anyone. Especially his wealthy family. "I'm more of an…acquaintance, I guess you could say."

"You're not crashing, are you?" Gracie asked in a horrified yet intrigued whisper. "Are you paparazzi? Does Houston even have paparazzi?"

"Houston does, indeed, have paparazzi and the Bartasavich family members are some of their favorite subjects. But I'm not crashing anything. I just thought saying I was an acquaintance of the bride and groom was easier than explaining that I'm the half sister of one of Kane's half brothers and am attending the wedding with another of Kane's half brothers, but am not, technically, related to Kane or anyone involved in the wedding myself."

Gracie stared at her for so long without blinking, Daphne wondered if she'd slipped into some sort of coma. Finally the girl nodded. "You're right. That was easier." Using a cookie press, she squeezed dough onto a tray, making irregular circles, her teeth nibbling her lower lip as she concentrated. When she was done, she raised her head. "Which half brother are you related to?"

"Zach Castro. So I guess Houston isn't the only place where the Bartasaviches are well-known?" she asked, as Gracie had obviously heard about them.

"Not sure how well they're known to the general public of Shady Grove but Ivy—Ivy Rutherford?—used to work here. Actually, she and I met while working at King's Crossing, a hotel by the river. That's where we became friends. And that's where she met Clinton Bartasavich, Jr."

"Ivy? You mean the goddess?" Daphne asked, remembering the gorgeous, confident blonde who'd gotten pregnant by C.J. and had, if Daphne wasn't mistaken, given birth to a baby boy not very long ago. They'd only met once, when Zach had been transferred to a hospital in Houston, but it was hard to forget someone like Ivy. She was blonde and had the type of beauty to bring a man to his knees, even while pregnant. Or maybe, that pregnancy glow had only added to her appeal.

Gracie grinned. "Goddess pretty much sums up Ivy. Yeah, she was the chef here before she decided to go have the billionaire bachelor's baby—which I told her would make a great title should she feel the need to write her memoirs. Not that I blame her for falling for the guy. He's nice. Is rich enough to own his own island and is super-handsome. Though I could do without the cowboy hats."

Daphne laughed. "He is handsome and I agree with you about the hats. Anyway, from what I understand, C.J.'s an all-right guy." Though Zach, of course, couldn't stand his eldest brother. But since he was biased, she tended not to take his opinions of his family too seriously. "He can be pretty arrogant," she said, remembering how, when Zach was in the hospital, C.J. had tried to boss the doctors and nurses around, tried to get answers. "But I think that's just his coping mechanism for being that wealthy and having so many people want something from him. There could also be some guilt thrown in there, too. For being born into a world of privilege and excess when so many others suffer."

"You sound like a psychologist," Gracie said, once again switching baked for unbaked cookies.

Daphne broke a piece off of the chocolate cookie. "Do I? Good. I'm actually starting grad school after the first of the year. I'll be getting my PhD in psychology."

"From what I've heard, you'll have your hands

full just with the Bartasavich family. But then, if you're just an acquaintance, maybe you won't have to deal with them that often. Except for your brother, of course."

"I wouldn't have to normally, but I'm hoping all that will change. You see, I'm not here just to enjoy an extravagant wedding celebrating the love between two people I barely know."

"You're not? Do tell." Gracie set the hot tray on the counter then circled around the island to sit on the stool next to Daphne. "This should be good."

"All right, I'm going to share a secret with you, Gracie."

Gracie raised her eyebrows. A pragmatic soul under all the fluffy hair and big, guileless eyes. "Do you think that's a wise decision? I mean, you've only known me for approximately ten minutes."

Daphne sat back, affronted. "Don't insult either of us. Of course it's a good idea. You're a very trustworthy soul. I can tell. I'm excellent at reading people. It's obvious you're honest and hardworking and you have kind eyes." She patted Gracie's hand. "No, I trust you completely. Which is why I can tell you that the real reason I'm here is to figure out if I'm in love with one of my dearest friends. And, if I am, I plan on getting him to fall in love with me, too."

Gracie didn't look shocked or disgusted, or as if Daphne had lost her ever-loving mind—she knew she'd been right to trust the teen. Her gut was never wrong.

That's why she trusted it when it told her that she and Oakes belonged together.

"Is this dream man a real, live person?" Gracie asked. "Or did you ask Santa to leave him in your stocking Christmas morning?"

"Oh, he's real, all right. He's wonderful. Smart, handsome, funny and so sweet. Seriously, once you meet him, you'll see I'm right and how good we will be together."

Gracie made a noncommittal sound, one that was way too adult for someone who resembled a Christmas fairy. "How long have you known this Mr. Wonderful?"

"Since I was thirteen, but it wasn't until I graduated high school that my feelings for him changed. That's when we became friends. Good friends."

Gracie sighed, took a turn patting Daphne's hand. "I hate to break it to you, but if you've been friends with a guy, chances of it becoming something more are pretty slim. Believe me, I know. Seems to me that with friendships like that, where one person has more than just friendly feelings toward the other, someone always ends up getting hurt. And I...well, it would just suck if that someone were you. I mean, you seem really nice."

"You're sweet. And I appreciate the thought and the concern, but Oakes—"

"His name is Oakes?" Gracie asked. "For real?"

"It was his mother's maiden name. Anyway, he would never hurt me. He couldn't. He's too kind. Too considerate."

"But...don't you think that, since you've known each other for so long, that if you two were meant to be together, something would have happened before now?" Gracie asked, seeming genuinely curious and not just trying to make a point.

Daphne pursed her lips. Considered the girl's words because it was obvious she meant well. "I understand what you're saying and normally, I would agree with you. And, if I had a patient who came to me with this problem, I'd tell them the same thing you just told me. But you see, the situation between me and Oakes is different. He's just too honorable. He still sees me as a kid. Treats me like a little sister, even though we are not related. At all."

She explained their unique circumstances to Gracie while the girl took another tray of cookies out of the oven. By the time Daphne was done, Gracie was wide-eyed and openmouthed. "And I thought my life was complicated."

"The situation is tricky, I'll give you that," Daphne agreed. "But that doesn't mean I can't make it work. We'll have almost four days together, which will give me plenty of time to confirm that my feelings for him are real. And it will also give him plenty of opportunity to stop seeing me as Zach's kid sister and to look beyond all the weird and wonderful ways our families are tied together."

"So he's staying here, too?"

"Yes. I was lucky enough to get the last available room here and not have to go to the hotel where the rest of the wedding guests are staying."

Gracie turned off the oven. "Come on, then."

Daphne slid off the stool when Gracie grabbed her hand and tugged her from the room. Daphne hurried to keep up with the teen—who knew legs that short could move so quickly? "You're not kicking me out for sampling a few cookies, are you? Just add them to my bill."

"Nothing like that. I'm going to help you—though I have to say, it's against my better judgment." They turned the corner into the dining room and Gracie knocked twice on the closed office door, then opened it before being bid to do so. "Fay, we have a guest here with a special request."

Fay was a thin, strawberry blonde with smooth hair and a kind, gentle smile. "Of course," she said as she stood and walked around her desk. "I'm Fay Lindemuth, the manager here. Welcome to Bradford House."

Daphne shook her hand then sent a quizzical

glance at Gracie. How was this woman going to help her and what did she mean they had a special request?

"Daphne needs to stay in a certain room, one next to a guest who hasn't arrived yet," Gracie told Fay as she gestured for Daphne to take a seat across from the desk. "It's all for the greater good," she assured the B-and-B manager. "And for love."

"Of course," Fay said immediately as she went behind her desk and started typing into her computer.

Stunned and grateful, Daphne sat there frozen. The best she'd hoped for was bumping into Oakes from time to time. Yes, the B and B was small, but if they'd been on opposite sides of it, she would have to spend more time lying in wait for the man.

"Fay's a sucker for a good love story," Gracie told Daphne.

"It's true," Fay responded, not upset to be called on her sentimental streak. "While our sweet Gracie is *not*."

"But you helped me anyway," Daphne said to the teen. She reached out and squeezed her new friend's hand. "Thank you."

"You're welcome," Gracie said, as serious as a heart attack. "I just hope, for your sake, this isn't a mistake."

"It's not," Daphne assured her. Going after Oakes was the best decision she'd ever made.

"ALL I'M ASKING," Rosalyn said to Oakes over the phone as he slowly walked toward the foyer of Bradford House, "is that you promise me you'll be here in time for brunch on Christmas morning."

"Mom," Oakes said, setting his bag down so he could squeeze the bridge of his nose. "I'll be home."

His mom was already nagging him to come home, and he'd only just arrived in Shady Grove twenty minutes ago. Had just registered for his room at the B and B, his preferred place to stay. He was happy to be away from the rest of his family, who were all booked into King's Crossing, a four-star hotel on the river.

"But what if something happens?" she asked, sounding worried and stressed. Ah, the joys of the holidays. "You never know about weather delays, especially this time of year and in the northeast."

"My flight home departs Pittsburgh before seven a.m. I'll be in Houston by ten." The time difference gave him an extra hour, plus he was taking a private charter so he wouldn't have to deal with airline delays. He would have promised he'd fly home Christmas Eve, the same night as the wedding, but the ceremony was to take place in the evening, and he didn't want to enable his mother any more than he needed to. The woman was a nervous wreck, worried she wouldn't have all three of her sons home for Christmas. Stressed over her annual Christmas day brunch. Still angry with Oakes for taking Daphne to this wedding.

He was crazy about his mom, but she tended to worry about each and every possible scenario. Including a few she made up.

"All right," she said, as if resigned to her fate of having an ungrateful, reckless son who'd ruin Christmas for everyone if he wasn't there for brunch at 11:00 a.m. "I'm sure you'll be fine. And I—I hope you enjoy yourself at the wedding. Please give Kane and his fiancée my best."

He softened toward her. How could he not? She knew he'd be at the wedding with Daphne, was still upset about it, but had wished him well anyway.

"I will," he told her. "You could have come, you know. Kane and Charlotte would have loved for you to be here."

While he wasn't sure that was completely true, as Kane kept most things—his thoughts and feelings, especially—close to the vest, his brother had invited Rosalyn to the ceremony. It was a considerate gesture, as Rosalyn had been his stepmother for ten years. But she'd declined, knowing that her being there would only upset Kane's mother, Gwen.

Oakes was pretty sure Rosalyn would have

preferred that type of consideration from Oakes when it came to Daphne, the daughter of one of the women Senior had cheated on her with. A pang of guilt hit him.

"It's better this way. Some things are just not meant to be." He had a feeling she was talking about more than her attending a wedding. He wasn't about to ask for clarification, though. Not when he could guess her true meaning.

Mainly that he was not meant to be with Daphne, in any way, shape or form. Not even as friends.

"Well, I have to go," Rosalyn said. "I need to pick up a few more things at the store. I love you."

She sniffed and he knew she was about to cry. Damn holidays always brought out her weepy side, but this time he knew it was more than that. "Love you, too."

He sat on the wooden bench to wait for the pretty, strawberry-blonde manager to take him to his room when his phone buzzed again.

He checked the screen. "Hey, Dusty."

"Swear to God," Dustin said in a harsh whisper. "If your ass isn't here on Christmas morning, I will kill you in your sleep."

Dustin, in his second year at college, had been home on Christmas break for just over a week and being home, away from his friends and the freedom he'd gotten used to during two years at school in another city, was obviously getting to him.

Oakes grinned. "How's it going at home, then? Enjoying being back?"

"Mom sobs at half the commercials on TV, but refuses to turn the damn thing off and keeps asking me to watch made-for-television Christmas shows with her."

Dustin's tone was bereaved with a healthy dose of irritation for good measure. "A man can only watch so many stories about women leaving their stuffy fiancé for an artist," he continued. "And why does every small town in those shows have their own Santa look-alike. There can't be that many old guys who look that way in real life."

His brother sounded like a desperate man. Never a good thing for anyone, especially not a twenty-year-old kid. "Tell you what," Oakes said as he stared out the front window at the gently falling snow, "get the key to my place from Mom. You can have a few friends over, hang out there for a night or two."

"Yeah?" Dusty asked, excited and eager. "Thanks, man."

"Hold on, I have a few conditions. One is that you don't wreck the place. Keep your friends in line. Two, clean up after yourself. I want it to look better than the way I left it. And three, don't even think about letting anyone drink while you're there."

"What? Come on. I'm in college. You remember college, don't you?"

"Vaguely," Oakes said dryly. "I mean it, Dusty. If you get caught drinking you'll not only get into trouble with Mom and Michael and the authorities, but *I* will kick your ass."

"Why do you always have to be such a freaking Boy Scout?" Dusty muttered.

It stung. Probably because he got it not just from his younger brothers, but his older ones as well. They all thought he was some sort of wuss. As if being a nice guy, being responsible and making good decisions, was equal to being spineless.

It didn't. And he was getting damn tired of them thinking it did.

"You don't like the rules? Stay home. I'm sure there'll be a really interesting romantic holiday special on this afternoon. You and Mom can string popcorn."

"Fine," Dusty agreed quickly—because as Oakes had noted, his brother was a desperate man. "No property damage, no messes and no alcohol. I might as well see if Greg and his buddies want to join us since we won't be doing anything illegal, immoral or enjoyable."

"Great idea." The manager stepped out into the hall and headed toward him. "I have to go, Dusty. Talk to you later."

After hanging up, he made small talk with Fay Lindemuth as she led him upstairs to his room. She was a quiet woman and maybe a bit on the shy side, so managing a bed-and-breakfast, where she had to welcome strangers all the time, seemed like an odd choice of a career.

She explained when breakfast was served, that there was coffee and tea service every afternoon and wine and cheese in the evenings. At his room at the end of the long hall on the second floor, she unlocked the door with a real key as opposed to a key card, showed him where everything he'd need was and then left him to unwind and unpack.

He considered flopping facedown on the bed, maybe taking a nap. But his conscience wouldn't let him. Not before he'd hung up his clothes.

And let Daphne know he'd arrived in Shady Grove.

He sent her a quick text then lifted his large suitcase onto the bed. He'd thought he and Daphne would be traveling together, but she'd been serious when she'd said she didn't want him to pay her travel expenses. She'd texted him about an hour after she'd left his house that night two weeks ago to ask about accommodations.

He'd told her that wedding guests were staying at King's Crossing but he'd decided to try Bradford House. A few minutes later she'd let him know she'd already booked a flight and reserved a hotel room. Then she'd told him she was swamped for the next little bit and would just see him in Shady Grove. The only other time he'd heard from her since was when she'd texted him over an hour ago letting him know she'd just checked into her room.

It was for the best, he told himself as he hung up his clothes in the closet. They weren't a couple and this wasn't a weekend getaway. There was no reason for them to spend every minute of the trip together. Besides, he had duties as brother of the groom. Tonight, there was a dinner hosted by Charlotte's parents, then later a small bachelor party. Tomorrow evening was the wedding rehearsal followed by another dinner. And, of course, the following day was the ceremony and reception, which was the only thing Daphne would be attending with him.

She'd be fine on her own. She didn't need him to hold her hand. She was probably already off exploring the town. He wouldn't be surprised if he didn't even see her until he picked her up for the wedding Saturday afternoon.

What *did* surprise him—and worry him—was the disappointment that followed that thought.

He enjoyed being with Daphne. And that made sense, as they were friends. But her showing up at his house drunk, wearing that damn dress, had triggered some overly friendly imaginings of the erotic kind. Starring the two of them.

They would eventually pass, he assured himself. They always had before.

But it kept getting harder and harder to push them back into the recesses of his mind. To ignore his attraction to her.

He was scared that one of these days he wasn't going to be able to fight it. That he would do something incredibly stupid, like kiss her. Or take her to bed.

And either of those things would destroy their friendship, ruin any chance he might have at getting closer to Zach and break his mother's heart should she find out.

He hung up a pair of pants, slapping the hanger on the rod with more force than necessary. No. It wasn't worth it. He had to keep things just as they were. He had his life mapped out. He just needed to stay on course. Sylvie had already agreed to attend his mother's New Year's Eve party with him, but he could definitely step things up where she was concerned. He'd call her, ask her out for Monday night when he got back to Houston.

Yes. When it came to Daphne, the best course of action was to leave well enough alone.

He was just bringing up Sylvie's contact information on his phone when someone knocked on the door. Expecting the manager again, he crossed the room and opened the door with a smile, only to feel that smile slowly fade away when he saw who it was.

His throat dried as he skimmed his gaze over Daphne. Her hair was down, the ends grazing her shoulders. Her sweater was all fuzzy and soft-looking and clung to her breasts and the indentation of her waist, the deep blue of the material bringing out her eyes. Her jeans were black, painted on and tucked into high-heeled, knee-high black boots. Her smile was wide, her mouth painted a deep and vivid red. She looked fresh and casual and sexy. Touchable.

Leaving well enough alone was going to be a hell of a lot harder than he thought.

Not because of the desire digging its sharp claws into his chest, stealing his breath. No, it wasn't his physical reaction to her that had his gut aching, his head spinning. Wanting wasn't the problem.

It was the need that was killing him.

The need to be with her, see her, talk to her

more often than a few times a month. To simply
be with her. A need that had grown slowly over
time, increasing each year, each week, each day
until it had become a part of him.

A need he was afraid would never go away.

CHAPTER EIGHT

"ARE YOU OKAY?" Daphne asked, frowning at him in concern. "You've been staring at me for like five minutes."

The back of his neck warmed, though he was sure he'd only been staring a moment or two. "Daphne. What are you doing here?"

She raised her eyebrows and cocked a hip, drawing his attention, once again to those jeans. "Well, I'm not getting much of a warm welcome, that's for sure."

He winced. Shook his head. "Sorry. I meant to say 'hello' then 'what are you doing here?'"

Her eye roll said that wasn't much better. "You texted me. Remember? Told me you'd arrived." She tipped her head to the side. Sent a pointed look behind him as if to ask if he was going to invite her in. He almost didn't.

Letting her inside his house two weeks ago was what had gotten him into this mess in the first place.

But then she took matters into her own hands, as she often did, and stepped forward with a sigh, forcing him to back up out of her way. But he hesitated at the door. It seemed like a bad idea, the two of them in what was, essentially, his hotel room together. Too cramped, even though the room itself was spacious. Too intimate with the huge bed there, as in "right there."

He closed the door, leaving it open a crack, as if that alone would ensure they didn't have complete privacy.

"No," he said, going for casual and unconcerned by sticking his hands in his pockets and leaning against the dresser. "I mean, what are you doing here, at Bradford House? Guests of the wedding are staying at a hotel on the river."

"Oh, that." She faced him, but even though she stood still, energy pulsated around her, seemed to vibrate just under her skin. "Yeah, I'm staying here."

He wasn't going to start repeating everything she said again, like he had in their last conversation, although he found himself wanting to. He had a hard time following her at the best of times, and now, with her scent invading his room, her eyes bright, that small, secret smile playing on her glossy red lips, he had a tough time gathering his thoughts. Making sense of them. Of what he wanted to say.

Of what he wanted, period.

"Why are you staying here?" he asked, knowing he sounded like a lawyer but unable to stop himself. "Instead of at the other hotel?"

She wrinkled her nose. "And take a chance of running in to Kane and C.J.'s mother? I don't think so. With my luck, we'd get stuck in the elevator together. The stress would kill me. From what I've heard, that woman is scare-eee."

That made sense. Gwen Bartasavich, the original Mrs. Clinton Bartasavich, Sr., was one terrifying woman. She hated each of her ex-husband's mistresses, ex-wives and two sons from other women with equal fervor—despite having been divorced from Senior for over twenty years. Now that he thought about it, that hatred would, more than likely, extend to Daphne, too.

Yes, her reasoning seemed sound. "I guess you thought it through. Though I doubt Gwen would have known who you were unless you went up to her and introduced yourself."

Daphne nodded. "True. But, like you said, I thought it through and realized it would be more convenient if you and I stayed at the same place."

"Convenient?"

She plopped down on the bed and had it—and her breasts—bouncing with the movement. "Mmm-hmm. I'm actually right next door." Straightening her arms behind her, she arched her back. She gazed at him innocently, but when she spoke, her voice was husky. Suggestive. "You know, in case you need me."

He bit back a flinch. *Need.* There was that word again, tumbling from her mouth, taunting him. Tempting him.

Just like the woman before him, smiling up at him from the middle of his bed, the ends of her dark hair swinging against her shoulders.

Damn her.

"What say we go out?" she continued. "Get some dinner. Then we can explore the town a little bit."

"I can't," he told her, relieved he had an excuse not to spend the evening with her when his feelings for her were so messed up. When she had on that sweater that made his hands itch to test its softness. "Charlotte's parents are hosting a dinner. Immediate family only."

"Oh." She sat up and scooted to the edge of the bed, her smile frozen as she obviously didn't miss his emphasis on "immediate family only." "Well, that sounds like fun." Her tone was cheery but she looked at him expectantly, waiting, he knew, for him to do the good-guy thing, to play his part as the nice guy and invite her along.

He didn't.

In this instance, protecting himself took precedence over everything else. He needed some distance, some space.

And he needed this weekend to be over with already so he could get back to Houston. Back to Sylvie and his plans. Back to pretending he wasn't attracted to Zach's little sister.

"You should still go out, though," Oakes said, pushing away from the dresser. He moved to his suitcase, blindly pulled out a pair of socks then ended up just holding them like a moron. "I'm sure Mrs. Lindemuth has some recommendations for restaurants."

"Good idea." Daphne stood. She hesitated, as if waiting for him to change his mind. To issue that invitation. When he didn't, disappointment crossed her face. He steeled himself against it. "I'll just go do that now," she said, sounding small and unlike herself. "Let you get ready. For your dinner."

He tucked the socks into a dresser drawer and nodded, avoiding her gaze. Hating the hurt in her voice.

"I'll see you later?" she said, making it sound like a question.

He met her eyes and immediately regretted it. She looked so lost. So…lonely.

And he remembered that other than him, she didn't know anyone in Shady Grove. Not really. She'd met both his brothers, as well as Charlotte, while Zach had been in the hospital, but they'd all been focused on Zach's care at the time. There hadn't been much room for niceties and in-depth, getting-to-know-you conversations. Now she was here, halfway across the country from everyone she knew, and he was leaving her to spend the night alone.

Part of him, the part that always wanted to help those he cared about, told him to change his mind. To suck it up and invite her to the dinner. To be the good guy he always was.

But another part, a deeper, darker part he was sure came from his father, wouldn't let him. It told him to be selfish. To just this once, put his own needs first.

"You'll see me later," he assured her. "You're right next door, remember?"

He wouldn't be able to avoid her until the wedding, even if he wanted to.

"Right." She crossed her arms. Nodded. Then cleared her throat. "Well, then…see you."

She turned and walked out, shut the door quietly behind her.

Oakes slammed the dresser drawer shut. He refused to feel guilty. He'd already gone above and beyond just agreeing to take Daphne to his brother's wedding. He'd offered to pay for her travel and hotel expenses. But he'd never agreed to entertain her for the entire weekend. He couldn't. He had family obligations.

And though he liked to believe otherwise,

though he desperately wanted to believe otherwise, Daphne wasn't family.

It wouldn't kill her to spend the evening alone, watching TV or reading in her room. Or she could take his suggestion and go explore the town on her own. She wasn't afraid to meet new people, to engage strangers in conversation. She'd probably end the night with a dozen new friends. Most of them male. And why not? She was beautiful, intelligent and funny. Guys would see her at a restaurant or a bar, by herself, and think she was fair game.

She'd be fine. No matter what she did, she'd be just fine.

And he'd have a break. A needed reprieve from his thoughts of her. A chance to plan how he was going to handle the rest of the weekend. A chance to breathe.

But breathing, it turned out, wasn't as easy as he'd thought it would be, not when all the air in the room left right along with Daphne.

LUKE PAUSED IN the hallway of Bradford House, his coat on and zipped, his favorite knit hat pulled down low over his forehead. He glanced out the window of the side door into the dark night. He should go out there, cross the back parking lot to his car, brush the snow from the windshield and back window, warm up the interior and go home.

He'd put in his time—four hours of cleaning bath-rooms, taking out trash and shoveling and salt-ing the walks. It was past seven. He was hungry and he still had to finish an English assignment.

He had no reason, none whatsoever, to linger at the B and B. No reason to go into the kitchen.

No reason other than the fact that Gracie was in there.

His inner voice told him to get the hell out of there before he made a fool of himself in front of her. Again. He should not, under any circum-stances, go anywhere near that kitchen.

But he did it anyway.

His brother was right, Luke thought with an in-ward sigh as he walked through the dining room as if being pulled there by an invisible force. He was an idiot. What other reason was there for him to be acting so pathetic over a girl? A girl who wanted nothing to do with him? Who refused to give him a second chance or even be his friend?

A girl who was seeing some other guy.

He pushed open the kitchen door, spied Gracie behind the island.

And there was his answer.

She looked as if she'd been in the middle of a Christmas cookie explosion. They were every-where, on every available surface—the large is-land, the counters, the huge farm table where employees ate.

"Hey," he said, stepping farther into the room, letting the door swing shut behind him. "Need any help?"

She blinked at him as if coming out of a deep trance. Or a sugar coma. She checked the time on the microwave. "I thought you only worked until seven?"

He shrugged, a nonanswer, but better than lying outright and saying he was scheduled to work until eight or nine.

Better than telling the truth. That he'd heard Damien's boyfriend was having an emergency appendectomy and Damien wouldn't be back tonight and that Gracie, being Gracie, had offered to finish making cookies for a holiday party being held here tomorrow.

The truth—that he wanted to help her. That he just wanted to spend some time with her.

That would have her closing off from him, for sure.

"Tell me what to do," he said. He'd helped his mom bake when he was younger, but that had been mostly stirring in ingredients and sneaking raw cookie dough.

Gracie studied him. Flour specked her shirt and she had a smear of red icing on her chin. Her eyes were bright, her cheeks pink from the heat of the stove, and several curls had escaped her ponytail to sort of...*sproing* around her face. She looked freaked out and tasty as hell.

"Umm, well, the cookies are all baked," she finally said, though so reluctantly, he figured she'd just waged a fierce battle with herself about whether or not to accept his help. "But I guess I could use some help with the decorating. If you want to."

He wiped the back of his hand over his mouth to hide what had to be a very self-satisfied grin. "No problem." He shrugged out of his coat, tossed it and his hat onto a stool. "Where should I start?"

"You can frost the sugar cookies," she said, while he washed his hands at the large sink. "I'll work on the gingerbread people."

When he came back to the island, she handed him a bowl filled with fluffy red icing.

"I know Damien would have used several different colors," Gracie continued, "but at this point, it seemed safer for my stress levels and mental health to keep things as simple as possible."

"That's smart." And that was Gracie. Smart enough to realize her limitations. Resourceful enough to somehow do the work of a professional chef. And kind enough to offer her help. Smiling, he added, "And it answers the question about that bit of icing on your chin."

She brushed her fingertips across her chin, not embarrassed to be less than perfect.

"Uh…you missed," he said, his heart rate speeding up. If this was one of those chick flicks Kennedy used to make him sit through, Luke would reach out, wipe the frosting away for her. Maybe let his hand linger on her face, his fingers caressing her soft skin. Their eyes would lock and they'd lean toward each other.

Except this wasn't a movie because when he murmured, "Let me," and reached for her, Gracie stepped back and rubbed the end of the towel draped over her shoulder across her chin.

"How's that?" she asked, sort of breathlessly.

A balm to his battered ego. "You got it."

They worked in silence for a solid five minutes. Him slathering frosting onto round sugar cookies while she used a piping bag to make faces on gingerbread men.

"Thank you," she finally said, "for helping me. Fay was going to but tonight is Elijah's Christmas program at school."

Their boss, Fay Lindemuth, had two little boys who usually ran wild around the B and B. Fay wasn't big on discipline, which was evident in the behavior of her older son, kindergartner Elijah. The kid was a bigger terror than Luke had ever even considered being—and according to his mother, he was the cause of every one of her gray hairs. Fay's youngest, Mitchell, was as easygoing and good-natured as could be.

"No problem." Luck winced. Shit. Hadn't he already said that? "I mean… I'm glad I could help. I…" He pressed his lips together before he said something he'd regret, something that would let her know that he was hung up on her. But he was tired of doing that. So freaking tired of holding back when it came to her. He turned toward her, touched her wrist so she looked at him. "I miss you, Gracie."

She blushed but she didn't back away, didn't pull her arm from his touch, just stared at him, eyes wide and wary. But also, he thought, hopeful.

He edged closer, kept his voice low. Sincere. "I know you're with Bryce now…" And it took all of Luke's willpower to say that without sounding angry. Or worse, jealous. "But I was hoping that maybe you could stop being mad at me and be my friend again." He rubbed his thumb lightly across the pulse at her wrist. Felt it jump under his touch. "It *is* the time of year for forgiveness and goodwill toward all, right?"

"I'm not mad at you, Luke," she whispered. "I was never mad."

He took the opportunity to move in even closer. So close he could see the freckles on her nose. Could feel her warm breath wash over his neck. "Never?"

Her lips twitched. "Okay, so maybe I was mad. But you apologized and I forgave you."

The day after he'd kissed her at his sister's house, they'd gone for coffee only to find Kennedy working at the coffee shop. He'd acted like an asshole, trying to get Kennedy into trouble for messing up Gracie's order, using Gracie to prove he was over his ex-girlfriend—and she'd noticed. Then he and Gracie had argued and that was when she'd told him she no longer wanted to be his friend.

But it was when she came to his house a few days later and admitted that she liked him that he'd ruined any chance he had with her by getting back together with Kennedy.

So, no, maybe Gracie wasn't pissed at him any longer. But he had hurt her.

And now he was closing in on a chance to be her friend again. He couldn't blow it by going too fast or asking too much from her.

He eased back. Let his hand drop from her arm. "Great. So there's no reason we can't hang out. Like we used to."

She chewed on her lower lip, looking so unsure, it killed him. "I don't know…"

"As friends," he added quickly. "Friends who help each other. Like staying late at work to frost cookies."

Her eyebrows rose. "Are you trying to make me feel guilty? Because you're the one who came in here and offered to help."

"Nope. No guilt involved." He frosted another cookie. Set it aside. "Though if you did feel guilty, guilty enough to want to pay me back in some way, I suppose I could let you go shopping with me when we're done. I still haven't bought anything for my nieces for Christmas."

"Why do I have a feeling you offering to help with the cookies was some sort of setup?"

"Because you know I have no idea what to get a couple of little girls?" Because she knew him, even if she didn't want to admit it. "In exchange, I'll help you pick out stuff for your brothers."

"I'm already done shopping. Bu-u-t," she said, drawing out the word long enough to make him sweat, "I suppose I could help you." She smiled at him shyly. "Since we're friends and all."

His own grin about split his face. "Right. Friends."

If wasn't exactly his end goal, but he'd rather be friends with Gracie than lose her altogether.

SHE WAS NERVOUS.

And that was ridiculous, Daphne scolded herself as she shimmied into a purple, bandage style dress. And stupid, too.

And she was not stupid.

Although thinking she and Oakes would be attached at the hip this entire weekend had been a rookie mistake. Of course he was busy. He had obligations—to his brother and the rest of his family. Yes, she'd been surprised when he hadn't invited her to tag along.

Surprised and, she could admit now, a bit hurt.

Not that she had any right to feel such a way, she rationalized, smoothing the skirt of the dress down her thighs. It was a family dinner. A time for Kane's and Charlotte's families to be together before the wedding. A kickoff to the festivities, if you will.

And, as she'd pointed out to Oakes time and time again, she wasn't his family.

She had no right wishing differently in this one instance, just so she wouldn't have to spend a few hours alone.

Still, it would have been nice if she could have gone with him. The more time they spent together away from Houston, the closer they could become. And he'd realize that them being together wasn't such a crazy idea after all.

This weekend was supposed to give them that time. The time Oakes needed to see her as a woman. An intelligent, fun, interesting woman he could be attracted to. One he could envision spending time with on real dates, having a real relationship with.

She glanced at her reflection in the full-length mirror. Too bad staying in the room next to his and barging into his personal space hadn't gotten the results she'd hoped for. Instead of the quiet,

romantic evening she'd imagined—dinner, followed by drinks, followed by their first kiss—
he'd gone off without her.

Leaving her to resort to Plan B.

And a plan was totally different from a so-called
scheme, no matter what Zach would say.

Plan B was to show up at O'Riley's, the bar Kane
owned, where she had learned on Facebook that
Charlotte's friends were throwing a bachelor/bach-
elorette party for the bride and groom.

Funny how Oakes forgot to mention that.

She'd also found out—thanks to social media—
that the party was open to any and all friends of
the couple, for a twenty-dollar cover fee. Well,
luckily, Daphne had twenty dollars and a dress
that showcased her curves to their best advantage. Oakes wasn't going to know what hit him.

She hoped.

Not that she wanted him to want her only for
her looks. But it might be a good place to start.
She'd caught Oakes watching her more than once
when he thought she wasn't looking. It gave her
courage. Gave her hope. Made her think he liked
what he saw—at least enough to keep right on
looking.

And told her that what she felt wasn't as one-
sided as he'd like her to believe. As he'd probably
like himself to believe.

Reaching behind her for the zipper running up

her back, she frowned. She twisted her other arm back there, her fingers waving as they tried to touch metal. With a sigh, she dropped her arms, looked over her shoulder the best she could and continued twisting around. When she realized she was basically chasing her own tail—like a dog—she stopped and mulled over her options, of which there was exactly one.

She needed to find help.

Pressing the fabric of her dress against her chest with one hand, she used the other hand to hold the material together in the back and stepped out into the hallway. Looked right. Then left. Empty. Where was everyone? Should she knock on a door or two?

If she was in Houston she wouldn't think twice. Texans were friendly folks, the kind who helped out a girl when she needed it. But who knew what these Pennsylvanians were like. East coasters were different, especially the northern variety.

A light, female laugh drifted up from a doorway and she tiptoed toward it. Saw a set of narrow stairs leading down to the first floor. Daphne hurried down, peeked around the corner and gave a huge sigh of relief to find the kitchen… and Gracie.

"My savior," she said, only then noticing the handsome boy with short brown hair and a swoon-worthy grin who stood on the other side of the counter. "Oh, not you," Daphne told him. "Though I'm sure you're a very nice person."

"Daphne," Gracie said, not the least perturbed to find a guest sneaking down what was obviously an employees-only stairway, or that said guest was now hiding behind said stairway wall like a creeper. "Are you okay?"

"I'm fine. Just having a bit of a clothing issue." She started to turn to show Gracie what the problem was, but then realized she would be flashing the boy, too, so she stayed very still. "I can't zip up my dress."

The boy raised his eyebrows but thankfully didn't get all weird about a strange woman saying she needed help getting into her clothing. "Guess that leaves me out?" he asked in a tone that sounded hopeful—as if he wanted her to disagree.

She laughed. She loved kids, teenagers most of all. And it was obvious this one was a charmer. "I think, in this situation, that would be best."

"All right, though I should point out, I've been zipping zippers since I was three." He grinned at her, then at Gracie. "I hate to brag, but I was really advanced for my age."

Gracie sent him a serene smile. "That must be why you couldn't tie your shoes until you were in the second grade. Too much studying up on zippering."

"I like to focus on one thing at a time."

And holy cow, but that was said intensely and the meaningful look he shot at Gracie had her blushing. Wowza. In a couple of years that kid was going to be mighty dangerous to a girl's heart.

Daphne studied Gracie. Then again, it looked as if he was already a danger to one particular girl's heart right now.

"I wouldn't mind someone focusing on getting this dress closed," Daphne said. "It's getting drafty in here."

"Oh, right," Gracie said at the same time the boy said, "I'll uh… I'll just go warm up the car, okay, Gracie?"

She bit her lower lip. "Are you sure you want to go shopping tonight?"

The boy seemed disappointed but shook it off quickly, sent Gracie a grin. "I'm running out of time. Plus, the stores are open late so…"

"Okay," Gracie said, though she still seemed indecisive about whatever they were discussing. "Yes. I'll be out in a few minutes."

He grabbed a coat and hat and loped off, the way handsome, charming teenaged boys did, all ease and confidence and grace. The world was his and he knew it, if only because he'd been blessed with the kind of good looks and friendly personality that appealed to the masses.

After he'd turned a corner, Daphne stepped into the kitchen and presented Gracie with her back. "Can I just say...wow. Your boyfriend is supercute."

When Gracie didn't answer, Daphne glanced over her shoulder to find the girl blushing so hard, Daphne worried her face might burst into flames.

"He's not my boyfriend," Gracie said, ducking her head. She grabbed the zipper's tab with enough force to pull Daphne back a step. "We work together. And he is a friend. My friend. Who is a boy. But we're not, we don't..."

"I get it," Daphne said gently, surprised to see Gracie so flustered. She'd been so composed earlier. "I'm sorry. I didn't mean to make you uncomfortable."

But if the way that boy had looked at Gracie was any indication, he was looking to upgrade from coworker and friend-who-is-a-boy to boyfriend with a capital *B*.

Unfortunately, Daphne had enough on her plate tonight without delving into her new teenage friend's love life.

It'd have to wait until tomorrow.

Gracie tugged on the zipper. And tugged. And tugged some more. "Don't take this the wrong way," she said, "but could you maybe hold in your stomach a bit?"

"It's the damn cookies," Daphne muttered, sucking in her stomach and holding it. "If we can't get me into this dress, I'm holding you and that chef... Douglas—"

"Damien," Gracie amended.

"Whatever. He's obviously the devil. And you're in cahoots with him. Letting me eat seven cookies like that. I knew I should have stopped at six. Yes, it was that seventh cookie that did this."

"Almost...have it..." With a final tug, Gracie pulled up the zipper the rest of the way. "There. It looks great from back here, by the way."

"I hope so," Daphne said. "Considering I'm giving up breathing. Mirror?"

Gracie pointed to a door off a short hallway. Daphne went through it, walking into a half bath with a full-length mirror behind the door, where she took in her reflection. The dress was perhaps a bit snug around the hips, but then she liked to show off her curves, her shape. She believed in embracing herself in all her forms—mind, body and spirit. And, if she did say so herself, she looked good.

Damn good.

Negotiating the stairs to her room would be tricky but she'd left her purse up there. Not to mention her shoes and coat. She had no choice.

"You're a lifesaver," she told Gracie when she reentered the kitchen.

"You're welcome. Though I'd like to point out that during the heat of battle—me against your zipper—you referred to me as the devil's assistant. Which wasn't very nice."

"It wasn't. My apologies. I'd offer to grovel for forgiveness but let's be honest, there's no way I'm bending over in this dress, let alone getting on my knees. So how about you do like that song and let it go?"

Gracie slapped her hands over her ears. "Don't mention that song. My brother watches *Frozen* every day. And I mean every...single...day. Bringing up that song is like an invitation to having it stuck in your head for the next twenty-four hours. It's like one of those brain-eating worms. It just stays in there." Her voice dropped to a horrified whisper. "Forever."

Daphne laughed and linked her arm with Gracie's. "Sorry. Or as you kids say, my bad."

Gracie rolled her eyes. "Don't make me regret liking you."

"Oh, don't worry. There's no chance of that happening. I'm extremely likable." She patted Gracie's arm. "Which is lucky for me because I'm going to need your help putting my shoes on, too."

CHAPTER NINE

SOMETHING WAS WRONG.

Oakes didn't mean just the fact that over two hours ago Daphne had waltzed into O'Riley's, Kane's bar, looking like sin in a deep purple dress and high heels. Or that he'd spent a good portion of the last hour distracted by her presence, by her bare legs and the questions running through his head like "how did she even knew about the party?" and "why was she here?"

He'd kept his distance but had also kept an eye on her, had watched her mingling with the guests. And he noticed that she was missing her usual ease, the part of her that seemed so comfortable in any situation. Worse, the last time he'd spotted her she'd been standing alone, watching the other guests with a smile on her face, but he knew it wasn't one of her real smiles, more like a polite, keep-your-distance smile. The kind he'd seen on plenty of people's faces at social events he'd been attending since he was a kid.

He took a step toward her when C.J. joined him. "You brought Zach's sister?"

C.J.'s tone was harsh. Questioning. Oakes didn't let it bother him. His eldest brother was a pain in the ass, but he really did mean well. He took after their father in many ways, but in that way of meaning well and actually caring about other people was where Senior and Junior differed.

"You know I didn't bring her," Oakes said. "You saw me at the Ellisons' dinner party."

"Then what is she doing here?"

Oakes didn't want to explain that she was his plus one to the wedding. Had hoped to avoid any and all discussion about it and just show up on Saturday with her on his arm. And that, he could see now, was a stupid plan.

"She and Charlotte got to know each other in Houston," Oakes said. "When Zach was in the hospital. Maybe she told Daphne about the party."

"No, that's not what I mean. I already asked Kane and he said they didn't invite her to the wedding. And, as you and she are friends, the question is what is she doing *here*, as in Shady Grove?"

Oakes sighed. Sipped his beer. "She's my date to the wedding."

"Oh." C.J. paused. "Do you think that's a good idea? Dating Zach's sister?"

"We're not dating," Oakes said. "I'm doing her a favor for the weekend. And in case you haven't noticed, she's over there and I'm over here. We're not together."

"I've noticed that you've been watching her most of the night."

Oakes frowned at his brother. "What the hell are you? A stalker?"

Kane joined them. Though they were full blood brothers and looked very similar, C.J. was broader, his blond hair cut short, his style conservative, more in tune with the CEO of a major American corporation. Kane, on the other hand, was leaner, rangier, with hair long enough to pull back into a ponytail and tattoos peeking out from under the edge of his shirtsleeves, his jeans dark and new, but his biker boots faded and worn.

"Who's a stalker?" Kane asked, sipping a bottle of water.

"C.J.," Oakes said. "He's been watching me all night."

"I'd think, if I had a woman who looked like Ivy," Kane drawled, "I'd have my eyes on her. And not you, Oakes."

At the mention of Ivy's name, C.J. scanned the room as if seeking her out. Oakes followed suit, finding the gorgeous blonde holding court in the corner surrounded by three men.

"You aren't going to put a stop to that?" Oakes asked. C.J. liked to control everything. And Oakes meant every damn thing.

"That'd be like trying to stop the sun from shining," C.J. said in an easygoing, accepting way that about knocked Oakes back two steps.

Guess being in love really had changed C.J. Or else he'd finally smartened up enough to realize that there were some things better left alone.

"Besides," C.J. continued, "Ivy can handle herself. Never doubt that."

Oakes didn't. Even though he hadn't spent all that much time with her due to the craziness of the past few months, what with Zach's injuries, Ivy and C.J. getting back together, her moving to Houston to live with C.J., then giving birth a few days before Thanksgiving, not to mention the ongoing medical issues with their father.

C.J. set his empty glass on a tray. "Kane, by the way, Estelle asked about seeing the baby tomorrow. Tell her she can stop by our room at King's Crossing in the morning."

Estelle was Kane's eighteen-year-old daughter. The baby being C.J.'s newborn son.

"I'll tell her," Kane said. "But she doesn't usually roll out of bed until around eleven. Although tomorrow might be an exception since she and Charlotte have plans, plans and more plans to do with this wedding."

Estelle had taken to Charlotte right away. Not surprisingly as Charlotte was great. She was sweet and smart and funny, and she didn't take any bullshit from Kane.

Plus, they were relatively close in age. And that fact, Oakes realized, made his niece and soon-to-be sister-in-law close to Daphne's age, too.

In case he needed reminding that she was too young for him. Though Charlotte hadn't been too young for Kane.

But just because Kane had fallen in love with a much younger woman, didn't mean Oakes was about to follow suit and pursue anything with Daphne. It was too close to Senior's behavior—taking advantage of young women, using his name and wealth and innate charm to draw them in, then tossing them aside when he was done with them.

"I was talking to Oakes about the fact that he brought Zach's sister halfway across the country for a weekend getaway," C.J. said.

"Ah, is that what this little powwow is about?" Kane asked. "I thought maybe Carrie had snuck in and was accosting him again."

Carrie, their father's now ex-wife, had had too much to drink at Kane and Charlotte's Valentine's Day engagement party and had come on to Oakes. "If I remember correctly, I was dealing with that situation just fine," Oakes said, irritated that C.J. had put his nose into business where it didn't belong. His brother had taken it upon himself to take

Carrie aside and tell her, in no uncertain terms, to stop hanging on Oakes.

Oakes might have appreciated the backup if C.J. hadn't acted as if Oakes couldn't handle the situation on his own.

"You're dating Zach's sister?" Kane asked. "When did that start?"

"It didn't start," Oakes said from between his teeth. "And her name is Daphne."

"We know her name," C.J. pointed out, though Oakes couldn't remember a time where C.J. had actually spoken to Daphne, other than to assure her when Zach was first brought back to Houston that he'd be all right, that he'd pull through. "Just...be careful there. There are too many ties between our families for you to start something with her. And Christ knows Zach is hard enough to get along with as it is—he'll be an even bigger pain in the ass and want even less to do with any of us if you sleep with his sister."

"We're not sleeping together," Oakes said, working to keep his voice casual, his growing irritation in check. "And even if we were, it'd be none of Zach's damn business. Just like it would be none of yours."

With that, he walked away. But not before hearing Kane say, "Good work, Junior. At this rate, you'll alienate both your youngest brothers before you even get your kid baptized."

Oakes kept walking, kept his gaze averted, avoided making eye contact with anyone. He wasn't in the mood for small talk or for being friendly—he wasn't interested in being the nice guy, or the easygoing, good brother. He crossed to Daphne, who was standing near the dartboard, smiling at something a small group of people were saying.

"Excuse us," Oakes said, not recognizing anyone in the group.

Without another word, he wrapped his fingers around Daphne's wrist and tugged her toward the corner. "Wow," she said, somewhat breathlessly, since they had walked pretty quickly across the room. "That was rude. I didn't know you even had it in you to be rude."

Wasn't that what everyone thought? That he was some pushover, always doing what other people wanted? He didn't know whether to be pissed or not. He *was* a nice guy. He liked being a nice guy. He didn't want to go around with a chip on his shoulder like Kane and Zach, didn't need a huge ego like C.J.'s to make him feel good about himself.

Hell, he was losing his mind.

"We're leaving," he simply said, instead of trying to explain what was going on in his head—which he didn't even understand himself.

She frowned. "Now?"

"No, in twenty minutes. I just wanted you to be prepared."

She raised her eyebrows. "Rude and sarcastic all in one evening? It is a banner day." She studied him. "What's going on?"

What was going on was that he was irritated and annoyed and ready to leave. His thoughts were racing, he was pissed at his brothers for giving him a hard time for bringing her. He was angry at her, too, for showing up after he'd purposely not invited her.

Plus, no matter how much he tried to deny it—to others and himself—he had sought her out tonight, had thought of her.

Lately he thought of her too much. Too often. And those thoughts were anything but brotherly.

"I'm ready to leave." He managed to keep his voice calm and collected, even forced a smile. "If you'd rather stay, I'm sure Kane or C.J. could see you back to the bed-and-breakfast."

"Well, considering that I'm more than capable of seeing myself back to the B and B—just as I saw myself here—I'd say I don't need either you or your brothers to haul me back there. And even if I did need to be taken home like a child, I sure wouldn't ask either of them. In case you haven't noticed, Kane is busy being an almost groom and

I'm sure C.J. and Ivy are anxious to get back to their baby."

He glanced at his brothers and saw that she was right. Kane was doing his best to look interested in some conversation with his future father-in-law and C.J. stood at Ivy's side while she spoke with Charlotte's older sister… Sarah or Sasha or something like that.

"There aren't any cabs in Shady Grove," he pointed out. "No public transportation—"

"That's not true. There's some sort of busing system. I checked. But it stops running at nine. Small towns. So…different than the city. Anyway, I'm sure I could find a ride."

"You're my responsibility this weekend," he pointed out to Daphne. "I'll take you home. Or at least, back to your room. If you want to stay longer, that's fine. It just looked to me as if you weren't having a good time."

"Don't be ridiculous," she said but wouldn't meet his eyes. "I've had a lovely evening. But I am tired so maybe leaving now would be best."

They thanked their hosts and said their goodbyes. And Oakes saw the pointed glance his brothers exchanged as he helped Daphne on with her wrap. To piss them off because he was feeling contrary, he kept his hand on her lower back as they walked out into the bitter cold to his car.

By the time they reached it, at the far side of the parking lot, they were both shivering.

"Good God." Daphne gasped as she slid into the passenger-side seat. "How do people live with this cold? And they actually *do* things outside in the winter? Skiing and sledding and skating? Makes no sense to me."

He turned on the car and blasted the heater, but all that came out was cold air so he turned it to low, prayed it would warm soon. He rubbed his hands together before placing them on the freezing steering wheel and slowly pulled out into the street.

Two blocks down the road, he cleared his throat. "I'm sorry if I was…short with you. At the party."

"Yeah, I figured. It's okay. It's actually sort of nice."

Following the directions on the GPS, he turned left. "So you like someone snapping at you?"

"Not particularly. What I meant was, it's nice knowing you're not perfect after all."

His fingers tightened on the wheel. "I never said I was perfect."

"You wouldn't, but let's face it, you're pretty darn close to it. I mean, look at you." Turning in her seat, she waved a hand at him. "Good-looking. Smart. Successful. Funny. You don't take yourself too seriously, you're easygoing and everyone likes you. You never get mad. Tonight was the first time since my high school graduation that I've seen you get even mildly irritated." He sensed more than saw her shrug. "Like I said, it's nice knowing you can get pissed or annoyed or just have a bad day or be in a bad mood. Makes you seem more...real."

He wasn't sure why her assessment of him bugged him, but it did. Was that how she saw him? As a bland, nice guy, always smiling like some idiot who didn't know any better? "Not everyone likes me," he insisted, not knowing how to refute her other points when he knew most of them were true. He was easygoing, but what was the point of being otherwise? Too many things were out of your control, namely other people. Why bother getting upset when they didn't live up to your expectations? "Zach doesn't."

"True," she said, as they pulled into the private parking lot of the Bradford House. "But that's only because he's a dumb-ass who blames you and your mom for the lot that was his life. Plus, he knows you care too much about it, about him liking you. That you want to be close to him, to have the same type of relationship with him as you have with your other brothers. When you give people that much power over you, when you try too hard, it gives them all the control."

He stared at her, stunned. He hadn't done that.

Had he? Yes, he wanted to have a relationship with Zach, but she made him sound like some damn puppy, overeager and desperate for approval.

Hell. This night just kept getting worse and worse.

IF PEOPLE DIDN'T want her opinion, Daphne thought as she climbed the B and B's stairs, with Oakes behind her like a brooding specter, why did they ask?

Okay, so maybe he hadn't specifically asked for her thoughts on his relationship—or lack thereof—with Zach, but he *had* brought it up. Had brought up their brother specifically. She wondered if he'd done it to make a point. To remind them both of the ties between them, the ones he probably saw as an obstacle. As too twisted and knotted to ever be unraveled.

At the top of the stairway she turned left, headed down the hallway toward her room. The building was quiet, a few lights burning in the hall. Funny how, only a few hours ago, she'd been so hopeful about this evening, so excited to be spending any amount of time with Oakes. But at the party, that hope had drained, that excitement had faded, and now all she wanted was to slip inside her room, wiggle out of this dress and go to bed.

She slowed her steps, glanced at his profile. He

was unsmiling, his hair flopping over his brow. He made her heart stutter and he kept as much distance from her as possible.

It was almost enough to make a girl want to give up.

Yeah, he'd been courteous and nice—up until when he'd been ready to leave. But he'd still treated her with the polite distance of someone looking after a friend.

Or a kid sister.

She pulled her key out of her clutch. Him taking her back to Bradford House was him being the nice guy he was, not wanting her to have to find another ride. Or not trusting her to be able to do so.

She shouldn't have gone to the party. Plan B had been a bust and she hadn't been able to come up with a Plan C.

Sometimes a girl just had to know when to cut her losses.

Even at the dive bar, where she *should* have felt right at home, she hadn't belonged, had been surrounded by people so far out of her social stratosphere she'd felt like a rock surrounded by stars.

And now those inner self-doubts, the ones she fought so hard to keep hidden, to pretend didn't exist, were roaring, trying to escape from the cage she'd locked them away in long ago.

She gave an inner eye roll. God. Dramatic,

much? She really needed sleep. It'd been a long day, filled with ups and downs and failed schemes, and the best thing she could do now was get some rest. Regroup in the morning.

Everything would look much better, much clearer and way more hopeful, in the light of a new day.

Facing Oakes, she smiled but kept her voice soft in deference to the other B-and-B guests. "Thanks for the ride." She wasn't deluded enough to think he'd do something as spontaneous, as wonderful, as kissing her good-night, so she unlocked her door. Opened it and stepped inside. "Good night."

"Do *you* blame me?" he asked quietly.

"Excuse me?"

He stepped forward, close enough that she couldn't shut the door without slamming it in his face. "Do you blame me? For the lot that is your life?"

Crap. Why had she said that about Zach? She'd always had a problem saying too much, giving away too many of her thoughts, her feelings. For the *most* part, she'd learned how to watch her words, how to hold some things back, lest they make a return trip and bite her in the ass.

Prime example right here. Right now.

She forced a light laugh. "Don't take it personally. Zach just needs an excuse to keep his emotional distance from you. From your entire family."

Oakes edged ever closer and she found herself backing up a half step. "I didn't ask about Zach. I'm asking about you. Do you blame me, Daphne? If I hadn't been around, if I hadn't been born, maybe my mother wouldn't have stayed married to my father. Maybe he would have married your mother."

"No. Oakes, I didn't say Zach's feelings were logical. Obviously, they aren't. If you hadn't been born, then my mother wouldn't have been hired to be your nanny and would never have met your father, let alone had an affair with him and gotten pregnant."

He shook his head. "Maybe *blame* isn't the right word. Do you resent me for having the life you didn't get a chance to have? I know Zach hates our father and that's his right. He took advantage of your mother when she was barely an adult, got her pregnant. Or maybe it's my mother you should place the blame on for staying with my father after she found out about the affair. For forgiving him and giving him a second chance. For believing he deserved a second chance. Keeping him tied to her instead of freeing him to be with your mother."

"Please. Do you really think my mom and your dad would have lasted longer than six months?

They had nothing in common. And I don't think she loved him. Not really. She was infatuated. Taken in by an older, handsome, charming, powerful man."

"Exactly. He took advantage of her youth. Her innocence."

"And she learned a valuable lesson." Because he seemed so upset, so angry on her mother's behalf, she touched his arm. "Oakes, she wasn't blameless in what happened. She knows it. She took responsibility for her choices long ago."

"If my father hadn't seduced her," Oakes continued as if he hadn't even heard her, "if he hadn't gotten her pregnant, she never would have felt as if she needed to marry your father."

Daphne went cold all over. Oh, no way was she going there. She was not about to let him delve into her history, wasn't about to share her past with him, the truth of it all.

She believed in truth and honesty and all of that—for the people she counseled at her internship. Not necessarily herself.

"If she hadn't married him," Daphne told him, forcing a grin she didn't feel, knowing it probably wasn't fooling him one bit, "I wouldn't have been born. And then the world would have missed out in the glory that is me, so really, it was a win-win all around for everyone. Now, look at the time," she said, checking an invisible watch on her wrist. "So late. No wonder I'm beat. Must be jet lag."

"It's only one hour difference from Houston to here, which means it's not even eleven o'clock in Houston."

How had he gotten so close to her? He now stood fully in her room, but that hadn't stopped her from holding on to the door handle even though the door was now wide open. "Yes, well, I'm not much of a night owl. Early to bed and early to rise and all that. So, once more, good night. Thanks for the ride back here," she added, in case he refused to leave until she'd used the top level of proper etiquette and politeness. But he just stood there and she needed to fill in the silence so she blurted out the first thing that came to mind. "The party was fun."

"No, it wasn't. At least, not for you."

"I didn't say *I* had fun. I said the party was fun."

It had seemed to be a success. Plenty of people had laughed and drank and ate.

"I knew you looked uncomfortable," Oakes said almost triumphantly. So glad she could help him get some sort of personal win for the old ego. "You didn't enjoy yourself at all. Why?"

She sighed. First the questions about her resenting him, blaming him for her childhood, her family, now he wanted to know why she hadn't had a great time at a party she'd essentially crashed?

"I did enjoy it," she insisted, though the lie seemed to fall flat. "It's tough, not knowing any-one—"

"Bullshit."

She could only stare at him. And her silence, unfortunately, gave him the opportunity to keep right on talking.

"You're one of the friendliest people I know," he continued, then shocked her again by simply tugging on the door until she released the handle and closing it firmly behind him. Leaving them, neat as you please, alone in her room. "You never have problems meeting new people or making friends."

What was with him tonight? First his being short and grumpy with her at the party and now this stubborn need to dig into her psyche, delve into her inner thoughts.

She'd thought she'd known everything about him, but now he was showing her there was much more to him than just a good guy who could al-ways be counted on to have your back. Not that these new traits were all that fabulous. Actually they should, reasonably, have her rethinking her feelings for him. Instead, they did the opposite.

Like she'd said, it was nice, discovering he wasn't quite as perfect as she'd always assumed.

He didn't have to be perfect to be perfect for her. Besides, knowing and seeing his faults—at least a few of them, and who knew what she'd find once she dug deeper beneath the surface—made him seem even more approachable. As if they were on a level playing field instead of him being on a pedestal.

One she'd lugged into the room and pushed him onto, she admitted.

Since it looked as if he wasn't going anywhere until he got some answers, she decided to give him a bit of the truth. Not about her family, not about her father or how bad it had been for her growing up. That was all history and she wasn't going to dig it up for anyone. Not even him.

But she could give him *something*, could try to explain what had happened to her tonight.

"I am extremely friendly," she agreed, crossing to the dresser and taking off her jewelry, sliding her bracelet off, then removing her earrings. "A big part of it is just my natural personality. I like people and enjoy getting to know them."

"You didn't seem to enjoy getting to know anyone at the party," he said, leaning against the door, his arms crossed.

"I introduced myself to a few people," she said, moving to sit on the edge of the bed and slide her heels off. She stretched her legs, pointed her toes then flexed her foot, did a few ankle circles. "It's just… I hadn't realized how I'd feel…being surrounded by so many obviously wealthy people."

He frowned. "What?"

This was why she hadn't wanted to tell him. It sounded so stupid, so immature, when spoken aloud. Giving him even more ammunition against them being together, as she acted like some insecure teenager.

"I regressed, okay?" she said, a snap to her tone that she hadn't meant to be there. She inhaled and held it for the count of five. Felt better once she exhaled. "It was like going back to high school, all the pretty, pretty rich kids with their designer clothes and expensive cars and huge homes. And then there was me, getting dropped off by my mother in her secondhand truck. You know, I used to ask her to drop me off at the corner," she admitted, ashamed at herself for being embarrassed, for caring what other people had thought. "So no one would see us. She must have thought I was embarrassed of her. I'll have to remember to tell her I wasn't. I just… I didn't want to be different."

"I can't imagine you not wanting to be different. You were born to stand out."

Nothing he could have said would have pleased her more. "Thank you." She had to clear the emotion from her throat. "You're right. I do like being different. Did. But I always wanted those differences to be my own, to be my personality and my style and the way I thought. Not my social or familial situation."

She shook her head, feeling foolish for letting her memories, her past, come back and cloud what should have been a very nice evening. An evening where she could have met new and interesting people.

"Zach paid for me to go to that high school," Daphne continued, talking about the private school she'd attended. "He and mom wanted the best for me. But mom drew the line at him supporting us fully. So I was a fish out of water. And you know, it wasn't even the other kids that bothered me. Most of them were decent. There were even some with similar backgrounds to me, those who'd earned scholarships or whose parents had somehow managed to afford tuition. And I didn't really experience teasing or harassment or anything. It was just me. Knowing I was so different from them. I was always friendly, but I never made any real friends there. I knew it would be too one-sided. But most days I felt as if I was playing make-believe, pretending to be upbeat and happy. Pretending it didn't bother me, that I wasn't envious of their wealth, the seeming ease at which they lived each day. And I just... I couldn't force myself to do that tonight."

"Why didn't you tell me?" he asked quietly.

She snorted. "Tell you that I was having a

flashback to adolescence and was freaking out that I was afraid no one would like me, or that they'd figure out I got this dress off the rack during Nordstrom's seventy-percent-off sale?" She shook her head. "No. This is my problem—one I am working on and will continue to work on. I promise, at the wedding, I will be my usual charming, effervescent self, bringing joy and spreading sunshine to everyone I meet."

To convince him of her sincerity, because it was obvious the man was concerned about her, she closed the distance between them with a smile. She needed to show him that she really was all right, albeit a bit embarrassed to have acted so insecure this evening.

She held up two fingers. "I really am okay," she promised him solemnly. "Scout's honor."

"I think Scouts hold up three fingers," he said. "Isn't the one you're doing the Vulcan salute from *Star Trek*?"

"No. That's like this…" She held up all four fingers and separated the ring and middle fingers. "Well, I guess two fingers can be the Lynch family salute. One meant to represent honor and honesty and all good things, like peace on earth, equal pay for equal work and justice for all. Amen," she added because it seemed to need a strong ending.

"I don't want you to feel insecure at the wedding," he said, obviously not believing she was as okay as she'd claimed. "If you're uncomfortable at all, at any time, just let me know."

"That's sweet and I'll take you up on it but honestly, Oakes, I'm good. And I'll be just fine at the wedding. *If* I can avoid all those death glares being sent my way by Kane's mother, that is." She shivered dramatically. "That woman is scary."

Gwen Bartasavich wasn't exactly a sweet, kind, cuddly sort of mother—Daphne doubted she would have been one even if her husband hadn't cheated on her and left her for another woman.

For Oakes's mother.

"Gwen's not that bad," Oakes said. The man was nothing if not kind and patient. Even with the woman who'd rather gut him with one of her spiked heels than look at him. "She's had a difficult life."

"Well, she hasn't helped herself by making bad choices, choosing to hold on to her feelings for a man who doesn't deserve them and blaming everyone else for her problems." Realizing what she'd just said, she grimaced. "Nothing personal against your father or anything."

Oakes grinned. "Believe me, I'm aware of my father's flaws. Hard not to be when faced with so many so often."

She returned his smile, but the lightened mood dimmed a bit when his gaze dropped to her mouth for a heartbeat. Then two. Her pulse skittered. She wanted to rise onto her toes, press her mouth to his. Wanted him to see how things could be between them. But she wouldn't make the first move. Wouldn't let him claim she'd pushed him into something.

He slowly uncrossed his arms and pushed away from the door, bringing his body within inches of hers. All she had to do was take that one step to bring them together.

She didn't move a muscle.

"I should go," he said, his voice soft and gruff.

Not trusting her voice, lest she say something stupid that guaranteed to set him running and not ever looking back, she nodded.

She waited, breath held, eyes locked on his. He didn't go. Didn't turn to break the spell that had been woven between them, that had the room suddenly warming. Shrinking.

"I'm not perfect," he said into the silence, a stark, blurted confession.

"I don't want you to be," she whispered. "Would never ask you to try and be perfect."

She would never put that pressure on him. Was that what had happened to him growing up? Had he felt the need to be the good guy, to play the peacemaker? Or was he simply tired of people only seeing a certain side of him?

"No," he said, thoughtfully, "you're not asking me to be perfect. Just to put my wants ahead of everyone else, ahead of everyone I care about most. Ahead of what's best."

Her heart started thumping so hard in her chest, she was afraid he could see it. He knew. He knew she wanted him to kiss her. That she just wanted him. "I'm not—"

"You are. And the worst part? When I'm standing here looking at you, smelling your perfume, having you so close to me, I'm not even sure why I'm fighting it. I can't even remember why I would want to fight it."

She couldn't speak. Couldn't think. He stepped forward and slid one arm around her waist, pulled her slowly, yet insistently, toward him. His other hand went to her neck, where he slid it behind her head, his hand in her hair. Cupping her head back, he lowered his head and kissed her.

His mouth was smooth and warm and firm and moved slowly, expertly, over hers. Oakes Bartsavich was kissing her. He was finally kissing her. It was like a dream come true.

And she was standing there like a ninny, her arms at her sides, her eyes wide open, her mouth unmoving.

Crap.

He lifted his head and sent her a quizzical look and she knew she'd blown it. She'd dreamed of their first kiss for so long, for so many years, and instead of it being the magical, perfect moment she'd always imagined, it'd been as awkward and strange as her cousins had feared it would be.

Not because they'd been friends, but because she was too nervous, too worried about making it just right. Because she'd been shocked he'd read her intentions so easily. Now it was ruined, the moment was over and he was already slowly backing up, his hands sliding from her.

He looked as if he wanted to say something, but then shook his head. "Good night, Daphne." He opened the door.

"Wait!"

He sighed, not looking back at her. "I don't think—"

"I need you to unzip my dress," she blurted, hating that she had to ask him to do it, but seeing as how there was no one else around and she wasn't about to sleep in this thing, she had no choice.

He faced her, his eyes narrowed. Suspicious. As if she'd just given him the worst kiss in the world and now wanted to lure him into bed by doing a striptease in front of him.

It wouldn't have been a bad idea, either, if her thoughts weren't racing, if she wasn't so confused herself at the moment.

"You want me to what?" he asked.

"My dress." She presented him with her back, in case he leaped out into the hall and ran to his own room before realizing she was in desperate need here. "Please."

She held her breath. She could sense him deliberating. It was obvious all he wanted was to go to his room and pretend that moment between them had never happened. Finally, she felt him shift toward her. He grabbed the zipper and tugged it down. It wasn't like in the movies, where the man pulled it down slowly, his fingers trailing against the woman's skin, his gaze following the movement, watching each inch of exposed back.

Nope, it was pretty much over in two seconds. Down went the zipper and out the door went Oakes.

Holding the dress up in front, she turned. Her hands trembling, she locked the door then wiggled the dress past her hips and let it fall to the floor. Gave it a kick for good measure. All her hopes. All her dreams of their first kiss had been destroyed. She needed a few minutes to absorb the blow. To accept it, as she had so many other disappointments in life. She'd curl up in bed, do some serious soul searching and figure out a way to fix this. A way to mend this setback and get them moving on the right track again.

She may be down, but she wasn't out. Not yet.

CHAPTER TEN

LUKE GRABBED HIS books and hurried out into the hall. It was packed with kids getting stuff from their lockers and hurrying to catch their bus or their ride home. They had early dismissal from school today to start Christmas break and everyone was amped up, excited to be going home early, ready for the two weeks off they'd get for the holiday.

It was so packed, he had a hard time finding Gracie, but luckily, he was a few inches taller than most of the kids. He rose onto his toes and looked left then right, spying her curly hair as she walked down the hall toward the cafeteria.

He made his way toward her. Would have called out her name but he doubted she'd hear him over everyone talking and laughing, the boys pushing and shoving, the girls with their high-pitched giggles. But he had to catch her before she left. Had to talk to her.

He'd been doing a lot of thinking lately, and while he wasn't exactly sure how he felt about her—his feelings were still too confused in that area—he did know that he missed hanging out with her and that last night when they'd decorated cookies then later, had gone shopping, he'd been happy.

He wanted them to be friends again, for real.

But first they needed to spend more time together to get back to how they'd been. It was the perfect solution. They'd be friends, spend time together, and in the meantime he'd be able to figure out exactly how he felt about her.

Proud of his rational thinking, his problem solving, he caught up with her by the band-room doors. "Gracie," he called, reaching out to touch her shoulder. She turned and his heart did one slow roll in his chest. His throat felt tight and funny so he cleared it. "Hey."

"Hi, Luke."

She looked so pretty, her hair down, a colorful scarf around her neck, for a moment, he forgot what he'd wanted to tell her. "Uh…are you working today?"

She frowned at him. "Yes," she said slowly. Probably because she knew he already knew she was working. Fay kept a schedule in her office with everyone's work hours listed. "From three until eight."

"Yeah? Me, too." He grinned. "Hey," he continued, as if he'd just thought of it this moment, "why don't I pick you up? There are so many peo-

ple at the B and B," he said quickly, in case she
was thinking of a good reason why she shouldn't
accept his offer, "and the parking lot gets so full
there's hardly room for all the employees' cars.
Plus, we're supposed to get a lot of snow today
and into tonight and I know you're not completely
comfortable driving your dad's truck or Molly's
minivan in bad weather."

She'd told him that a few weeks back when
they'd been leaving work and it had been snowing steadily. He didn't think it made him a bad
guy to use it against her, to get what he wanted.

"Umm...sure. Why not?" she said. "That's really nice of you." But she said it in a way that
made him think she wasn't quite convinced his
only motivation was kindness and consideration.

"Great," he said as they started walking again.
"I'll pick you up at two forty-five." He glanced
out the glass doors that faced the student parking lot. The vehicles were covered in snow and
it was still falling. "Do you need a ride home?"

At that moment, Bryce walked up behind them
and slung his arm around Gracie's shoulder. Gave
her a quick squeeze that was a cross between
"we're buddies" and "I want to get into your
pants." "Ready?"

"Yes." Instead of shrugging off Bryce's arm,
she smiled up at him.

Finally, Bryce seemed to notice Luke was there.

He took his arm off of Gracie and let it fall to his side. "Hey, Sapko. How's it going?"

"Good." He knew he should say more, ask about Bryce's plans for college or even the holiday break, knew he needed to be the nice guy and pretend that it didn't bother him in the least that Bryce stood so close to Gracie, and that she didn't seem to mind. He forced his brain to come up with something, anything, to say that wouldn't make him seem like an idiot, standing there staring at the two of them. "Got any plans for break?"

Lame, yeah, but at least it was something.

"Not too much. I think we're going to a Pens' game next week if my dad can score tickets. Man, too bad you couldn't have played for both the hockey team and the football team. The hockey team could've used you."

Luke just smiled but it was forced. He'd played hockey most of his life, had even thought he'd make a career out of it until his sophomore year, when a new coach had taken over the high school program and had moved Luke from the first line to the fourth. He'd quit and started playing football instead, had been the starting quarterback the past two years. "They did pretty well considering the number of players they had."

Because a lot of his friends had switched to football, too.

"We'd better get going," Bryce said to Gracie,

jingling his keys in his hand. "It's really starting to come down. See ya, Luke."

"Yeah. Later."

Luke watched them walk across the parking lot. Bryce took Gracie's bag from her, which Luke knew to be loaded with books, and laughed at something she said. Luke's hands fisted. Someone bumped him.

"Sorry," a freshman murmured and Luke realized he was standing in the way, staring at some girl like an idiot.

Shoving his fists into his pockets he turned, headed back toward his locker to drop off his stuff and get his jacket. He went up the back set of stairs, taking them two at a time. It was going to be all right, he assured himself. He had a plan. It wasn't as if Gracie and Bryce were an item. They were just talking, going to a stupid dance together. He wasn't breaking anyone up.

Not like his supposedly best friend had broken up him and Kennedy.

Luke turned the corner and groaned. As if just thinking about her had conjured her, Kennedy leaned with her back against his locker as she texted someone. His steps slowed. He felt the familiar reaction to her. What could he say? He was a guy, a teenaged guy who hadn't had sex in months, and she was gorgeous. Long, silky red hair, big boobs and long legs. Her tight, dark jeans molded to her hips and ass and the green sweater rode a few inches up her waist, showing her flat stomach.

She must have sensed him approaching because she looked up and over, her eyes meeting his. A small, smug smile played on her face. That was Kennedy. Secure and confident in her looks. Knowing what she could get just by using those looks. The sad part was she didn't have to use them. She was smart and could be really funny, but over the last few years she'd changed from the girl who used to make him laugh, had an easy smile and was nice to everyone, to a walking, talking clichéd mean girl who talked about people behind their backs and manipulated everyone around her.

Or maybe she'd always been that way and he'd been so into her that he'd ignored it. But when he'd walked in on her and Drew just after they'd had sex, he couldn't ignore it any longer.

"Hi, Luke," she said, her tone breathless though the only strenuous activity she'd been doing was typing on her phone. "Wow, can you believe all the snow we're getting? My dad will be thrilled. You know we're taking our annual ski trip during Christmas break and they're supposed to have even more snow up in Vermont. Remember how much fun we had there last year?"

He nudged her aside so he could open his

locker. That had been her MO ever since crying and begging him to take her back hadn't worked. She'd begun reminding him of all the good times they'd had together, the trips they'd taken with each other's families, the plans they'd made to go to the same college, their promise to make it work long-distance if they couldn't go to school together.

All those plans, like his dreams of playing hockey professionally, were gone now. He was starting to think that it was a waste of time, planning and dreaming and setting goals. It was fine when it was just you, when the only person involved in making those dreams come true, in achieving those goals, was yourself and it was a solitary endeavor. But when you brought in other people, when you relied on them, when your dreams or goals depended on them doing their fair share or them realizing your potential, everything fell apart.

"What do you want, Kennedy?" he asked.

She frowned, but it didn't make her any less beautiful. When they were together, he never would have talked to her like that, never would have used that impatient tone. He'd tried to make her happy, tried to keep her happy, but it had become increasingly difficult over the past year.

Now he couldn't remember why he'd bothered trying.

"I just wanted to talk to you," she said with a pout. "I miss you."

Grabbing his coat and hat, he sighed. "We've been through this."

He shut the locker, spun the lock. She should have thought about missing him, about not being with him before she'd hooked up with Drew. Her cheating on him was what had made it impossible for them to work things out after they'd tried getting back together. Luke couldn't forget what she'd done.

Couldn't forgive her.

"I know," she said, hurrying to keep up with him as he walked down the hall. "It's just…it's Christmas. I was hoping maybe we could…try and be friends."

He had enough friends, but telling her that wouldn't get rid of her. She was always around anyway. They hung out with the same crowd, which included Drew. That made lunchtime interesting, seeing how they always sat so that there were several other buffer friends in between the three of them.

Maybe she was right. Maybe they should try to be friends, or at least, friendly. It would make life easier in a lot of ways, at parties and lunch— whenever they all hung out. If he let go of his anger toward her, she might stop acting so desperate to get back with him. There were plenty of guys who'd love to be her boyfriend. She needed to move on so he could move on.

He stopped at the doorway. Faced her. "Yeah. Maybe."

Her eyes lit up. "Really? Oh, Luke, thank you. You won't regret this. And now that we're friends, we can go to the dance together."

She said all of this with a satisfied smile on her beautiful face.

He shook his head. "I should have known you were up to something."

"Wait. What do you mean?" she asked, catching up with him once more as they descended the stairs. She smiled and waved at one of her friends. "Luke, I'm not trying anything. I only meant that we could go to the dance with the group. Like we always do."

Like they used to do, he wanted to amend, but what would be the point? She thought nothing had changed except that they were no longer a couple. She obviously didn't want anything else to change. "Actually I hadn't planned on going to the dance."

"I know, that's why I wanted to talk to you. I hate that you're not going because I'll be there—which is exactly why we should all go together. Half the boys are saying they won't go since you're not going, you know how it is. Half siding with you. A few siding with Drew. Come on,

Luke. It's our senior year. Do you really want the rest of it to be how it's been so far?"

He didn't. It hadn't been all bad, but the tension amongst his friends wasn't cool. And it wasn't exactly how he'd wanted them to spend their last year together. He and Drew both tried to downplay it, the animosity toward each other, and Drew had attempted to reconcile with Luke more than once, but Luke wasn't ready to forgive and forget just yet.

Though maybe he should.

"Okay," he said. "I'll go. With the group," he added, in case she started thinking it was going to be the two of them, like a couple.

"Thank you, Luke! Thank you!" She looked as if she wanted to hug him, but he kept his arms at his sides, his expression clearly telling her not to even try it. "You won't regret it."

He thought of Gracie and Bryce walking side by side, of what it was going to be like, how hard it was going to be watching them slow dancing together.

"I already do," he muttered and walked away.

OAKES SOMEHOW KNEW who it was knocking on his door before he even answered it. Maybe it was the three quick raps followed by three more, the rapid knocks full of energy and impatience. Maybe it was because he'd thought of Daphne pretty much nonstop since leaving her bedroom last night. Had dreamed about what he would have done if he'd given in to his impulse and kissed her again. If she'd responded instead of staring at him shell-shocked. How he could have unzipped her dress slowly, relishing the feel of her warm skin against his knuckles. How he could have peeled away that material, turned her slowly to face him...

Three more knocks followed, then she said, "I know you're in there, Oakes. Don't make me beg."

With a sigh, he opened the door, found Daphne in a pair of jeans and a thick sweater, her coat hanging over her arm.

"I can't imagine you begging," he said.

His imagination immediately went to the image of her begging him—not to let her into the room, but to touch her, to move inside of her, harder. Faster.

Hell.

She grinned, looking so fresh and pretty, her cheeks pink. One part of him wanted to slam the door in her face. But the other part of him wanted to yank her inside and pull her against him. He settled for stepping back so she could come in.

"Well, to be honest, I probably wouldn't have begged," she told him. "I mean, that seems a bit excessive just to be let into a room. Anyway, you'd have to come out at some time. I could always just lie in wait for you."

That was the problem. He felt as if she was lying in wait for him. He'd already snuck out of his room at the earliest convenience, grabbed breakfast and coffee from downstairs and brought it up here to eat so he wouldn't run in to her. Even then he'd felt like an idiot, looking around the corner before stepping onto the second floor, just to make sure she wasn't in the hall.

"Get your coat," she said.

"Excuse me?"

She frowned at him. "I'm not sure how else to say that. Put your coat on. Your jacket? That piece of outerwear I'm sure you bought in some fancy boutique in downtown Houston that has a designer's name stitched on the hand-sewn label and cost what most people spend for a month of groceries. Put that on your person. Please."

"First of all, I'm not C.J. I don't shop at boutiques. Second of all, my jacket was regular price, so no families went hungry because of me and, before you can ask me where it came from, it was made in the good old US of A, which I'm hoping means that no child labor was used in the production of it." Although it *was* a nice jacket and, yes, designer. Should he apologize for owning a nice coat? "Thirdly, why would I want to put it on?"

"Because it's cold outside." She crossed to the small closet, opened it and pulled his jacket off the hanger. "I mean, I've seen some people walking around without winter coats—and a few kids in shorts, which is just really weird because it's below freezing out there—but I figured you'd want to wear one."

She tossed it at him, leaving him no choice but to catch it. "I'm not going out."

"Of course you are. It's lunchtime and I'm hungry. Plus, I'm pretty sure you haven't been out of your room all day." She eyed him shrewdly. "You're not hiding from me, are you?"

Because, *damn it*, he had been, warmth suffused the back of his neck. "I've been working." He indicated his open laptop on the small desk, along with files he'd brought from the office. "Not hiding."

"Sure, sure. Whatever you say."

Obviously she wasn't buying a word of it. She was too perceptive.

"Well, now it's break time," she continued, slipping on her coat. "And if you have any gloves, you're going to want to put them on, too. A hat wouldn't be bad, either."

And with that she tugged on a bright red knit cap over her hair.

"I'm not going to lunch," he told her.

"Sure you are. You have to eat. And I'm starving, so…chop, chop." She clapped twice. When he didn't move, she sighed. Rolled her eyes. "Oh, come on. What's the problem?"

"The problem is I have work."

"All work and no play makes Oakesy a grumpy boy."

"No, it made Oakesy a full partner before his thirty-fifth birthday."

She snorted. "Please. You're a Bartasavich. You could have just told them you wanted to be partner. I'm sure they would have jumped at the chance to have you without you putting in so much overtime."

"I don't use my last name to get ahead," he said coolly. "I earn my own way."

And it pissed him off that she'd think otherwise.

"See? Grumpy. And sensitive, too. Let's get you some food, some fresh air and some really excellent company in the form of *moi*. You'll come back full, refreshed and ready to tackle the rest of those law briefs or boring court transcripts or whatever it is lawyers read. And, best of all, it's my treat. Really, you're getting a great deal here."

"What if I don't want a great deal?"

She sent him a considering look. "Well, then I guess I'd just have to accept that." But something in her tone told him there was more to it than that. She walked over to him and patted his chest. He stiffened, his breath locking in his lungs. "Yes, I would have to accept defeat gracefully and just... hang out here until you change your mind."

With a whoop, she leaped onto his bed, landing on her back. She rolled over to her side, propped herself up on an elbow and grinned at him. "You go on," she said, waving the fingers of her other hand. "Get back to work."

Work with her lying on his bed, her coat open, exposing how well that sweater fit her, her cheeks now even more pink from wearing that hat and coat inside?

She sighed and rolled onto her back, her arms spread out, her face tipped toward the ceiling. "Fay said this house is over one hundred years old. How cool is that to think that some other woman stared up at this exact same ceiling in a time before cell phones and cars and planes?"

He sat down at his desk, determined to wait her out. Made a noncommittal sound, mulling over her words—he was pretty sure there were cars one hundred years ago. But he wasn't letting her drag him into a conversation. Especially one so inane and meant only to distract him. To manipulate him into giving her what she wanted.

"It must have been boring back then," Daphne continued, sitting up now. "Especially for a woman, as most weren't allowed to work or get an education. I can't imagine sitting around all day, doing embroidery or whatever it was they did. No wonder they had so many kids. I mean, yeah, birth control was pretty much nonexistent, but what else was there to do all day except have sex? At least it would help pass the time, would kill a good fifteen minutes or so."

As he reread the passage he'd already gone over twice, yet couldn't remember a word of, his jaw clenched. He would not fall for it. Would not even think about her and sex or the fact that if that's how long she thinks the act lasted, she's been with the wrong men.

And that only had him thinking of her being with another guy, which amped up his irritation.

Damn it.

She shifted again, the bed bouncing as she scooted to the edge, sat with her legs swinging, her calves *thump, thump, thumping* the bed frame, driving him to distraction. "Don't get me wrong, I like kids," she continued. "Just in case it came across that I don't. I'm all for them. Just in smaller numbers. I'm thinking I'll have two. Three tops, and that's only if the first two are the same gender as I'd like one of each." He felt her studying him, but that didn't stop the thumping sound. "Males seem to run in the Bartasavich family, huh? Other than Kane's daughter. I'll probably end up with a bunch of nephews first before I have my own kids since I still have so much schooling to get through, but who knows. Zach likes to pretend that he's too much of a lone wolf to ever get married, do the whole husband-and-father thing. Now he's using his injuries as an excuse to remain single but he lost his arm and leg, not his—"

Oakes slammed the laptop shut. Stood. "Okay. Let's go."

He went around the desk, grabbed his coat and shrugged it on.

"If I would have known that was all it would take," Daphne said, "I would have brought up Zach's penis earlier." She frowned. "Wait. Ew. That didn't come out quite the way I meant. Pretend I didn't say that last part."

"With pleasure." He held open the door. "One hour," he told her as they stepped into the hall and he shut and locked the door behind them. "That's all. I have work I want to get done before the rehearsal dinner."

"Well, I can't promise anything, but I'll do my best to make sure you are back here, safe, sound, fed and happy an hour from now."

They went outside and he turned to head toward his rental car. "Let's walk," she said. "The restaurant Fay suggested is only a few blocks away."

"It's freezing. And snowing," he pointed out.

"Come on," she said, linking her arm through his and tugging him down the sidewalk. "It'll be an adventure. And it's so pretty. If we walk fast enough, we won't feel the cold."

"Your nose is already red," he said, falling into step beside her.

She rolled her eyes. "Okay, if we walk fast enough, we won't feel the cold *quite* as much."

How could he resist? She looked so pretty and happy, snowflakes collecting on her hat, clinging to her dark eyelashes. *An adventure*. That's what she said. He felt like every moment with her was an adventure. He wished he didn't find the idea of it so appealing, didn't find her so interesting.

"So I've been doing some thinking," Daphne said after they'd managed to walk an entire block and a half in silence. "And I realize what the problem was."

"I'm almost afraid to ask. What problem are you referring to?"

"Our kiss."

He would have stopped—would have turned around and gone right back to his room—but she tightened her grip, as if sensing he wanted to bolt. "The only problem with that kiss, Daphne, was that it was a mistake."

One he regretted. If he could take it back, he would. But in the end, it had proved that there wasn't anything between them. The attraction he felt had fizzled when push came to shove.

"It was a mistake," she agreed, all at ease and cheerful, which immediately had him suspicious. "It never should have happened. At least not like that. But it's okay." She patted his hand with her free one. "I forgive you."

He stopped abruptly. She kept walking and was jerked back. "You forgive me?"

Facing him, she nodded sagely. "Of course. I was partly to blame. I wasn't expecting it, you kissing me. Not at that point. And, of course, I'd built up what our first kiss would be like, the magic of it, the imaginary music and little hearts dancing around our heads, the pure perfection of it all. It fell flat, of course, but as I said, I'm willing to accept my part in that. I should have known that nothing could live up to my fantasies. Plus, the more I thought about it, the more I realized what the real problem was. I was angry at you."

She'd thought of kissing him? Had fantasized about it? He really didn't need to know that. It made it that much harder to keep his hands to himself. To not kiss her again.

"I apologize," he said, though he wasn't sure he should since she'd just admitted she'd dreamed of his kiss. "If I came on too strong."

She waved that away. "You didn't. That's not why I was angry."

"It's not?"

She shook her head. "I was angry that you turned what should have been a magical moment into some sort of lesson in self-control. You definitely ruined my fantasy, but I realized that might just be a good thing. You made a mistake last night. A huge one. Now we're on even ground. I finally see that you're not perfect and that's good. If you were really perfect, you might expect the same from me and I am about as far from perfection as can be. But now that I know you're a regular, mortal man, complete with flaws, bad moods and capable of making horrible decisions, it's so much easier for me to be myself."

He considered himself a logical man. An intelligent one. A reasonable one. Yet around her, he couldn't think straight. "Let me see if I've got this right. You're angry with me because you think I kissed you to test my self-control?"

"Yes. But more than that, I think you've been wanting to kiss me and this was your way of getting it out of your system. A way of proving to yourself that it was just curiosity and that there's nothing between us except platonic friendship."

Either she'd taken a course in mind-reading, or she knew him well. Better, he worried, than anyone else.

He wanted, badly, to deny it. To tell her she was way off base. But he wasn't a liar. He'd dive headfirst into a snowbank before he admitted it, but she was one hundred percent correct. He had been hoping to get her out of his system. He'd gone back to his room last night telling himself he was relieved their kiss had been a miserable, awkward experience. That it only proved how unsuitable they were for each other.

Too bad he hadn't believed it. He'd wanted, more than anything, to knock on her door, take her into his arms and kiss her again. And again. Until they got it right.

"And what, exactly, was the horrible decision I made?" he asked, not really wanting to know, but it was the best way he could think to avoid commenting on her accusation.

"Not kissing me again, of course. I'm an excellent kisser, you know." She laughed. "Oops. Guess you don't know but believe me there are plenty of men—and one woman, but that was only that one time during freshman year at college—to attest to that fact."

She was killing him.

"Don't worry, it's okay." Another pat on the hand. "Although it wouldn't hurt for you to apologize for messing up what should have been a monumental moment between us."

"You want me to apologize?"

"It's only polite," she murmured. "And it'll make the next time we kiss all that much better. Like a clean slate between us."

"We are not going to kiss again," he said, trying to mean it, but he didn't even sound convincing to himself. He sounded desperate.

As if sensing his weak willpower, she smiled... a feminine, knowing smile. "Okay."

"I mean it, Daphne. Don't kiss me."

She widened her eyes. Blinked innocently. "I hadn't planned on it."

"I know what you're doing," he said, his voice harsh. Angry. "You're trying to lure me in, messing with my head. Trying to get me to break."

"Oh, Oakes." She cupped his face with her gloved hand. "I would never want to break you."

But she pushed and pushed with her bright smile and light laugh and endless chatter. She tempted with her curvy body and pretty face. Beckoned him to forget all the reasons he couldn't be with her, couldn't have her. Threatened his resolve and made him want to take a risk. Just once.

"I'm not going to kiss you," he told her gruffly. But he was pulling her toward him slowly. So slowly she could stop him at any time. Instead, she yielded.

"If you say so."

"If I do," he said, a desperate man fighting a losing battle, looking for a way to justify his actions, "it's only to prove, again, that there's nothing there."

But his words were weak. How could they be anything but when he was drawing her nearer, his arms wrapping around her waist, his legs spread wide to make room for her.

"If that's what you need to tell yourself," she whispered.

It was. He wished he could believe it, too. Eyes on hers, he lowered his head and pressed his mouth to hers. Her lips were cold, but he warmed them, moved over them and deepened the kiss as he pulled her closer. Wished they weren't wearing heavy coats, that he could feel more than just a hint of her curves against him, but then, maybe it was better this way.

He was in enough trouble as it was.

CHAPTER ELEVEN

THIS, DAPHNE THOUGHT, this was how she'd imagined it.

The world was silent and cold, snow swirled around them as Oakes's lips moved over hers. The kiss was sweet, almost reverent, but she tasted the desire underneath the lazy motions of his mouth, in the way his hands fisted her coat at her back.

It was...magical.

Pure and honest, he wasn't hiding from her now, wasn't holding back and it was all she could do to hold on herself. Her hands clutched his broad shoulders, her head spun, her blood warmed.

A car honked and she sensed Oakes coming back to himself, coming back to reality. She wanted to cry. Wanted to stamp her foot and demand he stay there, right there, in the kiss, with her, stay in that warm bubble they'd created, just the two of them. But she was already losing him. He lifted his head fractionally and then, as if he couldn't resist himself, kissed her again, a gentle brushing of his mouth over hers before he kissed her right cheek, then her left, then the tip of her very frigid nose.

He lifted his head but she kept her eyes closed for a moment longer, just a moment to fully capture what had happened, to memorize it, hold it close. Slowly, in a daze, she opened her eyes, found him staring at her.

She wasn't sure what she'd expected. For him to be angry? Honestly, she wouldn't blame him as she'd pretty much tricked him into that kiss. For him to be upset with her, that was a given. Possibly even regretful, now that she thought about it. But she didn't want him to feel any negative emotions. She supposed what she did want—for him to swoop her up into his arms and carry her back to his room, where he'd declare his love and devotion to her—was a bit too much to expect right now.

She'd never been much for patience or waiting for things to happen. But now, with Oakes? She'd wait because she had to. She'd wait because he was going to be worth it, no matter how long it took.

What she hadn't expected was for him to be staring at her, looking dazed and slightly punch-drunk, a crease forming between his eyebrows. Or for him to sigh, the crease to disappear before he grinned a small, self-depreciating smile.

"I guess I showed you," he said in his deep voice.

She blinked. Then laughed, her relief so great that he wasn't upset with her—or himself. At least not enough to act on it right now.

"You did. Anytime you want to teach me a lesson like that, you go right ahead. I'm a slow learner. But right now," she continued, knowing it was a lot for him, the kiss, the obvious connection between them throwing him for a loop, "let's get to the restaurant. I'm starving and we only have forty-five minutes left on your self-imposed lunch break."

Once again she looped her arm with his. Partly because, yes, she wanted that contact, but also because, yes, she wanted to test him. See what his reaction would be. Would he pull free? Try and pretend what had happened between them hadn't? That it had been an aberration?

She needn't have worried and felt guilty over wondering in the first place. He didn't pull away or even stiffen at her touch. On the contrary, he pulled her closer. Then again, she shouldn't have considered he'd act any other way. It wasn't as if Oakes would shove her to the ground or insist she walk two steps behind him after kissing the daylights out of her on a street corner.

She kept up a steady stream of light chatter the rest of the way to the restaurant that Fay had recommended. They found it easily enough, tucked between a pharmacy and the newspaper office.

They went inside the brick building and a sign at the bottom pointed them to the stairs. The second floor was a large dining room with wooden floors and cozy tables. The hostess seated them by the window overlooking Main Street.

"This is great," Daphne said, shrugging out of her coat and taking off her gloves and hat. "Oh, look, there's a bookstore." She glanced at Oakes across from her, saw him grinning at her. "What?"

"Your hair, it's sort of…" He waved his hands around his head. "Everywhere."

She glanced at her reflection in the window. Laughed. "It looks like I've been struck by lightning," she said, trying to smooth it out, but static electricity was stronger than her feeble attempts. With a shrug of defeat, she put her hat back on. "How's that?"

"You have a strand…" He reached across the table and tucked hair under the hat. "There."

"Thanks."

"You look good," he said. "Cute."

"Hooray. Just what every woman wants to hear. But considering this hat does have a pom-pom on top, I'll take cute and run with it."

The waitress came and took their drink orders, told them the specials and left them to study their menus. "I can't imagine many women being that carefree about their hair or what they looked like," Oakes said. "At least not the women I know."

"I can only imagine how the women you know would react to flyaway hair," she said, knowing his social crowd.

"You're very self-possessed," he said. "And I mean that in the very best way."

"I figured. Thanks. It took me a long time to learn how to be happy with myself. It was tough at school, being different from everyone else. Mostly I felt invisible, and for a while I did my best to fit in. Until I realized that I didn't want to fit in. And I didn't want to be friends with anyone who would pretend I didn't exist, so I went my own way, left people alone and they left me alone."

"That sounds lonely," he said, setting his menu aside.

She wanted to shrug off his concern but she wouldn't lie. Not to him. "It was. Luckily, I still had good friends from the grade school I used to go to, and from my neighborhood. They were always there for me, as was my family. I have several cousins around my age and I could always go to my mom and Zach if I needed anything. At least, until Zach joined the marines. That was when I really learned how to fend for myself."

The waitress came back with their drinks and took their food orders.

"It was tough," Oakes said, sipping his water, "when Zach signed up. Dad had a fit, threatened to use all his power, pull any string he had to make sure Zach never saw any action."

"I remember. Zach was furious. I think my mom would have allowed your dad to do whatever he wanted, whatever it took to keep Zach safe, but in the end, she knew she couldn't stop Zach from doing what he felt he had to do. His entire life, all he ever wanted was to protect others. Like he protected me and Mom."

"From your father?" Oakes asked quietly.

She pretended great interest in removing the wrapper from her straw. Nodded. Then cleared her throat. "Zach threatened to cut your father out of his life even more if Clinton Senior, made even one phone call," she said, changing the subject back to the one at hand, not wanting to talk about her father or her past. It was over. No sense dwelling on it. "I didn't think your father would back down but Zach got his way. He was sent right into the thick of it. Sometimes I hate him for it," she admitted. "All those days of wondering if he was all right, knowing he was putting himself in danger. Not very sympathetic of me, I guess."

"I know what you mean. I wondered if he wasn't putting himself in danger as a way to prove something to Senior. To the world."

She considered that. "Maybe. He's always had

that chip on his shoulder. There's something inside of him that pushes him, that's for sure. It's why he'll rarely accept help, even now when he needs it the most. I think he mistakes it for sympathy or pity when it's really just people wanting to support him. Needing to do something so we don't feel so helpless."

Oakes nodded. "We can't force people to accept help."

"I know. It was one of the toughest lessons I learned and one of the first things they teach psychologists. And it's too bad, really. Because I could help the crap right out of Zach."

Oakes laughed and she warmed all over. She liked making him laugh. The waitress returned with their lunches and they enjoyed a companionable meal of thick sandwiches on homemade bread and fresh, crisp chips. Despite Oakes's earlier insistence, they stayed past his allotted hour. She couldn't remember enjoying lunch or a date more.

Not that he'd classify it as a date—she was certain he wouldn't. But she was going to go right ahead and do so, if only in her mind. She liked him. She really did. When she'd first fallen for him, it had been all reaction. All feeling. And even she wasn't deluded enough to believe that a connection, one that lasts a lifetime, could be made in an instant. But the more she got to know

Oakes, the more time they'd spent together, the more she'd realized how much they actually had in common.

Yes, they had their differences, too. Enough to make their conversations interesting. And Lord knew they'd had completely different circumstances growing up, but those experiences had shaped them, made them who they were today, gave them each unique perspectives on life. She liked how he listened, really listened to her. To her opinions. Her thoughts.

They went back outside to find it was still snowing, the white stuff building up on the sidewalks, on cars and piling on tree limbs, bending them. "That was fun," she said as a group of teenagers passed them. "Come on," she teased when he remained silent. "Say it was fun."

His lips twitched. "It was fun."

"Say 'Thank you, Daphne, for tearing me away from my horribly boring law work and forcing me out into the fresh air.'"

"How about I just say thanks for lunch?"

"I suppose that'll do." She tugged her gloves on. "Do you know how to get back on your own?"

"I think I can manage," he said in a dry, I-am-male-and-therefore-superior-at-navigating-than-you-woman tone. "Why?"

"I thought I'd check out the bookstore. I need to get a gift for the happy couple."

"The wedding's tomorrow," he pointed out.

"Well, yes, I suppose I could wait and pick something up in the morning or early afternoon, but I figured since I'm downtown, why not just get it now?"

"No. I meant the wedding is tomorrow, as in, you haven't bought their gift yet?"

"Oh. You're one of those people."

"Those people?"

"Sure. There are two kinds of people in this world. Those who have a closet filled with gift wrap and boxes and gift bags and bows and ribbons all neatly organized. Who send back RSVPs the day they get them, who have a stack of greeting cards for every occasion, who buy gifts weeks, even months ahead of time. And those who mail birthday cards two days after the birthday, have perfected the art of wrapping gifts using whatever is handy including, but not limited to, garbage bags and the comics from the Sunday paper. You are the former. I'm the latter."

"I take it you haven't finished your Christmas shopping then?"

"Only because I had to. Usually I wait until the last minute. I love the energy, the excitement of going to the stores on Christmas Eve."

"You mean the panic."

She laughed. "That, too. I'm guessing that not only has your Christmas shopping been done since Thanksgiving, but that you bought your brother's wedding gift over the summer."

"You'd be wrong. I bought it the day after they announced their engagement."

"I'm not sure," she said, "but I think some-how during this conversation, we switched gen-der roles."

"Would it help if I said my mother actually chose the gift?"

"It does help."

"You know," he said, "I wouldn't mind check-ing out the bookstore myself. A lawyer can never have too many books. Maybe I'll find a boring one on some obscure law topic no one has cared about in two hundred years."

"If that's your way of saying you're enjoying spending time with me and don't want it to end, then I say, come on."

OAKES WAS GLAD Daphne hadn't expected an an-swer. He did enjoy spending time with her. He couldn't remember the last time he'd been so in-terested in a woman, so attracted. He'd like to blame the kiss. After all, a man can't be held com-pletely responsible for his reaction to a beautiful woman's kiss.

But it was more than that, more than just physi-cal, more than just his wanting to kiss her again, to peel that coat off her, to lay her on that huge bed back in his room at the B and B and make love to her.

It was her. Her laugh and her insightfulness and her intelligence and her humor. Her energy and spirit and zest for life, her enthusiasm for it.

She was appealing as hell and the more time he spent with her, the more he wanted to be with her. But he had to be smart. Had to be cautious. He couldn't make a mistake, couldn't make a misstep, not with Zach's sister.

As long as he kept things between them platonic, he'd be okay. They could be friends. He liked being her friend, wanted to continue seeing her in that role for years to come. He just couldn't sleep with her.

As long as he kept his hands to himself, he'd be all right.

The bookstore was a charming, homey place with a café in the back that filled the first floor with the scent of coffee and pastries. He and Daphne split up once they got inside, her going to the gift section while he browsed the stacks of the latest bestselling fiction.

He was adding a hardcover to the pile he planned on buying when his phone buzzed. He checked the caller ID. He thought of the kiss he and Daphne had shared, thought of what his mother's reaction to it would be if she knew and winced.

Damn guilt. Kept jabbing him in the gut, reminding him of what was important. Of how careful he needed to be.

He cleared his throat before answering, "Hey, Mom."

"Hi, honey." In the background, he could hear the strains of "Santa Baby" and the loud hum of conversation. "I'm at the store looking for that CD your father wanted, but I can't find it."

Not his actual father, but Michael, the man who'd helped raise Oakes, had treated him and loved him just as if he were his own. When other people spoke of his father, they meant Clinton Senior. "I'm at a bookstore that carries CDs right now," he said, crossing to that section. "I'll look for it."

"Oh, that's wonderful," she said. She must have gone to a quieter spot because when she spoke next her voice came through clearer and the background noise faded. "And I'm glad to hear you're not stuck in your room working. That you're getting out."

He glanced at the area where he'd last seen Daphne.

"I, uh…took a lunch break," he said, telling himself he wasn't really lying, that he was just withholding a certain detail to spare his mom's feelings. "The bookstore is across the street from the restaurant where I ate so I thought I'd stop in."

There. Not really a lie, just not all of the truth.

"Found it," he continued, tucking the phone between his shoulder and ear as he pulled out the jazz CD.

"Wonderful," Rosalyn said gratefully. "That's the last thing on my list, and I would have been done already if he hadn't mentioned wanting it the other day."

"He'll love it," Oakes assured her.

"Thank you for getting it. So what are your plans for the rest of the day?"

"Back to work then the wedding rehearsal and rehearsal dinner tonight." Though he wasn't sure why he was going to the wedding rehearsal when he didn't actually have a part in the ceremony.

"How's everything going?" she asked and he knew she was both interested and concerned. Though she never said a bad thing against Senior, never had any unkind words against any member of the Bartasavich family and had always made sure Oakes spent time with them, had shared her son with them as generously as possible, that didn't mean she liked it or was happy about it.

"It's good," he said, setting the CD aside with his books and heading toward the back of the store.

"How is Senior?"

"He's not coming in until this afternoon," Oakes said. Since his stroke, Senior had been wheelchair bound. His full-time nurse would be traveling with him.

"Well, I hope his condition improves," she said and he knew she meant it. She may not have gotten the best deal out of her first marriage, but she was kind enough to not want Senior to suffer. "And Zach, too, of course."

"Zach couldn't make it," he told her. "I think he thought it would be too difficult."

"I can't blame him. But he is progressing?"

"He is," Oakes said, spying Daphne sitting at one of the café's tables, two coffees and a pastry of some sort in front of her as she read a book. "Actually, his sister is here. At the bookstore with me."

Silence. He didn't want to rub his mother's nose in the fact that he was taking Daphne to the wedding, but he wouldn't hide it, either. Wouldn't pretend it was some dirty little secret. Something he was ashamed of. "Well, then," Rosalyn said, sounding strained. "I'll let you go. Although, Oakes…"

His hand tightened on the phone. "Yes?"

"Just… I know it's none of my concern, but Daphne might feel left out. She doesn't really know anyone there, other than you."

Leave it to his mother to dislike the idea of him being there with Daphne, but still be worried about Daphne's feelings.

He'd had that thought already and knew she was right. Daphne had come to the wedding only knowing a few people and those people were all already part of a unit—his family. "She's not the type of person to be intimidated by being some-where alone or where she doesn't know people," he said thoughtfully as he watched Daphne sip her coffee without taking her eyes from what-ever she was reading. She'd taken off her hat—it was really warm in the store—and her hair was all crazy like it had been at the restaurant, but she didn't keep playing with it, didn't try to smooth it. "She's extremely self-confident and aware. Es-pecially for someone her age."

Except she'd admitted to him last night how uncomfortable she'd been at O'Riley's. How she'd been insecure as a teenager surrounded by Hous-ton's elite.

The silence on the other end of the phone was loaded. "I knew you and Daphne were…friendly," Rosalynn said softly, "but I hadn't realized you two were that close. It sounds as if you've gotten to know her very well over the years."

"We're friends," he said simply.

And that friendship had definitely grown stron-ger during the time Zach was in the hospital. Oakes and Daphne would grab a cup of coffee or a bite to eat. Nothing major, nothing significant. Or at least, it hadn't been to Oakes. He'd been trying to keep her mind off of Zach and how dire things had looked. He'd known that Zach would want someone to watch out for his mother and sister and Oakes had naturally stepped in. Again.

"Well, she's incredibly lucky to have you in her life," Rosalynn said, sounding worried. Wary. "All I'm saying is that she'll probably be more comfortable having you close by."

Daphne seemed pretty comfortable no matter what the situation. Being around her, on the other hand, made him decidedly uncomfortable. Antsy and worried and confused.

But he didn't want to stay away. He didn't want to lose Daphne. He wanted to spend more time with her, forget all the reasons they shouldn't be together—all the very valid reasons—and just enjoy the moment.

He and his mother bade each other goodbye and Oakes put his phone back into his pocket as he walked over to Daphne. "I see you found the pastry section."

She looked up at him and grinned. "No pastry is safe around me. They can't hide."

"I hope it went that well finding a wedding gift?"

She gestured toward a picture frame. "Got it."

"That was fast."

"I don't waste time mulling over things. I know what I like when I see it and I get it. Or go after it," she added, giving him a small smile. She nudged one of the cups toward him. "I got you a black coffee that tastes exactly like coffee."

He watched her sip her own drink. "And what did you get?"

"A gingerbread latte. And you missed a spectacular whipped-cream mustache. At least, from the look that kid gave me, I'm guessing it was pretty great." She inclined her head toward a little boy two tables over eating a cookie. "I considered keeping it for a while but I wasn't sure when you were going to be off the phone."

He took the lid off his cup—those things were breeding grounds for germs—and sipped the coffee. "Thanks for this. And that was my mom," he said in explanation. "She was in a panic over a last-minute gift for my stepdad. Luckily, I found what she needed right here."

"Oakes to the rescue. But then, I'm sure you get that a lot. You seem to like saving people, the way you agreed to let me be your date for tomorrow. Not to mention how you swept in last night and took me away from that perfectly lovely bachelorette party because I was feeling self-conscious and having a bit of a pity party."

He shifted, felt uncomfortable even though he knew she was teasing him good-naturedly.

"I like helping people. I actually considered becoming a cop."

Her eyes widened and she slapped his arm. "No, you didn't."

He moved out of her reach, made a show of it to make her smile. "I did. My father wanted me to go into the family business, get a business degree, then an MBA and fall into line at Bartasavich Enterprises. My stepfather never told me in so many words, but I always had the feeling he wanted me to follow in his footsteps and become a lawyer. I thought I'd go my own way, get a degree in criminal justice *then* the police academy."

"What changed your mind?" she asked, seemingly interested, eager even, to know what he was thinking. To know him better?

"For one thing, my mom freaked every time she thought about me wearing a badge. I don't blame her. She comes from a sheltered background, where the men all have nine-to-five, safe jobs. But in the end what really swayed me was I fell in love with the law."

"Really? You mean that actually happens?"

He laughed. "It did for me."

"Do you regret it? Not following your own path the way you thought you would?"

He thought about that. "No," he finally de-

cided. "I don't. I still find what I do endlessly
fascinating, I enjoy where I work and the people
I work with. And I did go in my own direction
since I'm not some VP of marketing or finance
at Bartasavich Enterprises, don't practice criminal law and have no plans of ever becoming a
judge." He sipped his coffee then took the bite of
pastry she offered him. Caramel and cinnamon
in a flaky dough. "What about you? What made
you decide to become a psychologist?"

She leaned back, her eyebrows drawn together
slightly. He liked that about her. Liked how one
moment she was full of energy and spitting out
whatever thought came into her head, and the
next she was mulling over a specific question as
if her life depended on giving the correct answer.

"I want to understand what people are thinking, why they do what they do, why they make
the choices they make. I guess it started with my
constantly questioning why my father acted the
way he did, why my mother chose to stay with
him for so long. But I never got any answers to
those questions. That was when I realized that
some things just happen and it's not really our
circumstances that define us, it's how we react to
those circumstances. And if I can help some other
kid get through a difficult time, if I can give them

a safe place to go, then all the years of studying and hard work, will have been worth it."

She was amazing. Strong and resilient. She hadn't let her less than stellar circumstances affect her.

Suddenly she checked her phone. "It's getting late. You'll probably want to get back," she said in an obvious attempt to end their discussion. "Get that all-important work done before you head out to the rehearsal."

She was right, so he couldn't even argue with her, couldn't try to get her to open up more to him. Standing, he nodded at the book in her hand. "Are you getting that?"

"Yes. And a few more I left up at the counter."

"I have my own pile up there as well." They walked to the counter together. "Do you want a ride to the rehearsal dinner?" he asked after an internal debate.

One he wasn't sure he lost. Or won.

"Oh, I'm not going to that."

"Why not?" Quite a few out-of-town guests had been invited. Of course, Kane and Charlotte hadn't even known Daphne was coming until two weeks ago.

She looked at him as if he was crazy. "Mainly because I wasn't invited. The wedding rehearsal is just for family and people actually in the ceremony."

He needed to drop it, but he couldn't seem to let it go. "What will you do then?"

"I'll find something to keep myself busy. Shady Grove is small but it's still a town. It's not like we're stuck out in the middle of a desert somewhere. They have actual shops and restaurants and bars and maybe even a movie theater," she teased.

"You could come with me," he invited before he thought better of it. Before he had time to analyze why he'd been adamant about not taking her to the dinner and bachelor/bachelorette party last night only to want her with him tonight. "Be my plus one."

He hadn't wanted to bring a date to his brother's wedding because that seemed like too big of a commitment to make to a woman. In any other situation, traveling across the country to attend a family wedding pretty much guaranteed that things were serious in a relationship.

But he and Daphne were friends. Good friends. Just friends.

And if he kept telling himself that, he might go back to believing it.

"You're inviting me to spend more time with you? My, my, my—I did make a good impression today, didn't I? But, as much as I appreciate the invitation, I'm going to have to regretfully decline."

His gaze narrowed. What was this? Last night she'd wanted him to invite her along, had even crashed the party at the bar. What kind of game was she playing? "Why?"

He didn't usually ask women who turned him down to give him a list of reasons *why*. Then again, he didn't often get turned down. That smacked of the Bartasavich ego, but Oakes wasn't being arrogant. He just had a really good track record when it came to dating.

Mostly because he didn't like to take risks. There was no such thing as a sure bet, but he'd helped his odds by getting to know the women he asked out, reading the signs, gauging their interest in him before he made any overtures. Daphne paid for her books and the wedding gift and faced him again. "You're only asking because you feel sorry for me. You're worried about what I'll do all by my lonesome and you feel responsible for making sure I'm not all sad and lonely in my room. Or else you're worried I'll crash the dinner like I did the party last night."

"That is not why I asked," he insisted, handing over his credit card to the cashier.

"No?" Daphne asked.

"No. Well, maybe partly. But mostly, I asked because I like spending time with you."

Her grin blossomed. "Well, why didn't you just say that? What time is the rehearsal?"

"Seven."

"I'll be ready by six thirty."

CHAPTER TWELVE

"How was physical therapy today?" Daphne asked Zach over an hour later while she used Skype to chat with him from her room.

"Torture," he said in his growly voice, his dark brows drawn together as if just remembering pissed him off.

She'd gone to a few of his rehabilitation appointments with him, but it had been too hard on her to watch. The sessions were grueling and she knew they must be extremely painful—it was too much for her to handle. And she hated her weakness, especially when Zach never once complained. He just gritted his teeth and did whatever they asked him to do. He was a man bent on getting his strength back, on getting back to living his life with as much normalcy as possible, with all the independence he used to have.

"I still can't believe you went to Shady Grove," he grumbled.

"I told you I was going," she said. "Since when have I not done what I said I was going to do?"

"It was a mistake," he said simply. "You going

there. Do you really think the Bartasaviches are going to embrace you with open arms?"

She thought back to the way Oakes had kissed her on the street corner, how he'd held her so close, his lips warming as they moved over hers. She bit back a grin. "Oh, I think some of them are warming up to me."

"Stop smiling. I don't like it."

She rolled her eyes. "Most brothers would be happy their family is treating their little sister well."

"Most brothers have the same family as their little sisters."

"You got me there."

Yes, their situation was…unique. But not unheard of in this day and age of divorce, remarriages and blended families.

"Anyway," she continued, "I'm having a great time. It's snowing here and they play Christmas carols on Main Street and all the stores are decorated. The B and B is fantastic, too. When you come visit Kane and Charlotte, you need to stay here." She frowned. "I'll have to ask if they have an elevator to the second floor, where the rooms are. I haven't seen one but it might be in a different part of the house."

"Why would I visit Kane?"

"Uh, because he's your brother and because you missed his wedding." He opened his mouth but she waved away whatever he was about to say. "I know, I know, you have an excellent reason for missing it—"

"Thank you," he said dryly.

"But I'm sure you'll want to visit Shady Grove at some point, see how they're doing. Especially when they start having kids."

"Junior had a kid I haven't seen yet," Zach said.

"That's because you're incredibly stubborn. Especially when it comes to C.J."

Ivy, C.J.'s…well, Daphne thought she could be termed his girlfriend but someone who looked like Ivy, who looked as if she ate up men for breakfast and spat them out before lunchtime, didn't really fit the typical girlfriend mold. But who was Daphne to judge? Ivy might be perfectly happy being labeled C.J.'s girlfriend. After all, she seemed happy enough with him to get pregnant by him and have his baby last month, a boy they'd named Clinton Bartasavich the Third.

And that had to be the most pretentious name in the entire world. Thank God they'd decided to nickname the kid Trey.

"No," Zach said. "It's because C.J. is an ass. Takes after his father."

She had to bite her lip so she wouldn't point out that Senior was Zach's father as well. "He's here, you know. Senior. Oakes told me he got in around two."

Zach's eyes narrowed. "Why would Oakes tell you that?"

She lifted a shoulder, made herself more comfortable on the large bed and crossed her legs under her. "He got a text from C.J. telling him Senior had arrived so Oakes went over to the hotel to see how he was doing, how his flight went."

"You were with Oakes when he got the message?"

"Didn't I mention that?" Zach shook his head. "Oh. Yes, I was with him."

"Why?"

She didn't pretend to not know what he was asking. "Because we had lunch together. Which, may I remind you, we've done dozens of times before. And, before you start in on how he's a Bartasavich and therefore the spawn of Satan, et cetera, et cetera, let me tell you that we not only had lunch together, but he also invited me to the rehearsal dinner tonight."

"Daphne," Zach said, not sounding pissed, but more weary. "Just…be careful. They aren't like us."

"You mean they're not human? What are they? Alien? Zombies?"

"Be serious."

"It's tough to be serious when you're being so dramatic. They're people, Zach, just like us. They have good days and bad days, and they put their pants on one leg at a time." Horrified at what she'd just said, she slapped a hand over her mouth. "Oh, my God, I'm so sorry. I didn't mean—"

"Knock it off. I know you didn't. Besides, I have to put my pants on one leg at a time. It's all I have."

Her eyes welled. "Stop. I'm really sorry. I wasn't thinking."

"Nothing new there. Relax. It's a part of my life now. I have to live without my arm and leg. That's my life. No hiding from it."

"No, you wouldn't hide from it." Her brother was the strongest, bravest person she knew.

"You're not even the first person to make a stupid comment to me," he said. "And I doubt very much you'll be the last." He paused and his mouth quirked in a way that it used to, before he was injured. "I doubt it'll even be the last time *you* say something stupid."

He had her there.

"And while my family may, indeed, be humans, their good days are ones where they rake in a million dollars. Their bad days are when the cleaner didn't get the champagne stain out of their shirt. And for the record, they don't have to put their pants on one leg at a time—they can pay someone to put them on for them. Dress them. Bathe them. You name it."

She sighed. This was not going well. How was

she going to convince Zach that she knew what she wanted? He didn't usually doubt her. Didn't question her capabilities or her motivation. He was usually right beside her, urging her on.

"I realize your family is richer than Midas," she said, stressing that the people they were talking about, the people he couldn't stand, were his relatives. "But Oakes isn't some snob. You know that, even if you won't admit it. He works hard." She remembered what Oakes had said about earning his own way, about not using his father's name, his stepfather's reputation, to get ahead. "He's a good guy," she said softly. "Why can't you just admit it?"

Zach looked tired and she didn't think it was just from his rehab earlier that day. "I do know that." And it was a banner day when he said anything halfway decent about any Bartasavich except for Estelle, his niece. "He's a decent guy. But he likes his life tidy. Neat. No drama. No problems. Being with you would mean nothing but problems and drama and rocking that boat he's spent his entire life doing his best to keep calm and dry."

"I'm not a child, Zach," she said, her tone irritable, her mouth a thin line. "I'm not going to upset his life."

"How could you not? Do you really think he's going to be able to bring you to Christmas dinner?

The daughter of the woman who had an affair with his mother's husband? You're a constant reminder of what had to be the worst time in her life. Do you think Oakes wants to rub her face in that by bringing you into her life?"

Daphne shook her head, denial flowing through her, though a part of her went cold, wondering if he was right. "Oakes isn't like that. He'll get his mother to understand that I'm not Mom. That what happened was in the past. It's history."

Zach rubbed his hand over his face. "Yeah. But the problem with history?" he asked wearily. "It has a habit of repeating itself. It never really goes away. And while people can learn from it, they never, ever forget it. I don't want you to be caught in the middle when Oakes has to decide between you and the rest of his family. Because you and I both know what choice he'll make."

"Thanks for the ride," Gracie said as Luke pulled into her driveway. It was still snowing hard, but the salt trucks and plows had been out so the roads were pretty clear.

"No problem." He put the SUV into Park. "I can give you a lift anytime you want," he said. "I mean, so your dad doesn't have to take you to work and pick you up."

Even in the dim glow of the dashboard light, he could see she was looking at him as if he was nuts. "It's out of your way to come get me then go back into town for work."

"I don't mind," he said, shooting for casual and cool, but his plan was ruined when his throat cracked. Shit. He hadn't done that since he was fifteen and his voice changed. He was croaking like a freaking frog. He cleared his throat. Smiled at her. "What do you say?"

"I say exactly what I just said." She spoke slowly, as if he were someone of lesser intellect and needed her to dumb down her conversation. "It's out of your way. Besides, I'm not sure how much longer I'll be working at Bradford House."

He sat up. "What? Why not?"

She shrugged. Played with the strap of her purse on her shoulder. "I love working there, especially babysitting Elijah and Mitchell." Fay and her two young sons lived in an apartment on the third floor of the B and B and Gracie often watched the boys while Fay worked or ran errands. "But I don't get that many hours and they'll be even less once school is out and Fay puts the boys into summer camps and programs."

"You should talk to Fay," he said. Their boss was nothing if not accommodating. "I'm sure she'd be able to give you more hours." He didn't want Gracie to leave Bradford House. It was the only time he got to see her outside of school, and basically the only time she spoke to him anymore.

"It'd suck," he admitted, hoping he could get her to change her mind, "working there without you."

Her eyes widened slightly but then she dropped her gaze to her lap. "I need something that pays better, too." She laughed but it was forced, not light like her real laugh. "Not that I'll be able to find something that pays enough to cover the cost of college tuition or anything, but every little bit helps."

What could he say to that? Continue working at Bradford House making less than a hundred bucks a week so he could keep seeing her all the time and don't worry about your education? Your future?

"My brother might know if there are any openings at the hospital." Luke had an older brother and sister who were both married and had kids. His brother, Scott, was an RN there. "He mentioned a job opening in the cafeteria there to me before I started at Bradford House, but the hours weren't flexible enough for me to work and play football. I could ask him about it."

She smiled at him. Like she used to. Like she enjoyed being with him. "That would be great. Thanks, Luke."

He shrugged. Tapped the steering wheel. The silence stretched until finally Gracie undid her seat belt. "Well," she said, almost as if waiting for him to stop her from leaving, "thanks again. I guess I'll see you at the dance tomorrow night."

She opened the door and he finally got his brain working enough to say "Wait!"

He grimaced. Not the best use of what his English teacher called his advanced grasp of syntax and language. "I mean, uh…is Bryce coming over?"

She got out of the car. She was so small, her coat dwarfed her, and her hair was all puffy around her face. "N-o-o-o," she said, drawing the word out as if his question was the weirdest thing anyone could ask.

And, now that he thought about it, it kind of was.

"I mean…do you guys have plans. Tonight?"

He held his breath while she frowned up at him, the snow collecting on her curly hair, her cheeks turning pink. "Why the sudden interest in whether Bryce and I have plans or not?"

"No reason. I just… I thought if you weren't busy, maybe I could come in for a little bit. My parents aren't home," he said before she could tell him no way and slam the door shut. "They took my nieces' into Pittsburgh to see some holiday dance show and won't be home until later and I just thought maybe, if you weren't doing something, and I'm not doing something, we could… do something together."

Jesus, you'd think he'd never asked a girl out, let alone talked to one before. Used to be a time, before he and Kennedy started going out, when he was pretty good at this stuff. Now, faced with one curly-haired hippie chick, he was acting like an idiot.

And he didn't care. As long as it got him into her house, he didn't care at all.

"Why?" she finally asked.

"I told you. My parents aren't—"

"No, why do you want to hang out with me? I don't see how your parents not being home is a problem, as we both know you're capable of spending the night alone at your own house. So, why on earth would you want to come to my house, where you know there are six boys who run wild?"

He rubbed his fingers across the steering wheel. Back and forth. Back and forth. "I just... I miss you," he admitted softly, his throat tight. He forced himself to meet her gaze, steeled himself against the suspicion and wariness he saw there. "I miss being your friend and I hoped... we were getting back to that."

After last night, those hopes had only gotten bigger. He'd enjoyed being with her, shopping for his nieces. She'd helped him pick out a game for six-year-old Rainie and a puzzle set for three-year-old Lila. Then they'd gone to Panolis for pizza—minus cheese for Gracie's two slices.

He'd had fun. And he'd thought she did, too.

He waited, holding his breath. She was probably going to tell him to get lost, to go to hell, but in a nicer, Gracie-way that included something positive about them going their separate ways, about it being fate and if they were meant to be friends, they would have found a way back to each other long before this.

That if he'd really wanted to be her friend, he could have made an overture, an attempt to do so again at any time over the past four months.

And she'd be right. She'd be absolutely right and there would be nothing he could say to refute it. He had no excuse except that he was an idiot.

But he was going to save that bit of truth until he really needed to reveal it.

She opened her mouth, probably to put into words what he'd already figured she'd say, when someone pounded on his window. He jumped. Spun around to see Drew grinning at him from outside, snow covering his dark hair.

"Hey, dude, what are you doing?" Drew asked, his voice muted through the glass.

Luke begrudgingly rolled the window down. "Hey." He wasn't friends with Drew, didn't trust him anymore, but that hadn't stopped Drew from trying to make amends, to be pals again. "I was just dropping Gracie off."

Drew looked past Luke, his smile fading when he saw Gracie. Then he looked from her to Luke, then back again. "You were bringing her home? From work, right?"

Luke wasn't sure, but there was something in Drew's tone that bugged him. Pissed him off. Like Drew was Gracie's dad and was making sure some horny teenage boy wasn't trying to make time with her in the driveway.

"Yeah," he said. "From work."

"Oh." Drew seemed to relax but was still looking at them funny, as if he didn't like what he was seeing. "Hey, do you want to come in?" Drew lived next door to Gracie. "We can play some Xbox. Order a pizza."

"Actually," Gracie said, "Luke is coming to my house. He's going to help us string popcorn for the tree."

A grin split Luke's face. "Yeah. Sorry, man."

"No problem," Drew said, his eyes narrowed, but Gracie had sounded perfectly sincere, cool and collected, as if she lied every day. "See you later."

He walked away, across the yard separating his house from Gracie's. Luke rolled his window up, turned off the engine then got out of the SUV. He went behind the vehicle, meeting Gracie at the bottom of the steps leading to the porch.

"Thanks," he said as they started up the stairs.

"I didn't mean to overstep or anything," she told him. "I mean, I'm sure you're more than capable of telling someone *no* when you don't want to hang out with them, but you did ask if you could come in and I... I guess I didn't want you to make plans with Drew before I gave you my answer."

She turned and smiled at him and Luke's chest warmed. "Yeah. No, that's fine. Great. I'd much rather string popcorn with you and the boys than hang out with him."

She took another cautious step up—the stairs were covered with snow and ice. "You two haven't made up then?"

"I'm not interested in being his friend. I can't trust him. He tried blaming it all on Kennedy, said she came on to him...but he could have said no. Could have told me what was going on instead of screwing her behind my back. I just... I hate liars, you know?"

She slipped and he caught her arm, steadied her.

"You okay?" he asked.

"Fine." But she was breathless and wouldn't look at him. "Thanks."

He thought she looked as if she wanted to say

something more, but then she crossed to the door, pulled it open and they were greeted with boys shouting and Christmas music blaring and dogs barking.

"You sure you're up for this?" she asked.

He grinned. "I can't wait."

"I STILL DON'T understand why you didn't just come to the wedding rehearsal," Oakes said to Daphne when they were walking across the parking lot to the restaurant where the rehearsal dinner was being held.

"I didn't want to ruin the surprise."

"I hope there *aren't* any surprises," Oakes said, taking her arm so she didn't slip in her high heels. Why she didn't have on boots was beyond him, but he'd learned never to question a woman's footwear choice. "Unless you know something I don't and Charlotte has an ex-boyfriend who plans on showing up and not holding his peace."

"Nothing like that—though wouldn't that be exciting?" she asked and he did a double take, but she looked and sounded serious. "No, I meant the surprise of the whole thing. The music choices and the order of the bridesmaids and, I don't know, if there are going to be doves released or balloons…"

"Nothing quite so circuslike," he assured her.

"Shh…don't tell me. It was the only reason I

waited at the B and B for you to be done. And thanks for coming back to get me."

It wasn't a problem as Bradford House was on the way to the restaurant. "I'm pretty sure we can expect a surprise-free wedding tomorrow," he told her as they entered and checked their coats. "Kane couldn't care less about such things and is probably only going through with the whole ceremony-reception for Charlotte, and she doesn't seem like the type to go for big, or fancy."

"She's not," Daphne assured him and she would know. She'd spent more time with Charlotte than Oakes had, though he liked his soon-to-be sister-in-law and looked forward to getting to know her better. "I'm sure tomorrow's ceremony is going to be lovely and without any drama."

"Is it possible to have a wedding without any drama?"

"Sure. If the bride and groom are both certain this is what they want and they're both relaxed and excited about starting their future together, instead of worrying about putting on some big show that will be talked about for years to come."

"That sounds like my father's third wedding." He frowned. "No, his fourth. His third they got married on the beach in Hawaii, which wasn't all that bad except we weren't allowed to get in the water, even after the ceremony. So Kane and C.J.

and I snuck off and went for a swim, then got into trouble for getting the bride's dress wet."

"Hawaii? I think I remember that… Zach refused to go. Or at least, he tried."

"And we all wished he would have stayed home he was such a brat the entire week. I thought Kane was going to drop him into an active volcano. But at least the party afterward was fun. Very traditional, complete with roasted pig and hula dancers. Dad's fourth wedding was the one with the dogs. His bride had two purebred Pomeranians and they went down the aisle first, except for the one that was old and had a problem with incontinence. Pissed right there on the statue of Saint Joseph. I think that's when Dad decided no more church weddings."

She laughed. "Well, here's hoping there's no spit pig, no bratty kids—like Zach—and no poorly trained dogs at tomorrow's nuptials."

"With my family," he said softly as they entered the room where the dinner was being held, "there are no guarantees."

The entire room didn't stop as one, go quiet and turn to look at them.

But it sure as hell felt that way. Probably because C.J. was glaring at him, while his beautiful, blonde niece Estelle was looking at them in surprise. She was the one who came over first, an excellent hostess like her mother and taking over for Kane, who'd been raised with manners and pomp and circumstance, but had stopped acting that formal years ago.

"Uncle Oakes," Estelle cried, giving him a big hug, complete with teenaged-girl squeal and a little bounce. "Isn't it great?"

He wrapped his arm around her waist. He couldn't believe she was eighteen already, that next year she'd be going to college. "Yes, it's great," he agreed, knowing that Charlotte's parents had indulged Estelle and let her help plan this party. At least she'd finally managed to get a decent set of grandparents, even if they were far away. "You remember Daphne Lynch, don't you? Zach's sister?"

She gave him a *duh* look, but then smiled at Daphne. "Hi. I'm so glad you could make it. Come on, you two are sitting with us."

And Estelle pulled Daphne into the room, chattering the entire time. Oakes followed more slowly and hoped he hadn't made a mistake bringing her here.

CHAPTER THIRTEEN

BY THE END of the night, as Oakes and Daphne walked up the stairs of the quiet B and B, he couldn't remember what he'd been worried about. His family had been too busy and too involved with the toasts and mingling to have much to say about him bringing Daphne. And she'd been wonderful. Any unease she'd felt last night had disappeared. She fit right in with his crazy family, had made many new friends among Charlotte's family and friends, chatted with the bridal party, held Charlotte's toddler niece and charmed everyone.

There had been one tense moment when Senior had seen Daphne. Unable to speak, he'd made the noises that he makes when he was upset, his upper body rocking slightly with agitation—the only movement he could make. It was actually Daphne who figured out what was wrong.

She looked very much like her mother at that age, she'd explained. Senior must have recognized her immediately.

Instead of being cowed or upset by his behavior, she'd gone over to him, sat next to him and just...talked to him. Oakes had no idea what she'd said, but she'd stayed there for quite a long time, smiling and chatting as if it was the most normal thing in the world to have a one-sided conversation with the now disabled man who'd seduced her mother, gotten her pregnant and made her life miserable. Oakes had watched her—how could he not? Had seen how she would point out someone or something, then lean toward Senior to speak so he could hear her.

Oakes wasn't sure how much his father understood, but he had a feeling that despite suffering the stroke, Senior's mind was still as sharp as ever. It was his body that had let him down—the communication between that quick mind and his body had gone silent. So when Daphne had finally stood up to leave, giving Senior's hand a pat in goodbye, Oakes could have sworn that his father had tried to move his hand. Not to brush off her touch, but to hold on.

He glanced at her as they went down the hall. Something he and his father had in common. Oakes couldn't get enough of her touch, either. Wanted to hold on to her, her laughter and spirit— the pure energy and joy she found in life.

He wanted to hold on and never let go.

Oakes frowned and shoved his hands into his pockets. No, that wasn't right. He wasn't falling for her. Yes, he was attracted to her, but it could never work, could never last. Even without their families, without their histories and all the complications brought on by those families and their histories, he and Daphne were too different. She was so young. She still had to finish her education, had to follow her dreams.

At her door, she faced him. "I suppose if I invited you in for a drink, you'd find some convenient excuse to decline?"

He studied her. She sounded like her usual confident self, but there was worry in her eyes, as if the thought of his rejection scared her. "You have drinks in your room?"

There were a few benefits to staying at Bradford House—mainly being separate from the rest of his family—but the conveniences of a B and B differed greatly from that of a four-star hotel. And a minibar wasn't one of them.

She switched her key from one hand to the other. "I asked Fay to set up a minibar," Daphne said, as if it was no big deal that she'd gone to the trouble of having drinks ready for them upon their return. "Just in case I could tempt you."

That was the problem. She tempted him too much. Made him forget all the reasons he should keep his distance from her. That he should tell her good-night and go to his own room. Alone.

"I suppose I could have one drink," he heard himself say.

Way to stand tough, buddy.

But she looked so happy, so relieved, he couldn't regret his words or his decision. "Come on in, then."

They went inside and she turned on one lamp, then another, and he was glad she hadn't left the room dimly lit. It would've made it too cozy that way. Too intimate. He noticed the bar set up to the side and crossed to it while she freshened up. Poured himself a drink and sipped it, and when she said she was putting on something more comfortable, he prayed like hell that she didn't mean a negligee.

This was a mistake, he thought, staring so hard at the closed bathroom door—he was surprised he didn't burn two eye holes into the wood. Yep. A really bad idea, and he prided himself on only making good decisions—unlike his father, who'd spent a lifetime making bad decision after bad decision. He set his drink down, turned to go when the door opened.

And Daphne came out in a pair of black yoga pants and a thick sweatshirt that fell off her shoulder.

It was almost worse than a slinky, lacy nightgown because she looked so pretty. Her hair tucked behind her ears, her face washed. Pretty and natural and completely at ease.

He looked at the door leading to the hall. So close. And yet so far.

"I'll have a soda," she said, crossing to the seating area near the window. "If you're pouring."

He opened a bottle of cola. Added ice to a glass. "No tequila tonight?" he teased.

"I promised my mother I'd be on my best behavior, and I try not to make promises I can't keep." She sat on one of the armchairs, tucked her legs underneath her. Smiled in thanks when he handed her the drink. "It was a nice dinner. Estelle was glowing. She's so happy for your brother."

Small talk. Oakes relaxed enough to smile. "She loves Charlotte and can't wait for her and Kane to start having kids. She's even talked about applying to a few colleges on the East Coast once that happens but I don't see her going through with it. She's really close to her mom."

"She might surprise you," Daphne said. "She's an adult now."

"Don't remind me."

He was always going to think of her as a little girl. He'd been lucky to spend as much time with her as possible while she was growing up. She lived in Houston with her mom, and Oakes had made it a point to see her at least once a week, to call or text her every few days, especially when Kane was in the army.

"You can sit down," Daphne said, a grin playing on her lips. "I don't bite. And, no, I'm not going to add 'unless you want me to' because that would be too obvious. And while I don't mind making myself clear, I try to avoid clichés as much as possible."

He sat, but found himself on the edge of the chair, his shoulders rigid.

"Wow," she said, setting down her glass. "You really are nervous, aren't you? Don't worry—" she patted his knee "—I didn't invite you in here to seduce you."

"I never thought you did," he said quickly, because if he did admit to that he might as well admit to having a gigantic ego.

"Liar," she said, but without heat. "Look, I don't want to trick you into bed *or* seduce you. When we make love—and I have no doubt it'll happen because I am an eternal optimist—it will be because we both want to. And not because I happened to wear a tight dress or you've had too much to drink or I tossed rose petals on the bed and lit a bunch of smelly candles. I don't want you that way, Oakes. I want you to be with me, fully, in the moment. One you won't be able to say I orchestrated."

He wasn't sure what to say. He wasn't shocked by her words and that surprised him more than what she'd said. Maybe he'd known, deep inside, that she felt more for him than friendship. She was so honest. So open. Traits he thought he had in spades. Or ones he used to think he could claim. But he knew he hadn't been open with her. Hadn't been completely honest. He'd been too busy trying to hide from her, keeping his distance.

He wasn't sure how much longer he could keep that up. "You have to know I'm attracted to you," he said slowly, wanting her to hear the truth, as much as he could give her.

"That's a good start," she said with a smile.

"I'm not so sure. I don't want to be attracted to you."

"That is a problem."

He stood. Began pacing. "It's a problem because you're Zach's sister. I'm his brother. It's too...complicated."

She sat back, relaxed and unruffled, when he felt like a ticking time bomb. "I don't mind complicated. Complicated makes things interesting."

"Or it ruins everything." He wanted a calm existence. One he was in control of. "I don't want to use you, Daphne."

Wouldn't use her. Wouldn't take advantage of her feelings for him the way his father had taken advantage of her mother.

"Oh, Oakes. You could never use me." She stood, approached him and took both his hands in hers, forcing him to stop prowling the room like a damn caged lion. "Why don't we back up a few steps? Do you like spending time with me? Take sex off the table—which just made me think of us having sex on a table, but you know what I mean."

He couldn't help it. He grinned. Mainly because he'd had the same thought. "How about, take sex out of the equation?"

"No, that makes me think of us having sex in a classroom, on a desk this time, with math equations written on the board. Let's just say...no sex. It's not there. And if that's gone, the question is, do you like spending time with me, as a friend?"

He lifted his hand, touched her hair. "How could I not? You're bright and funny and *fun*."

"All good things and, I might add, very well said. So we put all of this other stuff on the back burner for a while. I'll lay off with the flirting, and you can stop acting like I'm about to attack you at any moment and maybe we could go back to being...friends? Just friends."

He squeezed her hands. "I love being your friend."

"Then it's a plan. And as your friend I have to tell you that you don't have to worry about me tomorrow at the wedding. I'll be fine. I want you to enjoy your day with your family. Then, the day after, we both go back to Houston, and if you find yourself missing me, thinking about me, wanting to spend time with me, you can give me a call.

We'll step up our friend game by hanging out more. Do the kinds of things serious friends do."

He raised his eyebrows. "Serious friends?"

"Yes. The kind who do more than have coffee once in a while."

"My friends and I usually drink beer, play pool and watch football."

"As I happen to be a big proponent of all three of those activities, count me in."

He couldn't imagine her at his house, shooting pool, the large-screen TV on the wall turned to the game.

But then, he *could* imagine it. All too clearly. Her, in his place, with her dark, tight jeans and a baggy sweater, one of those soft ones that begged a man to touch. To see if the skin beneath was softer.

"Now that that's settled," she said, taking his drink from him and setting it down. "It's time for you to say good-night."

"You're kicking me out?"

"As your friend, I'm telling you it's late and we both have a big day tomorrow and I, for one, need my beauty rest."

Irritated for some reason, he frowned. "You're the one who invited me in for a drink in the first place."

"I'm well aware of what I've done and what I've said," she assured him, ushering him toward the door. "Now I'm saying I've changed my mind and think it's best if you go on your way and I get some sleep." She opened the door and practically pushed him out into the hall. Smiled at him and even gave him a little wave. "Good night."

And she quietly shut the door on his face.

What the hell?

He stared down the hall to the left. Then the right. But there were no answers there, so he stomped to his room, unlocked his door and went inside wondering if he hadn't just gotten the bad end of a worse deal.

THE CREDITS OF the movie Luke and Gracie had watched rolled across the screen. Luke stared at them, his heart racing. He wasn't sure what to do. What to say. He slid a glance at Gracie, who sat primly next to him on her bed, her hair down, her fingers twined together in her lap.

Gracie clicked the remote, shutting off the TV, then reached over to the bedside table. "Thanks again," she said softly because it was late—past midnight—and everyone else was sleeping, as far as they knew. Though her older brothers had been so amped up, they might still be awake somewhere in the huge house. "It was nice of you to help string the popcorn and play with the boys."

"It was fun," he said, not knowing what else to do but to slide to the edge of the huge bed, let his legs hang over the side, his feet on the hardwood floor. "I've missed hanging out with the boys," he admitted.

She had six younger brothers ranging in ages from toddler to eight and they were all energetic and really tough to handle. If *his* mom saw how they ran around and destroyed things, she'd have a fit. But then, his mom didn't need to know everything that went on at Gracie's house, such as the fact that after they'd strung popcorn and played with the boys and watched a Christmas special with the entire family, they'd come up to Gracie's room to watch a movie.

Her room was really a couple of rooms. She lived in a rambling old Victorian house, not like Bradford House, which was all glossy wood and had been renovated to look like some showroom. Her house was lived-in, with toys scattered all over, dirty dishes on the kitchen counter, chipped paint on the walls.

She had a suite, she called it. Two large rooms, one for her art stuff and one for her bedroom. She even had her own bathroom. Compensation for being the only other female in the house besides her stepmother.

They'd come into her bedroom and shut the door, as easily as you pleased. Her dad hadn't made any issues about it, her stepmom hadn't warned them to behave. Gracie said her parents trusted her, which he guessed was good in theory, but his mom always said trust had to be earned and kids needed structure and discipline. But Gracie was one of the best people he knew, so he guessed not having either structure or discipline hadn't hurt her any.

And it meant he got to sit on her bed with her, watching a movie, for the past two hours, her leg sometimes brushing against his. He could smell her scent, could sneak looks at her from the corner of his eye, see her smile when something amused her, watch her bite her lower lip during the tense moments.

He'd wanted, badly, to take her hand in his. To edge closer and maybe even put his arm around her. Or, better yet, have her make the first move. Have her slide over and lay her head on his shoulder, but that hadn't happened.

Being just friends sucked.

But he figured he was lucky to be friends with a girl who didn't have any curfew, didn't have rules about a boy being in her room or how long that boy could stay.

He stood and she did, too. "Well," he said, "I should probably go."

"Oh. Okay. I'll see you later?"

She made it sound like a question. "Yeah. At the dance, right?" And that only reminded him that she was going with Bryce.

And not him.

"Right. And at work on Monday."

He nodded. "Okay, then. 'Night."

"Good night."

They were friends now so he could hug her. He remembered the first time, the only time, really, that she'd hugged him. It had been right here, in her room. He and Kennedy had already been broken up, and he'd seen her snuggling up with Drew on Drew's back deck. Luke had been upset and Gracie had tried to comfort him.

Except he'd felt more than comfort. He'd felt... attracted. To Gracie. To the girl he'd thought was just a friend up until that point, a coworker he enjoyed hanging out with. And those feelings had grown until he'd gotten confused over his lingering feelings for Kennedy.

All in the past, he assured himself and just followed his instincts and bent over, wrapped his arms around her and held her close. She seemed surprised at first, stiff, as if she was going to push him away—which would be freaking humiliating—but then she went soft all over and wrapped her arms around his waist, laid her head against his chest.

She was so tiny. The top of her head barely reached his chin. He lowered his head and inhaled the sweet scent of her shampoo. She wasn't like Kennedy, who was tall and built, a walking wet dream to torment him, to keep him under her spell, always pushing him until he was ready to break, and then luring him back with her kisses and her body.

He fell for it every time, which meant he was a schmuck. Just like any other teenage boy. But he hadn't fallen for it, hadn't taken her back for good after she'd cheated on him. He'd broken free of her and now he could move on.

Now he was ready to move on. With Gracie.

He lifted his head and she stepped back slightly, but he held on and he noticed that she did, too. "Good night," he said, his voice gruff. He winced, realized he'd just said that two minutes ago.

Maybe he should just not talk. He didn't want to anyway, not when she was looking up at him, her eyes wide, her lips parted. He bent his head, slowly, giving her plenty of time to back away before he fully committed. But she didn't move so he brushed his mouth against hers.

Her lips were warm. Soft. So he kissed her again, this time settling his mouth on hers. This wasn't like the other time when he'd kissed her at his sister's house while they were babysitting his nieces. That had been quick. He wanted this to last.

He felt her sigh against his mouth, felt her mouth soften under his, her fingers gripping his shirt. He deepened the kiss, sweeping his tongue into her mouth. He wanted to take his time, knew he should, but she responded so openly, so honestly and fully, he couldn't hold back. Couldn't resist pulling her even closer, and then when that wasn't close enough, stepping back, with her still in his arms, and sitting on the bed, bringing her down with him so she straddled his lap.

He had no idea how long they stayed that way. He kept kissing her and as long as she was kissing him back, he was happy. Told himself that was enough. But then, the weight of her on his lap, the sweet scent of her skin, her softness, the warmth of her and her slight curves, tempted him to slowly draw his hands up and down her back, to touch her curling hair, to kiss the nape of her neck.

She touched him, too, her hands hesitant as she slid them up to his shoulders, her fingers cool as they caressed the back of his neck, delved into his hair. She shifted and his fingers flexed on her waist. He went back to kissing her mouth, slowly, ever so slowly, slid his hands to the hem of her sweater, ran his fingers underneath it, across her back, feeling the slight bumps of her spine. He waited to make sure that was okay and when she continued to kiss him, her hands playing with his hair, he tugged her even closer, slid his hands higher.

He moved his hands to her stomach, felt her

muscles quiver under his touch. God, she was soft. He knew he should stop. Should tug her sweater back down, should gently set her back on her feet and leave, but she wasn't stopping him and she felt so good, tasted so sweet.

He moved his hands up higher, trailed his fingers across her rib cage. She stiffened so he kissed her deeper, lowered his hands again. Up and down, around to her back and then to her waist. Keeping one hand on her waist, he smoothed his free hand up her side, touched the silk of her bra under her arm and then down again. He repeated the motion several times then, heart racing, he gently cupped her breast.

She leaped off his lap.

Or she would have, if he hadn't had a hold of her waist, if his other hand hadn't been up her shirt, trapping her.

"Let go," she said, sounding upset, shoving his shoulders.

He immediately let go and stood. She stepped back so quickly, she almost fell, her arms windmilling to keep her balance. He reached out to steady her and she slapped his hand.

"Don't touch me."

He held up both hands as if in surrender. "Okay. Okay, I won't. I swear." His heart was racing. Sweat was forming at the base of his spine.

"Gracie, I… God…" He wiped the back of his hand over his mouth but he could still taste her.

And she was staring at him, big-eyed and wounded, as if he'd attacked her.

"Look, I'm sorry," he said, using the same tone he'd use to calm one of his nieces when they got hurt. "I'm really sorry. I didn't mean for that to happen. I swear."

She crossed her arms in front of her, as if protecting herself from a blow.

As if protecting herself from him.

"I want you to leave now."

Her words, whispered in a raw, ragged voice he'd never heard her use before, swept through him. Burned him. "I'm not leaving when you're so upset. I swear, I didn't mean to scare you or—"

"You planned this."

The accusation, stark and ugly, had his head snapping back. "What? No. No, of course not."

"Do you think I'm easy? Cheap?" She looked horrified, her face white. "Oh, my God, did Drew tell you…"

He went cold all over, some weird premonition making him not want to know what she was talking about. "Did he tell me what?"

She shook her head.

"All that talk about wanting to be my friend, about wanting to hang out with me again because you like me was just an excuse to try and have sex with me. Why? Why me? We both know you could get just about any girl you wanted," she whispered. "Why did you have to do this to me? Why couldn't you just leave me alone?"

"I don't want any other girl," he heard himself admit. "I want you."

She laughed harshly, a sound he'd never heard from her before. "You've barely spoken to me in months. Now you want me to believe you...what? Suddenly, you have feelings for me?"

"I do. I always have," he insisted, stepping forward, but that only made her back away like a scared kitten so he stopped. Fought to keep his voice calm and low so they didn't wake anyone. "I swear. I was just...confused last summer...with everything that had happened with Kennedy and between us." He swallowed. "But when I saw you with Bryce, I realized how much you mean to me."

Instead of swaying her into believing him, his words only seemed to make her more upset. "When you saw me with Bryce? So you only want me so another boy can't be with me? Or is this just some stupid plan to make sure Bryce and I don't grow closer? Then I'll always be around, waiting for you to decide if you want me or not."

"I do want to be with you," Luke said. "It was just...losing you to someone else, to some other guy, forced me to see what I'd done. What a mistake it was to let you go."

Wasn't that what girls wanted to hear? The truth? Except she just shook her head again. "It's too late."

"It's not. You kissed me back," he said desperately. "I know you still like me, Gracie. Just give me a chance."

"I would have given you a chance. Two months ago I would have jumped at the chance to be with you again, but now it's too late. I don't want to be your second choice or the girl you go to because it's easier than moving on. If you really wanted to be with me, you wouldn't have waited this long." She looked weary and sounded exhausted. "Now please leave. Please."

Because her eyes had tears and her mouth was trembling, he did as she wanted. But as he silently made his way through her dark house, he couldn't help but wonder what he'd done to lose her before he'd even had a chance to win her back.

CHAPTER FOURTEEN

THE WEDDING WAS BEAUTIFUL.

Not that Daphne expected anything less, at least not from a Bartasavich. Except, this wasn't about the Bartsaviach family—not like it would have been in Houston. There were no reporters covering the event for the newspaper society pages, no paparazzi present to capture live video or snapshots of the bride and groom to flash across the local evening news. No reports on what dress the bride wore, who all attended or what kind of flowers made up the bouquets.

This was Charlotte's big scene, her day. Most of the guests in the church had been seated on the bride's side. The ushers had finally started putting people on the groom's side, just to balance things out. But the ceremony itself had been lovely. Not quite as traditional as Daphne wanted for her own wedding, but lighter. Fun.

Who knew scary Kane Bartasavich, with his grim countenance and rebellious past, could be brought almost to tears by the sight of the woman he loved walking down the aisle?

It had been a revelation to say the least.

"Did you enjoy the ceremony?" Oakes asked as he offered her a glass of champagne at the reception. A band was playing softly in the background and people were milling about, conversing and eating appetizers while waiting for the bride and groom and bridal party to arrive from the church.

"It was lovely," she said on a sigh and accepted the drink. Just one glass, she promised herself. Ever since her slip with the tequila a few weeks ago she'd been careful to watch her alcohol intake.

She just wished it was as easy to watch her tongue. She still had a bad habit of blurting out most of what popped into her mind. The alcohol just made it easier for her to speak faster and with more fervency.

"You were crying," Oakes said, sipping his own champagne. "At the church."

She smiled. "Were you watching me, Oakes?"

"I couldn't help but notice."

She made a humming sound and sipped her drink. He'd been watching her, all right. He'd been seated up front, in the first pew with his family, his father's wheelchair at the far end, then Oakes, then, after a huge empty space, Kane's mother. The only way he could have known she was crying—since she was sitting near the back—was if he'd been glancing over his shoulder trying to find her.

"Weddings make me emotional," she said, getting a warm feeling from knowing he'd sought her out. "And when Charlotte recited her vows and said that she wasn't expecting Kane, wasn't expecting to fall in love with him but was so glad she'd opened her heart to the wonderful man he is, well, let me tell you, we were all bawling."

Oakes frowned, looking right at home in his expensive suit, the champagne flute held lightly in his hand. This was his scene, she realized. What he'd been born into. High-end, catered events with fancy drinks and food and classy music in the background. Men and women dressed to the nines all chatting about stock prices, or how difficult it was to find a gardener who knew how to prune gardenias properly, or if they were going to spend their summer traveling across Europe or at the summer house in Maine.

She frowned, the champagne she'd sipped turning sour in her stomach. That had been a bit judgmental of her and not exactly the kind of thoughts she wanted to have for the man in front of her. Yes, he was used to fancy parties and small talk and high society events. But he wasn't a snob.

"What do you mean, you were all bawling?" he asked.

"Me and the women sitting in the pew with me. I tell you what, we were all wrecks. It started when Charlotte's dad started crying before he'd even walked her down the aisle and it only got worse from there. Luckily, we were well stocked with tissues." She accepted a chilled shrimp from a server. "What did you think of it?"

"Of you all crying?"

"No. Of the ceremony."

He'd looked so handsome pushing his father's wheelchair up the aisle, his smile warm and welcoming to everyone. But she hadn't been able to see his face, hadn't caught his expression to see what he'd thought of his brother's wedding.

Oakes had invited her to sit with them but she'd declined, not wanting to intrude on his family. She'd been perfectly fine on her own, had chatted with her pew-mates and enjoyed being at the wedding.

"It was nice," he said.

She almost choked on her drink but didn't want to waste one drop of the delicious liquid so she forced herself to swallow. "Nice? That's all you have to say?"

He shifted. Looked uncomfortable, like a schoolboy being called on when he didn't know the answer. "What else is there to say? Every wedding I've ever been to has been pretty similar. The location might change, the participants sure did, but they all follow the same format. Play a few songs. Recite vows. Exchange rings. Kiss. This one was as nice as any other."

"Men," she said with a sigh. Even Oakes, who she'd thought to be above such typical male behavior, was clueless when it came to such things. "It was lovely. Sentimental and personal and special."

He nodded. "Yeah. Like I said. Nice."

"Well, at least there weren't any peeing dogs," she said, earning herself a sharp look from an older woman as she passed them.

Oakes's lips twitched. "And I haven't seen any pigs spinning on a spit."

They clinked glasses in a silent toast. She slid closer to his side so a couple could pass. "Were you upset about not being asked to be best man?"

She'd wondered if his feelings had been hurt, if that was why he didn't think the ceremony had been anything other than just *nice*. Everyone who knew the Bartasaviches knew that Oakes was a favorite among them. His easygoing personality, kindness and natural charm made him a favorite. So it had come as a surprise to some that Kane had asked C.J. to stand beside him on his wedding day when those two were usually butting heads.

"Why would I be upset?" Oakes asked.

"Well, I just thought you were…closer to Kane." Not that Zach had said so specifically, but it was pretty clear that C.J. wasn't the easiest person to get along with and could definitely rub people the wrong way with his arrogance and bossiness.

"Kane and C.J. grew up together," Oakes pointed out. "They're closer in age and spent more time together than I spent with either of them. Remember, we were only together on every other weekend and alternating holidays—and during most of those, my father was working, leaving us to our own devices. Which enabled C.J. and Kane to take off and hang out with their friends. So, no, I wasn't upset. I was glad Kane asked C.J. They've had some problems and it's nice knowing they're at least working through them, especially now that Kane's married and C.J.'s a dad."

He nodded toward Ivy, who was stunning in a cobalt-blue dress, her blonde hair loose around her shoulders. Not even the newborn in her arms could make her look less sexy, and it was a toss-up to say which one of them was getting more attention. "Your nephew is adorable," Daphne said. She'd had a chance to hold him while Ivy used the restroom.

Oakes grinned and it was pure delight and pride. "Yeah, he's pretty great. It's fun being around a baby. We weren't around Estelle when she was that age so we missed that stage."

"You like kids," she said, her heart—already so full for him, of him—threatening to overflow.

"Who doesn't?"

"My sixth-grade gym teacher for one, but let's not get into that as it only gives me nightmares.

I think my mom wanted more kids but…" She stopped. Swallowed. But her dad wasn't exactly the type of person who should be around adults, let alone children. She shook her head. "Of course, it didn't happen, but I love when my cousins bring over their babies and little ones. Mom does, too—she dotes on them. I think she's already pining for grandkids, though I've told her not to hold her breath waiting for me as I have years of schooling to get through." After she got her Master's degree, she planned on going for her doctorate.

"What about Zach?"

"I used to think he'd settle down someday, quit the service, find a nice girl—Catholic if my mother had any say, Mexican would be even better—buy a house next to Mom's and raise his own family of dark-haired kids, who'd be as silent and grumpy as their dad, but now… I don't know. I wouldn't say the bombing changed him, but that's what scares me. He's so determined to act as if *nothing* has changed, as if what he went through was some minor setback and he'll be back on his feet—God, no pun intended—again in no time."

Oakes touched the back of her hand, just a light, gentle caress of his fingertip, but it told her that he cared. "He'll be okay. He needs time to work through it. On his own, in his own time."

"I know. It's so annoying. I want to help him. I want to force him to turn to me, to talk to me, to open up and tell me what he's thinking, how he feels. But all I get out of him is that he's fine and then he takes off, doing his rehab, pushing himself to get better faster."

"He knows you're there for him. He'll come to you when he's ready. You can't force someone to accept help."

A man with an honest-to-God handlebar mustache approached Oakes and started a conversation. Daphne kept smiling politely but all she could think about were Oakes's last words. How she couldn't force Zach to come to her.

And she realized the same held true for Oakes. She'd backed off on the flirting, as she'd promised, realizing that going too fast would only hurt her chances of him taking her seriously. She'd thought if she backed off, let him take control, he'd come to his senses and see how good they could be together.

But what if she was wrong? She couldn't force him to come to her, to think of her as something other than Zach's little sister.

For the first time since she decided to go after him, to pursue a relationship with him, she had the most horrible, heart-wrenching thought.

What if she failed?

SOMETHING WAS GOING on with Daphne and Oakes didn't like it one bit.

She'd refused to sit with him and his family during the dinner. Had insisted on sitting at a table with two of the women she'd met at the church—all the way across the room. He'd tried to tell her that she was more than welcome to sit with them. Had told himself that the only reason he'd asked her was because she was Zach's sister and he was looking out for her. Because no matter what the circumstances leading up to it, she *was* his date. But as the reception went on and he found himself searching her out time after time, he realized he was lying to himself.

He didn't like it. Didn't like that he'd taken to fooling himself. Didn't like that he was making excuses to want to be near her, to spend more time with her.

He was a grown man. A grown successful man, he reminded himself. One who'd gotten everything he'd ever set out to get. Achieved any goal he'd sought. And now he was going crazy over Zach's little sister, questioning himself and his motives, trying to talk himself out of approaching her because she'd been smiling and talking to some man almost all night. A guy closer to her own age, who apparently made her laugh. One who couldn't possibly have any ties to her family.

The guy leaned in and said something that had

Daphne laughing. The man's body language made it clear he found her interesting. Attractive.

Not surprising given Daphne's personality and wit. Not to mention how gorgeous she looked in a sequined, low-cut black top and frothy black skirt.

This was what he'd wanted, he reminded himself as he stood in the dimly lit corner near the bar nursing a beer. What she'd offered him last night and he'd taken hold of—her friendship. Nothing more. At least, not at this moment.

Oh, he knew what she was up to, what she'd thought would happen when she offered it. She'd thought that by going back to how things used to be between them—platonic friendship—by giving him space, he'd realize what he was missing out on with her. That he'd miss her. That he'd be the one to do the chasing.

Damn her. She was right.

He set down his beer and crossed the room, his gaze never leaving her face as she laughed at something the other man said. When he reached her, she sent him that same warm smile, the one he wanted her to give *only* him. "Oakes. Do you know Justin? He works with Charlotte at the hospital. He's an ER doctor. Justin, this is one of Kane's brothers, Oakes Bartasavich."

Oakes shook the doctor's hand but wasn't happy about it. "Nice to meet you. I hope you don't mind," he continued before the doctor could say anything, "if I steal Daphne away for a few minutes? Family business."

Before she could object or ask what type of family business, Oakes had taken her drink from her, handed it to the doctor and swept her away, his palm on her lower back.

"What's going on?" she asked as they maneuvered their way around the tables. She was breathless, probably because he was walking so quickly, expecting her to keep up in those high heels of hers. "Is something wrong?"

He stopped at the far end of the dance floor. A slow, melodic song was playing and he swept her up in his arms. Started dancing. "No."

"No?" she repeated, her eyes narrowed. She wasn't dancing so much as swaying because he was holding her so close, she had no choice but to follow his lead. "What do you mean *no*?"

"I wanted to dance with you," he said, sounding as curt as Kane, as arrogant as C.J., as uncommunicative as Zach.

Now she crossed her arms, right there on the dance floor while he continued moving, his hands on her waist. "You could have just asked, you know."

He tried smiling at her, charming her. "I didn't want to take the chance of you saying no."

She sighed, her shoulders relaxing, and she finally unbent enough to slide her hands up to his shoulders and start dancing for real. "Nothing ventured," she reminded him, "nothing gained. And it's good for us to be told no once in a while. Especially a Bartasavich."

"That's what I keep hearing."

But she was right—he'd rarely experienced being refused anything from anyone. If his last name didn't get him what he wanted, he could always count on his intelligence and his charm to work. Or, if the situation called for it, hard work and lots of it. He wasn't afraid to fail in most areas of his life maybe because he hadn't experienced true failure before.

And he didn't want to start here, tonight, with Daphne.

"Have I told you how beautiful you look?" he asked, his voice low.

"Nope. I figured even if you did think I looked good, you wouldn't tell me so I wouldn't get the wrong idea or get my hopes up that you were ready to take our relationship to the next level."

He stared at her and she smiled knowingly. How the hell could she read him so clearly?

"Well, you do," he said, not sounding happy about it.

"I do what?"

He shook his head but couldn't stop a smile. Held her gaze. "You look beautiful."

She swallowed, her fingers tightening on his

shoulders for a moment. "Thank you," she said softly. "I was hoping you'd think so."

He did. And that was the problem. He needed to stop thinking about her, needed to put some distance between them, get them back on solid ground as friends.

Instead, the more he was around her, the more he wanted to be with her. She'd cast a spell over him. One he couldn't break, even if he wanted to.

STROBE LIGHTS FLASHED, the lights giving Luke a headache, and the music thumped through his veins as he slouched against the wall and watched the people on the dance floor. There weren't many. A Christmas Eve dance was good in theory but most people hung out with their families the night before Christmas. Still, it was a Shady Grove High tradition, one started before even Luke's parents had gone here.

One he wished he'd skipped altogether.

His friends had long ago stopped trying to get him out there, had given up on trying to get him out of his rotten mood.

That was fine. He didn't want to ruin their nights, was considering taking off anyway. His folks wanted him home early so they could all go to midnight Mass together. He wasn't having any fun here anyway, and he doubted that would change. But he didn't move, just kept scanning the crowded dance floor, his gaze skimming over Kennedy's bright hair even though she looked incredible in a short, tight green dress and high-heeled boots that showed off her toned legs. But he didn't want Kennedy.

He wanted Gracie and he'd blown it. He didn't even know what he'd done. He frowned. Slouched even lower—pretty soon he'd be doing a damn squat—and huffed out a breath. Okay, so he knew what he'd done. But he'd apologized and she'd thrown it back in his face.

Now he didn't know what the hell he should do.

But he did know what he *wanted* to do.

So when he finally spied her dancing with a group including Bryce, he straightened. Watched her like some damn stalker until the song changed—as did his luck, because she started walking toward him. No, not him, he realized when she didn't so much as glance his way, but toward the doors that led to the hallway.

He followed, taking his time, trying to be supercasual about it. Too casual, it turned out, because by the time he reached the hall, she was nowhere in sight. He glanced around, figured she went to use the restroom and waited, nodding as people passed, saying hello to those he knew. Finally, she came out, headed toward him. Her steps slowed when she noticed him there, her mouth turned down at the corners.

And he hated the way she looked—Gracie should always be smiling. Happy.

"Hey," he said, walking right up to her, knowing if he didn't, she'd brush past him without a word. Without giving him a chance to talk to her, to apologize again. But the one word had come out like a croak and he winced, clearing his throat. "Hey," he repeated, forcing her to respond because Gracie was too nice not to.

"Hello, Luke," she said in a calm, cool tone he didn't like at all, that he'd never heard her use before, not with him.

"You…uh…you look really pretty," he blurted, because it was the truth. Her hair was down and her cheeks flushed from dancing. She had on a long, gray skirt and lacy black top.

She frowned, as if being complimented was a bad thing. "Thank you."

"Are you enjoying the dance?" he asked quickly in case she thought she could send him a cold greeting like that and be on her merry way.

"Yes."

He nodded. "I thought so. You looked…you look like you're having fun."

Her eyes narrowed. "Is that supposed to mean something?"

"No. No, just that you seem to be having fun. That's all." She'd been laughing and dancing with her friends and Bryce. The slow dances Luke had

witnessed, where the two of them had swayed
to the music, had just about killed him. "Look, I
didn't mean anything by it. I'm just... I wanted
to talk to you."

"Obviously," she said, indicating him waiting
for her to come out of the bathroom. "Well? What
do you want to talk about?"

"I want to apologize," he said, tugging her over
to a corner when a group of giggling sophomore
girls came toward them. "*Again*, for what happened at your house last night. I'm really sorry,
Gracie. I didn't mean to move so fast. You have
to believe me. It's just...when I kissed you and
you kissed me back like that—"

"Like what?" she asked sharply.

He felt as if he was walking into quicksand
and sinking fast. "Just...like you liked me, too."
She didn't deny that she liked him and that gave
him hope so he continued. "I didn't mean to take
advantage of you, I swear." He edged closer. "I
just... I really like you, Gracie, and you were
right, it was stupid of me to wait so long to tell
you. I don't have any excuses except that I was
really messed up after Kennedy cheated on me
and I didn't want to use you as a rebound. And I
was scared of falling for someone else when I'd
just been ripped apart by my last girlfriend."

She seemed to soften. "I can understand that.

But…it doesn't matter. I'm talking to Bryce and I'm not sure where things are going with him."

"That's fine," Luke said quickly because at least she was listening to him and not yelling at him. "But, I mean…you guys aren't exclusive yet, are you?" She shook her head slowly. "And he doesn't seem like the kind of guy who'd get mad if you were friends with another guy so you and I could still…hang out. I've really missed that, Gracie."

"Okay," she said after a pause. "I guess that wouldn't hurt anything."

His chest loosened. "Great. Maybe…maybe we could do something after Christmas. We could take my nieces sledding or something. They keep talking about you." Rainie and Lila had fallen in love with Gracie when she'd babysat with him that night last summer and still bugged him about when they'd see her again.

She smiled hesitantly. "Sure. That would be fun."

"Great," he said, realizing he sounded like a parrot repeating that word, but he was too damn relieved and happy to care. "We can figure it out at work on Monday."

But she wasn't looking at him. Worse, she was no longer smiling. He glanced over his shoulder to see what the problem was, but only saw Drew walking toward them.

"Brandon is looking for you," Drew told Luke. "He wants to know if you can give him a ride home." Drew faced Gracie as if turning toward a firing squad. "Hi, Gracie."

"Hello, Andrew." If possible her tone was even cooler for Drew than it had been for him. "I'll talk to you later," she told Luke, then walked away.

Drew shifted. "What did she mean, she'd talk to you later?"

"Just what she said. We're friends." Luke didn't like the tone Drew had used. "Why?"

"Just wondering."

But then something Gracie had said the other night floated through Luke's mind.

Did Drew tell you...

"You and Gracie are neighbors," Luke began. "Do you ever...hang out?"

Drew looked at him sharply. "Why would you ask that? What did she say?"

"Nothing—"

"Did she say I was embarrassed by her?" Drew continued as if Luke hadn't spoken. "Because that's not true. And I didn't use her, either. She was the one who invited me to her bedroom, who asked me if I wanted to kiss her. She let me sneak into her house late at night so if she tried to tell you I used her or tricked her, she's lying."

But Luke couldn't answer. He couldn't even breathe. Though he wasn't sure what Drew was talking about, he had a pretty good suspicion and it made him go cold all over. "You and… Gracie?"

"Look," Drew said, lowering his voice. "I could have handled it better. I didn't mean to hurt her feelings. And no matter what she said, I did like her. A lot. I didn't lie to her. Not really. And I sure as hell didn't trick her into sleeping with me."

"You slept with her?" Luke asked, feeling his world implode. First Kennedy and now Gracie. His anger built like a fire, threatened to burn him alive. "You slept with Gracie?" he repeated louder. Loud enough for a few people lingering in the hall to glance over at him.

"Chill," Drew said, frowning. "She didn't tell you?"

No, she hadn't told him. Wasn't withholding the truth the same as lying? It had to be. "When?" he asked, fighting to get the word out past the lump in his throat.

"When what?"

"When did you and Gracie hook up?"

"Last fall. I swear, we haven't been together since then, so if you want to try and get with her, you have my blessing."

His blessing? Furious, Luke's hands fisted. "I don't need your permission."

Drew held up his hands. "Right. Right. I didn't mean it that way…hey, where are you going?"

Luke walked away. He stormed into the gym,

waited for his eyes to adjust to the flashing lights, ignored the thumping bass as he pushed past people, jostling them as he went. He found Gracie dancing with her group of friends and Bryce and a couple of his buddies. He broke through and took a hold of Gracie's arm, swung her to face him.

"Hey, Sapko," Bryce said, frowning, "what's the problem?"

Luke ignored him. He kept his eyes on Gracie, on her face. He thought she was so open. So honest. What a joke. "You screwed Drew?"

She went white and a few of her friends close enough to hear his ugly, harsh accusation gasped. Bryce came over to stand beside her.

"Did you?" Luke asked, giving her arm a little shake.

Her lower lip trembled but when she spoke, it was with great dignity. "That is none of your business."

"You did. Jesus." He felt as if the world tipped, as if he'd lost his footing.

"Let go of her, Sapko," Bryce said in a threatening tone. "Now."

Luke eyed up the soccer player. They were pretty evenly matched and Luke could sure use a way to get rid of some of his building anger, his fury. But fighting Bryce wouldn't solve anything.

And he told himself Gracie wasn't worth it.

A crowd had gathered, though the DJ continued playing music. It was only a matter of time before one of the teachers or parents chaperoning the dance came over to see what was happening.

He made a show of peeling his fingers off of Gracie's arm and stepping back. Though he spoke to Bryce, he kept his eyes on hers. "She's all yours, man."

Luke walked away, straight out the side doors and into the cold, dark night.

CHAPTER FIFTEEN

DAPHNE KNEW SOMETHING had changed. Maybe it was the romance of the wedding, or the magic of the holidays, but when she and Oakes walked up the stairs to their rooms at Bradford House after all the festivities, anticipation filled the air. Oakes hadn't just danced with her, he'd stayed with her the rest of the evening. Had touched her—her elbow, the small of her back. He'd taken her hand to lead her onto the dance floor again and again and again.

Yes, something had changed. She just wished she knew if it was something that had pushed him into seeing what they could be to each other. Or something that was pushing him away from her.

As if in silent agreement, they stopped between the doors to their rooms. She cleared her throat, her fingers clenched around her clutch. She held her breath, hoping, praying he'd say something, that he'd make the first move. If he didn't, she knew there was no hope for them.

She needed a Christmas miracle and she needed it now.

"Thank you," she said, keeping her voice soft, not only because it was so late and she was conscious of the other guests, but because the moment also seemed to call for it, for a reverent, quiet tone. "For taking me to the wedding. For everything, really. You came to my rescue, agreed to take me to your brother's wedding just because I asked. I'll never forget how you were there for me, always have been, really. No matter what you decide to do next, I'll never forget that, Oakes."

He frowned. Looked so handsome in his dark suit, his hair slightly mussed and damp from the falling snow. "What do you mean, what I decide to do next?"

She looked at him, had never found it so difficult to meet his eyes, to speak the truth. "Whether you decide to walk away from me and go into your own room. Pretend there's nothing drawing us together. Or..." she continued, stepping closer and laying her hand lightly on his chest. She felt the erratic beat of his heart. "You could decide to come into my room and spend the night with me, Oakes. You could decide to be with me, make love to me. That's what I want you to do."

He stared at her, his gaze intense, his jaw tight. "If I do, everything will change."

"Change is good."

He shook his head. "No. Change means people leaving. Marriages falling apart and parents getting divorced. It means the end of the way things are. It means chaos and uncertainty."

Her heart went out to him. He'd been entitled and blessed, certainly, but he'd also had upheaval in his life, the kind that had taken its toll. Had left him afraid to step outside of his comfort zone. "Oakes, the world won't come to an end if we're together," she promised. "The only thing that will change is how we view each other. Which isn't a bad thing at all. We can finally stop pretending. Stop fighting and finally have what we both want."

He looked tempted, so tempted, and she held her breath, waiting, hoping. And then her dreams came true when he kissed her, long and hot and deep, the kind of kiss that wasn't just sweet, that didn't say he was holding back. So she poured herself into the kiss as well, wrapping her arms around his neck and holding on, pressing against him.

He leaned back, his gaze intense and heated, and then he smiled, a warm, sexy grin that curled her toes and warmed her in all the places in between. He lifted her hand to his mouth, placed a warm kiss on her palm. Then he turned and, still holding her hand, unlocked the door to his room and tugged her inside. She'd barely crossed the threshold when he pressed her back against the door and kissed her again, his hands gliding up her sides before delving into her hair.

She arched into him, into his kiss, his touch, but it wasn't enough. She shoved him back far enough that she could slide out of her coat, then pushed his coat from his shoulders. While he shrugged out of it, still kissing her, she yanked at his shirt, pulled it from the waistband of his pants and skimmed her hands over the hard ridges of his stomach.

His muscles quivered under her touch. He worked her top from her shoulders, kissing her collarbone, then making a trail down her throat and across her shoulder. Their breathing grew rapid, their hands more adventurous as they sought the contact of skin on skin. The slow, languid kisses turned heated and carnal, their hands now hurried, their touches frantic.

Oakes tugged up the hem of her skirt, his fingers hot, his hands insistent as they skimmed over her thighs, seeking her heat. He slid her panties down then laid the flat of his hand against her core. She moaned and lifted her hips.

He growled. Oakes Bartasavich actually growled, and whirled her around, pressing her chest against the door. She sought purchase but there was nothing to hold on to, just the cold, hard wood. Reaching around her, he cupped her breast through her top with one hand, his thumb rubbing her nipple. His other hand went back to her center. She pressed her rear against him as he worked his magic, the sensations building inside of her. As much as she wanted to see him, as much as she wanted to be face-to-face with him, she craved his touch too badly to stop him now.

His breath was warm on her skin as he placed openmouthed kisses along the side of her neck. "Come for me, Daphne," he whispered, his husky, erotic tone combined with his clever fingers causing her stomach to clench pleasantly. "I want you to come for me."

She couldn't resist. Her orgasm hit her hard, taking her breath as she rode wave after wave of pleasure. When she came down, he slowly withdrew his hand and set it on her waist, kept kissing her neck, her cheek. She smiled and turned, saw the doubt in his gaze, the worry.

"None of that," she said, leaning forward to kiss his unsmiling mouth. "It's too late to turn back now, Oakes. Tonight, you're mine. And I'm yours."

HER WORDS BLEW through him. For one night, just one, he could put his own needs first. He could have what he wanted, what he craved more than anything. He could have Daphne. With no regrets. No recriminations.

As long as he told himself it was just this once,

as long as he knew that this was the only time he could be with her, they could finish what they'd started.

And that was good, as he wasn't strong enough to refuse her any longer, though his mind urged him to. His want was too strong. His need ran too deep. This was his one and only chance.

And by God, he was going to take it.

"No turning back," he told her, his voice husky. "Not tonight."

"Thank God," she murmured, then threw herself into his arms and as soon as their mouths touched, the heat between them flared. Desperation clawed at him. Fear that if he didn't have her now, something would happen to take her away from him. An inner sense that this was his only opportunity. His kiss was hot and hungry, his hands clumsy as they ran over her curves, reached around to tug the zipper down the back of her top.

Memories of the other night flowed through him. Had it only been two nights ago? Two nights ago that they'd shared their first disastrous kiss? But he wouldn't think of that because it made him wonder if he'd been an idiot to wait this long and he wasn't going to let any thoughts of the past or the future interfere with this moment. Tonight was all about the present. Period.

He pulled back and gently, slowly, slid her shirt down, the stretchy material giving way to expose her shoulders and upper arms. He took his time, loving how each slow inch revealed more of her smooth, golden skin, her breasts plump over a silky black strapless bra. The slight ridges of her rib cage and the indentation of her waist. Her chest rose and fell heavily and she didn't try to cover herself, but stood before him, watching his reaction.

Kneeling, he dropped the top then unhooked her skirt, loosening it enough to draw the material past her hips, revealing a silky scrap of underwear the same color as her bra. Lower he went, smoothing the material down her thighs and knees until he let it pool around her ankles.

"Hold on to me," he ordered and then lifted her right foot. Her hands went to his shoulders, her fingers digging in as he helped her step out of the skirt. He trailed his fingers over her ankle, up the backs of her legs as he stood, his fingers brushing against the sexy slope of her belly, then up to graze the sides of her breasts.

He stepped back, raked his gaze from the top of her mussed hair to the tips of her high heels then back up again. "You're so beautiful," he told her, unable to believe his good fortune. She was here. She was his.

At least for tonight.

Keeping his eyes on her, he reached around, unhooked her bra and let it drop away, the sight of her in only her panties and those high heels almost his undoing. He yanked her to him, loving the feel of her curves, her warm, soft skin, but it wasn't enough. He needed to be closer, to feel her against him, skin-to-skin.

She must have had the same thought because she started yanking at his tie, almost choking him in the process. He saved himself by nudging her hands aside and loosening the knot in the silk. While he slid it over his head, she was already working on the buttons of his shirt. He shucked his pants aside as she shoved his shirt from his shoulders, her hands racing over his chest and across his abdomen.

He kissed her and tugged her toward the bed but she pulled back. "Wait," she gasped.

He immediately let go but knew if she'd changed her mind, he might not recover. "Is something wrong?" Was he going too fast? Being too rough?

She walked back to where she'd left her coat, and the sight of her strutting away in nothing but her shoes and underwear was a sight he would never complain about. "No, nothing's wrong, Oakes," she assured him, much as she had that night when all this had first started, with her showing up on his porch, assuring him she was fine. "But we're going to need these."

It was then he realized she'd dug through her clutch and pulled out not one, not two, but three condoms.

He blinked. "I'm not sure whether to be flattered or scared to death. I'll go with flattered since I don't want my ego—or anything else—deflating before we've used even one of those."

She laughed and he swore he'd never forget the sight of her standing there, the brilliant moon illuminating the room, her laughter washing over him. "Let's just say I like to be prepared. We'll just have to see what…comes up…the rest of the night."

He grinned and pulled her toward him, their need having calmed down enough that they fell onto the bed together, a tangle of arms and legs. They kissed, slow and deep, explored each other's bodies with their hands and mouths. He wanted to touch and taste every inch of her, but touching her, tasting her, only made his need for her grow.

He took a condom from her, opened it and rolled it on, then rolled on top of her, holding his weight on his elbows as he looked down into her face. He watched her eyes as he slid inside of her wet heat. The feeling of completion, of being home, almost took his breath. Gazes locked, fingers entwined, he began to move, slowly at first, wanting to make it last as long as possible, but she was so tight. So responsive to him, her hips moving to meet his every thrust, her eyes dark with want, and she made these husky little moans in the back of her throat that had him moving faster. And faster. Taking them both higher and higher until she shattered beneath him, convulsed around him, pushing him over the edge as well.

Breathing hard, his body still shaking from the force of his release, he collapsed on top of her. She held him close, her breathing ragged in his ear, her hands smoothing back his hair as if she couldn't get enough of him. And he realized that this hadn't started that night on his porch when she'd arrived drunk. He actually wasn't sure *when* their friendship had turned into something more, but he knew one thing—he was going to take full advantage of tonight.

Because tomorrow, everything between them would change.

"WHAT SCROOGE PUT coal in your stocking?" Luke's older brother, Scott, asked him Christmas morning.

Luke frowned at him. "What are you talking about?"

Scott sat down next to him on the couch, watched his toddler son rip wrapping paper into confetti under the lit Christmas tree. Scott, his wife Dee Dee, their two kids, four-year-old Ruth and one-and-a-half-year-old Jacob, had invited Luke and his parents over for Christmas morning to watch the kids open their presents.

Too bad Ruth had gotten up at four demanding to open her presents. Scott and Dee Dee had held off as long as they could but here it was, barely five a.m. and the presents had all been unwrapped.

Luke just wanted to go home and go back to bed.

He couldn't. His sister Amanda and her husband, Jeff, along with Rainie and Lila, would be over for breakfast a little bit later.

Ruth had ripped through her presents then demanded more, putting a damper on Dee Dee's Christmas spirit as she took her cranky daughter into the dining room to explain the true meaning of the holiday. Luke and Scott's parents were in the kitchen starting breakfast, but Luke hadn't felt like offering to help, opting instead to stay in the living room and watch Jacob toddle around and try to eat everything that wasn't nailed down.

"I mean you're awful cranky for a kid who got a brand-new smartphone and a laptop for Christmas," Scott said.

Thirteen years older than Luke, Scott was always ragging on him about how spoiled he was compared to how tough he and their sister had had it growing up. It was like having three sets of parents: his own, Scott and Dee Dee and Amanda and Jeff.

One set was more than enough.

"I'm fine," Luke muttered. "And considering your wife got you that flat-screen smart TV, you shouldn't be bitching."

As if magically tuned to words he wasn't supposed to hear, Jacob stopped eating paper and brightened. "Bitchin'! Bitchin'!"

"Scott Sapko!" Dee Dee yelled from the other room—bionic hearing must run in the family.

"It wasn't me," Scott yelled back, having no problem throwing Luke under the bus. "It was Luke."

"Luke!"

This time it was their mom yelling.

Luke just sank lower into the couch. Scott offered him a cup of coffee. "Here. You look like you need this. Now, tell me what's the matter?" he asked, crumpling wrapping paper into a ball. "Stay up too late waiting for Santa?"

"Nothing's the matter," Luke grumbled.

"You're moping around, acting like your best friend moved away." Scott threw the paper ball at his son, hitting him in the head lightly. Jacob laughed and ran to pick up the paper. That kid was easily amused. "Which means it must be girl problems."

Luke sipped his coffee. He wasn't crazy about the beverage, unless it was mixed in a caramel macchiato, but he could drink it. And Scott was right about one thing, he hadn't slept well. Hadn't been able to get the image of Gracie and Drew out of his mind.

He opened his mouth to tell his brother he didn't have girl problems but what came out instead was, "Gracie slept with Drew."

Scott, in the middle of throwing more paper balls at his son, turned and looked at Luke in surprise. "Gracie? The hippie?" Luke nodded, his mouth pressed together. Scott tossed the paper high in the air, Jacob laughed and held his hands out to catch it. It hit his head and bounced onto the floor. "I'm sorry, kid," Scott said, giving Luke's shoulder a squeeze. "I never would have pegged her for someone who'd mess around on a boyfriend."

Scott knew all about Kennedy and Drew. He even knew that Luke and Kennedy had had sex. Luke trusted him not to tell their parents, but Scott was the one who'd told him to always use protection and not to use a girl just to get off.

Maybe having three sets of parents wasn't so bad after all.

"I'm not her boyfriend," Luke said. "I mean, I wasn't when she and Drew...when they..." God, he couldn't even say it. "It happened last fall, when we were juniors. I just found out about it last night at the dance."

Scott rubbed his unshaven chin. "You're upset that a girl you like *now*, was with another boy a year before you even started dating her, when you had a different girlfriend?"

"It's not like that. I mean, yeah, I like her. I did like her. But she lied to me."

"You asked her if they'd hooked up and she denied it?"

"No," Luke said. "But she didn't tell me. She should have told me."

"Why?"

Luke blinked then stared at his brother. What kind of question was that? "Because...because she knows how I feel about her and she knows how I feel about Drew after what happened with him and Kennedy."

"Maybe that's why she didn't tell you. Because she didn't want you to judge her or get mad at her."

Luke sank down farther into the couch. Pretty soon he'd be under the damn cushions. "She should have told me." Now he just looked like an idiot, chasing a girl who'd been with Drew. Who'd been with Drew first.

"So let me get this straight," Scott said, "you're mad at Gracie for having a life before you decided you liked her?"

When he put it that way, it sounded stupid. "I'm mad that she kept it from me."

And he had a right to be. Didn't he?

"Kid, I hate to break it to you, but the world doesn't revolve around you. People live their lives without your input each and every day. Is she still hung up on Drew?"

"I don't know," Luke grumbled.

"Ah."

He glared at his brother. "Ah, what?"

"You're scared she has a thing for Drew and not you."

Luke wanted to deny it but the truth of it hit him full force. What if she did have a thing for Drew? And even if she was over Drew, what about Bryce? What if she chose him over Luke? Why shouldn't she—he hadn't exactly given her a reason to want to be with him, had he? He'd gone back to Kennedy after Gracie admitted she liked him, then kept his own feelings to himself for months. And last night, he'd been really mean to her. Had said some ugly things. His words came back to him full force, how she'd looked as he'd said them and his stomach turned. "Shit," he whispered.

"Shit," Jacob whispered as he tore apart the paper ball. "Shit, shit, shit."

Scott just shook his head at his son. "Look, the truth is, you've always had it easy. Good looks—like your brother—that famous Sapko charm, brains, athletic ability. But when the going gets tough, when it seems as if you might lose, you give up. You quit playing hockey because you got a new coach and he was making you work harder than you'd had to work before. I think the real reason you went from wanting to play professionally, from living and breathing the sport, to abandoning it, was that you were scared when the time came, you wouldn't make the cut."

Luke didn't want to admit it, but his brother was right. He'd been afraid he wasn't good enough for the travel hockey teams, the ones where the best guys ended up playing for the minor hockey league teams. And now he was scared of Gracie choosing another guy over him. Of her not wanting him.

"What do I do?" Luke asked him.

"Well, grasshopper, since you're smart enough to ask for my sage advice on how to win back a female and gain her forgiveness, let me share my wisdom with you." Scott nudged Luke's head with the flat of his palm. "Grovel. If she's worth it, you need to grovel as hard as you can, for as long as it takes."

CHAPTER SIXTEEN

DAPHNE WOKE SLOWLY, her body loose and warm and well-used. Though they hadn't gone through all three condoms, they had made love a second time during the night, their bodies moving slowly, taking their time to get to know each other. And when he'd moved inside of her, their gazes locked, their bodies slick with sweat, she'd felt so complete, so cherished, as if she was something special.

If that wasn't love, she didn't know what was.

She stretched, the sheet sliding down her naked body. She reached for Oakes but found his side of the bed empty. Her eyes opened and she frowned at his dented pillow, the bed cool where he'd once been. Apparently he'd been up for a while though the clock on the nightstand said it was just after five.

Panicked, afraid he'd left for his early flight home, she bolted upright only to sigh in relief. He sat in the chair in the corner of the room, his feet and chest bare, a pair of jeans on, his hair messed. She smiled at him.

He didn't smile back.

That wasn't good. He was already thinking, regretting what had happened between them.

"Merry Christmas," she said softly.

He nodded. Her stomach dropped. No, this wasn't good at all.

Using the back of her hand, she brushed her hair from her eyes. "Are you all right?"

She hadn't wanted to ask because asking would only open them up to recriminations. But she hated seeing him so tormented. So unhappy.

Leaning forward, he linked his hands between his knees. "What happened last night…"

"Oh, no." She scrambled to her knees, dragging the sheet up to cover herself. "Don't you dare tell me that what happened between us was a mistake or that you regret it."

He lifted his head, met her eyes in the dim light from the lamp on the table. "I don't regret it."

She believed him. How could she not? This was Oakes. Honest and honorable Oakes.

And she knew, he was about to break her heart.

"You don't regret it," she repeated, "but you still think it was a mistake."

"It *was*."

Did he have to sound so weary? Speak to her so gently as if she was a child and not the woman he'd made love to last night? Frustrated, she yanked the sheet around her and climbed to her feet. "It wasn't a mistake," she insisted. "It was what we both wanted. How can it be wrong?"

"Not wrong," he hedged, "just not...something that should have happened. I'm attracted to you, Daphne. You're beautiful and smart and funny."

Tears clogged her throat and she cleared them away. "If I'm so wonderful, why don't you want to be with me?"

He flinched, either at her straightforward question or the thickness of her voice, she didn't know which. He stood and crossed to her, taking her hands in his. "You're a remarkable young woman. You have your entire life ahead of you. And someday, you'll meet a man who can give you everything you want. Everything you deserve."

She went cold all over. He didn't want her. "I don't want any other man," she told him, giving him her heart. Giving him the truth. "I want you. I've always wanted you, Oakes." When he tried to step back, she held his hands tighter. "Don't you see? It's always been you. You're the reason I couldn't marry Ricky."

Oakes frowned and pulled free of her hold. "What are you talking about? You said Ricky broke up with you."

"I just... I knew if I told the truth, everyone would want to know why I broke things off. It was you," she told him, praying she could get through to him. That he'd choose her, put her first in his life. In his heart. "I couldn't marry him because I couldn't let go of my dream of being with you. Don't you see? Each step we've taken in our lives has led us to this moment. To each other." Gripping the sheet with one hand, she laid her other on his chest. Held his gaze. "I love you, Oakes."

He shook his head, denying her words. Her declaration.

Rejecting her.

"You don't love me."

It wasn't just what he said, but how he said it. As if he was some teacher, giving her a lesson. She dropped her hand, her fingers trembling. "Don't you dare try and tell me what or how I feel. I know how I feel. God, I know myself better than you know yourself. Do you think I jumped into this blindly, without thought? Well, I didn't. I've had feelings for you since I was seventeen years old. But I didn't act on them. I even waited for them to go away, but they never did. They got stronger."

"You had a crush—"

Hurt, infuriated, she shoved him. Hard. Enough to have him backing up a step. "Don't." Her voice shook. With anger. With tears. "Don't you dare reduce my feelings to some childhood infatuation. I love you. And you love me, too. You have to."

Why couldn't he admit it? Didn't he know

she needed the words? That she needed him to love her.

"Daphne, I do love you," he said. "You know that."

But the way he said it, his tone gentle and regretful, was wrong. All wrong. He wasn't a man declaring his feelings for the woman he loved.

He was a man telling a good friend that he cared about her, but that it would never be anything more.

"You're not going to pick me," she whispered, her heart aching, her stomach turning. "Are you?"

He shoved a hand through his hair. "I can't. We can't pretend there's nothing in the way. Zach. Your mother. My mother." He shook his head. "It's too much for me."

Too much for him? And she wasn't enough. She'd never be enough.

Another man leaving her—the only man she wanted.

No, she thought, embracing her anger, shoving aside the hurt—the pain she could concentrate on later. She was the one doing the leaving this time. She picked up her purse, not bothering with her clothes and shoes and coat, and shoved past him.

He grabbed her arm. "Daphne, we should talk about this."

She looked into his eyes and her heart simply broke. "You can't fix this," she told him. "You can't make it all right. I won't forget the choice you made here today, Oakes." She wrenched free and opened the door, stopped, and forced herself to meet his eyes. "I put everything on the line for you. I put myself out there for you and you still turned your back on me. That makes me a fool, but it makes you a coward."

She stepped out into the hallway and shut the door behind her.

LUKE SHOVED HIS hands into his coat pockets and waited on Gracie's front porch. If her stepmother, Molly, thought it strange that he was there just after noon on Christmas day, she didn't say anything, but she did raise her eyebrows when he told her he'd wait for Gracie out here instead of inside.

That decision, he thought as he hunched his shoulders because the wind had picked up, may have been a mistake. But he'd known that once he stepped inside, her six little brothers would have surrounded him, giving them no chance to be alone.

Finally, the door opened and there she was, Gracie, frowning at him, her arms crossed defensively, her hair loose, all curly and huge around her face. "Luke," she said in a flat tone he hated hearing from her, "what are you doing here?"

"Uh…merry Christmas," he blurted, trying to smile but knowing it probably looked strained.

"Merry Christmas," she told him begrudgingly.

"Is that why you're here? Because you could have texted that, you know."

"I—I wanted to see you," he said. "Could you—could you come out? Just for a minute," he added quickly.

She sighed and stepped out onto the porch and he saw his mistake immediately. She didn't have any shoes on, just thick, wool socks over a pair of gray leggings. And she wore a dress, one with a high neckline and tight, long sleeves.

"Here," he said, shrugging out of his coat. "You must be freezing."

She stiffened when he reached around her to put his coat over her shoulders—at least she didn't refuse it. That was a good sign, wasn't it? His hands shook so badly—from the cold, he tried to tell himself, but his inner voice laughed at that and he knew it was nerves—it took him two tries to zip the coat.

When he stepped back—now he was freezing—he couldn't help but smile, she looked so cute in his coat, the sleeves hanging well past her hands. "My family is waiting for me," she reminded him, still using that tone that gave the cold weather a run for its money.

"Right. Sorry. I'm just... I'm sorry."

"It's okay. But if you could tell me why you're here—"

"No, I mean, that is why I'm here. To apologize for—for what happened at the dance. For what I said." He held her gaze. "Gracie, I'm so sorry for what I said. I didn't mean it, I swear."

She tipped her head to the side. "Funny, because it sure sounded like you meant it. You humiliated me in front of my friends, in front of half of the school. You basically called me a whore and a liar."

He felt sick, remembering what he'd said. Seeing the hurt in her eyes now. "I was wrong. I was just… I was jealous," he blurted, his face heating. "God, Gracie, I was so jealous, thinking of you with Drew. It made me crazy. It still does, to be honest. The idea of you two…together…" He swallowed. "I was an idiot. A complete asshole. I had no right to judge you like that. Could you…do you think you could ever forgive me?"

He held his breath, terrified she'd say no. She was one of the strongest, most self-assured people he knew. She didn't need him in her life. But he needed her in his.

Wanted her in his.

"Please," he said, stepping closer. "Please, Gracie."

She studied him and he kept his expression open, his eyes on hers, let her see what was in his heart. "Why?"

He blinked. "Why what?"

"Why is it so important to you that I forgive you?"

"Because I was wrong." He edged even closer. "Because I hurt you and I hate that I did. Because I can't stand the thought of not having you in my life."

"So you want us to be friends again?"

"No. I don't want to be your friend, Gracie. I like you. I've liked you for months and I'm sorry I keep messing up. That I rushed you in your bedroom, that I acted like such a jerk about you and Drew. But I want to be more than friends." He took a chance and lifted his hand, brushing a loose curl back. Leaving his fingers to trail against her cheek. "I'm sorry it's taken me so long to realize it, but I love you, Gracie. And I hated the thought of you being with anyone else, especially Drew, but more than that, I hated the thought that you…cared…about him so much that you'd…that you and he…"

She reached up and covered his hand. Held on to it. "I thought I loved him. But it was too fast. I let myself believe in something that wasn't there and I rushed into something I wasn't ready for."

He remembered how upset she'd been when they'd kissed in her room. "I won't rush things with you. I swear to God, Gracie, we don't have to do anything…" He glanced around but they were, of course, totally alone. He lowered his voice. "You know. Sexual. I just want to be with you. I was scared, these past few months, afraid of getting hurt again, of making another mistake like the one I made with Kennedy, but I don't want to live that way anymore. I want you, Gracie. Please, please say you want me, too."

"I do," she said softly, squeezing his hand and giving him the best Christmas present ever. "I want you, too, Luke."

"Now I HAVE to kill him."

Daphne, sobbing into Cyrus's neck, glanced up at Zach. He'd said it flatly, almost in resignation. "Don't start with me, Zach," she said, hating that she'd kept it together all morning while packing, saying goodbye to Fay at Bradford House, during the drive into Pittsburgh and the flight back to Houston. She'd even been composed seeing her mother and receiving her hug and Christmas greeting.

But as soon as Cyrus ran up to her, tongue lolling out, tail wagging ferociously, she'd lost it.

"I'm not starting anything," Zach said, his face drawn, his mouth a flat line. "I'm just stating a fact. Oakes hurt you and now I have to kill him." He lifted his good arm. "Of course, I'll have to figure out how to do that as a lefty, so it might be a year or two before I'm able to."

She sat on the floor with her dog, the lights on her mom's Christmas tree twinkling merrily. The sight of it, the scent of pine made her think bitterly of how in a year's time Oakes would probably be celebrating the holiday with some other woman. He'd have his perfect life with someone with no complications. "You were right," she muttered to Zach. "Are you happy now?"

"Ecstatic."

She rolled her eyes at his sarcasm. Sniffed mightily. "Look, I should have listened to you, okay? I went after Oakes, no holds barred, and I got hurt. Just like you said I would. He broke my heart. So, congrats. You tried to warn me but I didn't listen."

"Yeah, I was right," Zach agreed. "Just as I'm right about this—whatever happened between you and Oakes wasn't only Oakes's fault."

Her eyes narrowed to slits. "Whose side are you on?"

"Your side," he said simply. "Always. But being on your side doesn't mean pretending I don't see your flaws. No one is perfect. Not even Oakes. You made the decision to change the dynamic between you two, and now nothing between you will ever be the same. That's not on Oakes. That's on you."

"He's the one who's not brave enough to go after what he wants."

"It's not about bravery. You know Oakes. He doesn't do risky. He doesn't rock the boat, and you in his life is like riding a tidal wave in a dinghy. You pushed him, you expected him to fall in line because you wanted him so much. But you didn't consider what he wanted."

Zach's words hit her like a slap. Her throat tightened. She shook her head but the denial wouldn't come. Oh, God. She *had* done that. She'd pushed and pushed, had manipulated Oakes and every possible situation to get the result she wanted.

And it had backfired. Now she'd lost him for good.

CHAPTER SEVENTEEN

IT WAS SNOWING.

Well, that only added to the surrealism of this situation, Daphne thought as she carefully made her way up the walk toward Oakes's mother's house. The lights blazed, the large, ornate house welcoming and decked out in gold twinkle lights, the Christmas evergreen wreaths still hanging on the door and windows. It was like something out of a magazine, the perfect home with the perfect family.

How could Daphne compete with that? Her imperfections made her who she was and if she had her way—if she could convince Oakes to give her a chance—she'd be asking him to risk losing his family.

She stumbled on the first step leading up to the front door. She was asking him to risk a lot. And what was she giving up? Nothing. She'd be getting everything.

She'd come here because she couldn't stay away. Had planned the whole thing out, had practiced her arguments but now...now she wasn't so sure.

She forced herself to ring the bell. The long driveway was filled with cars, expensive vehicles that cost as much as one year of her grad school tuition. She heard faint music from the other side of the door, something jazzy and fun.

But the festive mood—the laughter and chatting—dimmed the moment Oakes's mom pulled the door open. She smiled at Daphne, looking confused. "Yes? May I help you?"

She'd only seen Oakes's mom a few times, never this close. There was no reason to. By the time she'd divorced Senior—and stopped being around during Zach's visitation with his father—Daphne had been only three years old. During the time Oakes came into Daphne's life, he was nearly an adult and hadn't had his mother hanging around.

She was, as Daphne had imagined, beautiful and classy in a sparkly silver top and black pants. "Hello. Happy New Year," Daphne added, seeing as how it was getting close to midnight. It had taken her a week to decide what to do, hours to work up the courage to come here and now that she was here, she wanted to turn and run like hell. "I'm looking for Oakes."

As if sensing she wasn't going to like the answer to her question, Oakes's mom's expression tightened. "And you are?"

"Daphne Lynch."

She flinched slightly. "I see."

"I'm sorry to interrupt your party," Daphne added hastily, anticipating having a door slammed in her face for the first time in her life. "But I really need Oakes. I need to see him," she amended. "Please."

Mrs. Moore nodded. "Of course." She opened the door wider. Gestured inside. "Won't you please come in?"

Daphne shook her head. "I'm fine waiting out here."

"Don't be ridiculous. It's freezing and…" She leaned out, to peer up at the sky. "Snowing. Come in. I insist."

Daphne stepped inside. "Thank you."

"I'll just go find Oakes."

Daphne nodded and waited in the foyer, with its tile floor and vaulted ceiling. The sounds of the party drifted toward her, the music and conversation, along with scents of whatever food was being served.

"Daphne?"

She turned to find Oakes standing in the doorway, a frown on his face. God, he looked so handsome in dark pants and a deep green shirt that brought out his eyes, the sleeves rolled up.

He was perfect.

And if she got her way, she'd completely mess up his life.

"Are you all right?" he asked, maybe concerned she hadn't said anything yet. "What's wrong?"

She almost laughed but figured if she let loose, she'd wind up hysterical. What was wrong? Everything. "I… I'm fine. Nothing's wrong. I—I missed you. And I didn't want to… I mean, you hurt me and I thought that was it. I'd just sort of purge you from my mind but it didn't work. Then I waited. I waited all week, hoping, praying you'd come for me. That you'd call or text or just…show up at my door like some guy from a romantic comedy, make some grand gesture to show me you regretted losing me. But you didn't."

He stepped toward her and she knew he hated that he'd hurt her. "Daphne, I—"

She held up her hand, stopping him and his words. "So I got the brilliant idea that I'd come to you. That I'd show up here and you'd see me and realize what a mistake you made." She knew his mother threw a New Year's Eve party every year, which he never missed. "That you'd take one look at me and realize how much you love me. That you'd tell me I was worth giving up anything— everything." She swallowed, felt hot with her coat on, but she didn't dare even undo one button. "I was wrong. All this time I was so wrong and I only just realized it. I tricked you, manipulated you into taking me to Kane's wedding."

"Daphne," he said, his tone gentle and understanding, which just about killed her. "You didn't trick me or manipulate me."

"Oh, but I did. I used your goodness, your kind, giving nature against you, making you think you were doing me some huge favor. But it was all part of my plan. My *scheme*, as Zach called it, to get you to fall in love with me. I'd had feelings for you for so long, and I thought if we spent some quality time together, I'd know for sure if what I felt for you was real. And I tried everything to get you to fall in love with me, too. It backfired. I came here tonight wanting one thing, but now I know it's the wrong thing. Because manipulating you and the situation in Shady Grove was selfish—and so was me coming here tonight. I ruined everything between us and now we can't even be friends. I've lost you and I'll have to live with that. I hope you can someday forgive me."

"Oakes?" a female voice asked as a slinky blonde came up beside him, linking her arm through his. She smiled at him then turned that perfect grin on Daphne. "Hello. I'm Sylvie."

Oakes hadn't taken his eyes off of Daphne.

"Sylvie," he said, giving her hand a pat. "Would you excuse us for another minute?"

"No," Daphne said. "That's okay. I was just leaving." She turned and walked to the door, looked back at Oakes. "I hope you get everything you want," she said quietly. Then bolted, not even daring a glance back when he called her name.

OAKES STOOD THERE like an idiot, a beautiful blonde at his side, his mother and the rest of his family and closest friends inside celebrating the last night of the year.

And all he wanted was the woman who'd dashed out into the night.

This wasn't working. His life wasn't working. He'd tried so hard to keep it controlled and calm, no bumps in the road, no wrong turns. But how could what he feel for Daphne be *wrong*? He hadn't been able to stop thinking about her. The past week, knowing he'd never have her in his life, had been hell.

He couldn't spend another minute without her. Wouldn't deny himself, not any longer.

"Sylvie," he said, turning to the blonde. "I'm so sorry but this was a mistake."

Sylvie inclined her head. She was brilliant and it only took her a moment to realize the woman who'd been in the foyer was the reason for this. "I see. I can't say I'm surprised. I'm assuming that woman was your date to your brother's wedding?"

"Yes. I'm sorry."

"No hard feelings, Oakes," she said. "We made no promises to each other. However, I'm no longer in a party mood so I think I'll just head home."

"Let me walk you to your car," he offered.

"No. I can manage. I think you'd be better off going after her," Sylvie said with a nod at the door. "Don't you?"

He squeezed her hands and then ran out into the night. Luckily, there were so many cars to weave through, he was able to catch up with Daphne at the edge of the driveway. She'd just hit her key fob, had the lights on her car flashing as it unlocked.

"Daphne!" he called, his feet slipping on the slick pavement. "Daphne!"

She froze then slowly turned and the sight of the tears on her cheeks almost undid him.

"What are you doing?" she asked, frowning and looking behind him as if she expected his mother to call on the dogs to chase him down. "Go back inside, Oakes. Please."

"No." He took a hold of her arms, turned her to face him. "I'm not letting you get away."

She sniffed, looking defeated. "Don't you see? It was a trick. You didn't want me. Not really."

He laughed, the burst of air forming a small cloud before disappearing. "You may have set things in motion but you didn't trick me into anything. I've wanted you for so long and I thought that if I could have you once, just once, I could walk away. I was wrong. Sure, I can live without you, just as you can live without me. We could both move on, find someone more suitable or easier, someone who won't make waves in either of our families, but I don't want to."

Because she didn't look as if she believed him, he kissed her. Poured his heart into the kiss, wrapping his arms around her and holding her to him tightly. He never wanted to let her go.

When they broke apart, she was crying again.

"Please don't cry," he said, his voice unsteady.

"I can't help it," she said. "I don't want you to give up anything for me. Your mother—"

"My mother will understand. Eventually. And once we get through a few unpleasant moments, she's going to love you as much as I do. It won't be easy, there will be some rocky and rough times, but we can get through them. Together." He cupped her face with his hands, the snow falling gently to sparkle on her dark hair, reminding him of their first real kiss over a week ago in Shady Grove. "Please give me another chance."

With a happy sob, she threw herself into his

arms. "I love you," she whispered, hugging him fiercely.

"I love you, too." He leaned back so he could look into her eyes. "I love you and I choose you, Daphne. I promise, I will always, always choose you."

* * * * *

LARGER-PRINT BOOKS!

GET 2 FREE LARGER-PRINT NOVELS PLUS
2 FREE GIFTS!

⚜ HARLEQUIN®

Romance

From the Heart, For the Heart

HRLP15